MW00488519

The Flavors of the Caribbean & Latin America

ALSO BY ALEX D. HAWKES

South Florida Cookery

The Shrimp Cookbook

Tropical Cookery

Encyclopedia of Cultivated Orchids

Orchids: Their Botany and Culture

Cultural Directions for Orchids

The Major Kinds of Palms

Guide to Common Plants of the Everglades National Park

The Four Arts Garden of Palm Beach: A Catalogue

A World of Vegetable Cookery

The Rum Cookbook

The Flavors of the Caribbean & Latin America

A Personal Collection of Recipes by Alex D. Hawkes

Drawings by Lynda West

Preface by Elisabeth Lambert Ortiz

THE VIKING PRESS New York

First published in 1978 by The Viking Press
625 Madison Avenue, New York, N.Y. 10022
Published simultaneously in Canada by
Penguin Books Canada Limited

LIBRARY OF CONGRESS CATALOGING IN PUBLICATION DATA
Hawkes, Alex D 1927–1977
The flavors of the Caribbean and Latin America.
Includes index.
1. Cookery, Latin American. I. Title.
TX716.A1H38 641.5'98 77-27513
ISBN 0-670-31755-1

Printed in the United States of America
Set in Linotype Bodoni Book

ACKNOWLEDGMENTS

M. Evans and Company, Inc.:
Recipe for "Huachinango à la Veracruzana," from
The Complete Book of Mexican Cooking by Elisabeth Lambert Ortiz.
Copyright © 1967 by Elisabeth Lambert Ortiz.
Reprinted by permission of the publishers,
M. Evans and Company, Inc., 216 East 49th Street,
New York, N.Y. 10017.

Prentice-Hall, Inc.:
The recipe for "Mole de Guajolote" on page 110, from
Elena's Secrets of Mexican Cooking by Elena Zelayeta.
© 1958 by Prentice-Hall, Inc.
Published by Prentice-Hall, Inc., Englewood Cliffs, New Jersey.

Simon & Schuster:
Recipe for "Feijoada Completa," from
A World of Vegetable Cookery by Alex D. Hawkes.
Copyright © 1968 by Alex D. Hawkes.
Reprinted by permission of Simon & Schuster,
a Division of Gulf & Western Corporation.

This book is dedicated to
Mr. Vincent Campbell, an admirable Jamaican cook,
without whom it would never have been written

Acknowledgments

I would like to express my sincere thanks to the following persons, organizations, and periodicals for their generous assistance through the years: Sra. Hermilia Casas de Almeida, Santiago de Cuba, Cuba; Mrs. Elizabeth Backman, New York, New York; Mr. Vincent Campbell, St. Andrew, Jamaica; the late Mrs. Katherine Hawkes Chatham, Coconut Grove, Florida; *Gourmet* magazine, New York, New York; Mrs. Winifred Gaskin, High Commissioner of Guyana, Kingston, Jamaica; Mr. Calvin Grant, St. Andrew, Jamaica; the late Mr. David A. Hawkes, Rapallo, Italy; Dr. and Mrs. P.M. Jackson, St. Andrew, Jamaica; Mrs. Doreen Kirkcaldy, Grace Kitchens, Kingston, Jamaica; Winston and Daphne Lee, The Golden Dragon Restaurant, Mona Plaza, St. Andrew, Jamaica; Dr. Gilberto Pereira do Nascimento, Rio de Janeiro, Brazil; Mr. John H. Nelson, Surinam Tourist Bureau, New York, New York; Mrs. Elisabeth Lambert Ortiz, New York, New York; Mr. John Schaffner, New York, New York; Uruguayan Embassy, Washington, D.C.; Division of Tourism, Government of the Virgin Islands, St. Croix, Virgin Islands; Mrs. Olive Whyte, Kingston, Jamaica; Mrs. Elena Zelayeta, Los Angeles, California.

—A. H.

Contents

Preface

Alex Hawkes and I first met when he sent me a copy of his *Cookery Notes,* a small publication about food and cooking that he produced monthly for a group of subscribers. In it was a review he had written of a Caribbean cookbook I had done for *House and Garden* magazine. He was warmly generous in his praise, and it was characteristic of him that he took the trouble to send me his publication. That was the beginning of an affectionate friendship I shall always cherish, especially now that Alex has left us, far too soon. We were friends by mail for months before I met him, when he came to New York from Florida, where he was then living. Then he was off again, moving to Jamaica in the West Indies, where I was lucky enough to see him when I visited my old school in Kingston. Though he was from northern Maine, he loved the islands, and this was the first bond between us, for I learned to love the islands when my family moved for some years to Jamaica from London.

Alex was a greatly talented man. He was, professionally, first and foremost a botanist-horticulturist, with orchids, palms, and bromeliads his botanical specialties. He was an author of distinction in these fields, with a dozen or more books to his credit. Had he done nothing else he would have left behind an enduring monument. But when he was a boy, his Scottish grandmother pushed him into the kitchen. She believed, Alex told us, that every young gentleman should learn to cook, and cook well. She saw to it that he did. I can see how, after that start, botany led him to a continuing interest in cooking, since botany has been an important part of my education, though an early desire (never quite abandoned) to be a botanist was overridden by journalism. It made an extra bond between us, since he knew how deeply I cared about the world of plants, and we were never tired of complaining to each other about the misuse of the names of fruits and vegetables and the difficulties this created for the cook shopping for unfamiliar ingredients. That was another aspect of Alex. Academically impeccable, he was at the same time intensely practical, always aware of other people's problems and eager to help solve them.

But for the great many of us who will miss him sorely, his greatest talent was a gift for friendship, and this is reflected here in his last book, which we are so lucky to have. I shall miss Alex a great deal, especially when I have some piece of botanical obscurity I want to discuss, and I feel very privileged that he wanted me to write this introduction. More than that, I am immensely glad we have this last book of his. It is such a warm, personal book that it is like having him with us again. It is a book full of very good things and wonderfully packed with the sort of information that widens one's horizons and excites one's imagination. All the aspects of his character have gone into the making of the book, which is based on his travels when he went on orchid-seeking or other botanical expeditions. These travels took him all over the Caribbean, Mexico, and Central and South America. As well as seeking orchids and bromeliads, he sought out new dishes, tasted with a critical palate, and because of his gift for friendship was able to acquire recipes for the dishes he enjoyed. Then he tested the recipes back at home and put them down on paper for us to enjoy. Welcomed everywhere he went, he had insights into foreign cuisines one can only gain through personal contacts. I always find that it is in the kitchens of friends and from friends one makes in the markets of foreign lands that I learn most when I am studying a cuisine. Alex found this, too, whether it was friends in a fine house in Jamaica overlooking the intensely blue, sun-drenched Caribbean or from villagers high in mist-wreathed mountains in Belize.

His travels took him to an area where so many culinary influences jostle one another that it is sometimes hard to know where to start unraveling the tangled skein of influences, but no kitchen was too small or too large to interest him. He found things he enjoyed to eat in tiny Barbados and in vast Brazil, and he includes not only these but new recipes from inventive cooks, as well as invented favorites of his own. It is a wonderfully eclectic collection reflecting the author's tastes.

In the early days of my friendship with Alex his book *A World of Vegetable Cookery* was published. It is at one and the same time a fine botanical treatise and a splendid cookbook in which he combined his talents magnificently. I don't suppose a working day of mine passes without my consulting Alex through his book, to check an origin, a scientific name, a common name. Whenever in the course of my own researches —which very much involved plant origins, especially in Latin America—I discovered something new, I would write to Alex, and I always received an enthusiastic response. He found learning a permanent excitement, and to him discovery was a wondrous thing. I would like to think I was sometimes helpful to him. He would get in touch to tell me about a lunch or dinner party he had given using recipes of mine, and he insisted he had learned a lot from me about Mexican cooking, about the multitudinous family of Mexican peppers, and about this and that. The truth is I am enormously in his debt. Whenever I asked for help, whether about an obscure herb from the Andes or a tropical root vegetable I could not track down, he managed to find the answer. Indeed, what made Alex so special, apart from his great knowledge, as a botantist, of the world of plants and his great knowledge of that world in the cookpot, was his generosity, not only in sharing his knowledge but in his eagerness to praise the work of others he admired. All of these qualities are evident in this new book. I know his old friends will welcome it to their bookshelves and kitchens along with his other books. I also hope it will make new friends among cooks who as yet have not had the pleasure of meeting Alex, good cook, good writer, good friend.

Elisabeth Lambert Ortiz
London, 1977

The Flavors of the Caribbean & Latin America

The Countries & Islands & Their Cuisines

Antigua

This smallish Caribbean island has been very much in the news in recent years and was even "invaded" by British troops at one regrettable juncture. It is now independent, fiercely so, and today I find it a most pleasant place—not necessarily because of its politics, but for its good, inventive cooking.

Antiguan cuisine is one that artfully combines the legacy of its lengthy British domination with tropical ingredients which are to be found on all parts of the island. Green papaya is cooked as a vegetable; the best shepherd's pie I have ever eaten was in Antigua; and such dishes as guava blancmange may well appear at the end of a hearty meal. Seafood, of course, is used considerably in indigenous cookery and usually is much better than the generally imported beef, lamb, and poultry.

Argentina

One of the largest South American countries, Argentina is a marvelously scenic land, its terrain ranging from endless flat pampas to the high Andes, from the incredible lake country to the chill extreme south. In large cities, where one often finds Italian names outnumbering Spanish ones, the diversity in cuisines is fantastic. Pizzas and pastas are almost as commonplace as the magnificent, hearty *asado*—huge slabs of grilled meats served with spicy sauces—and odd vegetables such as cardoons.

Argentine wines, cheeses, and meats are world famous. All generally known temperate-zone fruits and vegetables, plus a number of more unusual indigenous species, are available with happy frequency. Game, ranging from wild boar to ducks and geese, may be offered in private homes and in certain select restaurants, particularly those of Buenos Aires. Of course, superb seafood of infinite variety is almost always available.

Because of extensive populations of Italian and German extractions, there is a marvelous diversity of sausages. Spanish culinary heritage is also prominent, often with a special Argentine touch, and the stew-like Locro and the stuffed corn husks called Humitas are perfectly delicious—especially with a bottle of the proper wine.

Trout fishing is a popular pastime, particularly in Argentinian Patagonia; seldom have I encountered tastier fish anywhere in the world. A dinner of freshly caught, beautifully prepared rainbow trout, with a mushroom risotto, creamed green beans, and for dessert a sublime assortment of cheeses and fresh crisp apples, pears, strawberries, and other fruits is a meal to be remembered.

Argentina is an exceptionally bountiful country, one in which just about every culinary desire can be fulfilled. The interested visitor surely will add several pounds to his or her weight during even a brief stay—and enjoy every ounce of it.

Bahamas

The Bahamas, off the Florida coast, extend southward a considerable distance. The capital and only sizable city, Nassau, on the island of New Providence, is a cosmopolitan place whose restaurants offer native cookery as well as the cuisines of Europe, China, and many other parts of the world.

Because of the paucity of tillable soil on the majority of the islands, the Bahamas import most of their food. Of course they also depend on the largesse of the sea to provide conchs and oysters, red snappers and groupers, octopus and squid, and many other varieties of marine life. Using that superb seafood, Bahamian cooking can be marvelous, even though it is sometimes a bit too peppery for me. Conchs, those large, rather rude-appearing mollusks with the handsome shells, are used in many delectable dishes, such as raw salads, fritters, and chowders. Fried, broiled, or roasted stuffed fish of infinite variety generally are perfectly prepared and may be served with, of all things, a glorious Greek salad.

Whether using indigenous ingredients or imported ones, the Bahamian cuisine is distinctive and well worth the attention of visitors to these attractive islands. And please don't limit yourself to New Providence Island; visit some of the others to see the Bahamas as they really are.

Barbados

This is a very "British" island in the opinion of many visitors, including myself. Yet it is a pleasantly tropical, relaxing spot, with many unique native dishes that make the trip worthwhile.

The specialty of the island is flying fish, a graceful piscine species whose enlarged side fins enable it to swoop for considerable lengths across the waves. Flying fish generally is fried. I find it sheer delight, especially when served with fried ripe bananas and a sort of hash made of potatoes, chopped onions, and a touch of garlic—and maybe a couple of admirable Badjan rum drinks along the way.

Barbados is a major producer of sugar cane, and its rums are almost as internationally famous as those of Jamaica, Cuba, and Puerto Rico. Elegant hostelries offer wide arrays of rum drinks, but on my visits I found that the best drinks, and certainly the finest food, are to be had in the more modest guest houses and, of course, in private homes.

Belize

This country, athwart the peninsula of Yucatan, was long known as British Honduras and still retains a considerably British patina, although Latin American and Mayan Indian heritages are evident everywhere. Belize City, the former capital, is a sprawling, hot, rather cluttered place. The seat of government was transferred to Belmopan, away from the often hurricane-wracked coast and nearer the geographical center of the country.

Belizean cuisines, and they are certainly plural, are unusually interesting. Despite its size, the country is exceptionally scenic and diversified. One may encounter good English cooking or superb seafood creations on, for example, the cays off the coast, where some of the finest skin-diving in the Western Hemisphere yields fascinating edibles. In the interior, the dishes may have a decidedly Mexican—specifically Yucatecan—flavor, and in the high cool mountains one discovers odd and tasty wild game dishes of the Mayan Indians.

On my visits to Belize, I have enjoyed such esoterica as green, mint-flavored rum; an insidious home-brewed wine made from ripe cashew fruits; stewed sting ray; roast armadillo and paca (a strange, disgruntled little mammal, very common along the Hummingbird Highway); and fiery cassava fritters.

Belize is a country neglected by most tourists, but I suspect when they discover it they will find the orchid-laden forests and extensive ruins of Mayan cities as fascinating as I did. And they are certain not to go hungry.

Bolivia

Bolivia is a fascinating land with very high altitudes—dangerously high for me, it seemed—and chill air and also low-lying jungles that are terribly hot and muggy. On the whole, I preferred the tropical lowlands and their cookery, for here marvelous dishes are made with coconuts and a fascinating array of nuts, fruits, and vegetables, including cashews, sweet potatoes, and cassava. In contrast, a large percentage of Bolivians, the mountain dwellers of Indian ancestry, seem to exist mainly on potatoes of many varieties, prepared by simple boiling.

Everyone who travels to Bolivia should journey to Lake Titicaca (the fried fish is good there) and to the incredible ruins at Tiahuanaco, whose origin is still highly problematical. But do not neglect the tropical districts, for there one encounters an entirely different sort of Bolivian—and a distinctive cuisine as well.

Brazil

To me, and to a great many other people, Brazil (I prefer the Portuguese spelling, "Brasil") is just about the most wondrous country on earth. I know of no other place which induces such fond regrets from everyone who has ever paid even a casual visit there—the Portuguese word is *saudades*, "memories imbued with longing." Brazil was settled from Portugal and because of its huge population, more South Americans speak Portuguese (or its Brazilian variants) than Spanish, which seems surprising in view of Latin American history.

Food in Brazil is always a fascinating affair. Many international authorities rank its diverse cuisines along with those of China, Italy, and France. The ancestral influences in Brazilian cooking were the aboriginal Indians (gradually being exterminated by the depredations of civilization); the colonizing Portuguese; and ethnic groups such as the Japanese who settled primarily in the state of São Paulo and the populations of German extraction in the southern states of Santa Catarina and Paraná. African accents prevail around Salvador da Baiá and in the states of the often disastrously arid *sertão* of the northeast. There, instead of Vatapá sukiyaki, or sauerbraten, one encounters volcanically hot dishes and some of the best seafood in Brazil. *Dendê*, palm oil, is a popular ingredient of this cuisine.

Almost every edible imaginable can be obtained in this immense country. An astounding supply of subtropical and tropical fruits, including many generally not known outside of Brazil, thrive here—tropical crops in the torrid north and interior, and grapes, apples, pears, and peaches in the temperate southern regions. The sea off the extensive coastline is incredibly prolific in the variety of its largesse, while innumerable rivers and streams abound with fish, crawfish, and more esoteric species.

The Brazilian national dish is the overwhelming Feijoada Completa and a well-prepared version of it is a most memorable culinary experience. Brazil also produces excellent cheeses and wines (which are almost as popular as the famed coffee and maté), and the rather potent beer is first rate. Cachaça, Brazilian white rum, is highly flavored and will curl your hair when drunk straight. And to be able to drink Guarana, which I consider the best soft drink in the world, is alone well worth the trip to this country.

British West Indies

The varied islands comprising the British West Indies are scenic and singularly fascinating for the culinarily inclined person. In this respect, I would consider the following to be worthy of mention: Anguilla, Barbuda, the Grenadines, Montserrat, Nevis, St. Kitts, Turks and Caicos Islands, and the British Virgin Islands. (Also part of the United Kingdom are Dominica, St. Lucia, and St. Vincent, described later.)

Several of these have an extensive British heritage; hence their cuisines may feature such delights as steak and kidney pie with a touch of Coconut Milk, or a jam made with small, flavorful strawberry guavas. In the British Virgin Islands many of the restaurant and hotel dishes have an American flavor because of the proximity of the U.S. Virgin Islands and Puerto Rico. Marvelous reminders of Puerto Rico's indigenous and Spanish cooking also have been transplanted. The British Virgin Islands import a great deal of their edible materials; I do not think they use tropical foods as extensively as they could.

Cràpauds, huge bullfrogs best known from Dominica, are also found in Montserrat. In the seldom-visited Turks and Caicos Islands one can find some of the finest seafood (including conch and turtle) of the Caribbean area (technically this isolated group is in the Atlantic Ocean). In fact, diverse oceanic specialties are found everywhere in the British West Indies; some exciting dishes are created in the lovely Grenadine Islands in particular.

Cayman Islands

The Cayman Islands lie south of central Cuba and northwest of Jamaica. The trio of isolated islands is increasingly popular with visitors who appreciate not only the essentially tax-free life but the abundance of fresh seafood. Green turtles are raised on an extensive scale on Grand Cayman, and there this relatively scarce delight is frequently available in various forms. Conchs and a tremendous range of crustaceans and fish also are found in the Caymans, well prepared and often memorable for their high quality.

Since few animals or crops are raised on these rather sere islets, most food items are imported. But one special local treat is the Caymanian species of iguana, a reptile which, when cooked well in a spicy sauce, tastes much like a superior type of chicken.

Chile

Chile is the longest and skinniest country in the world, and its terrain ranges from incredibly arid deserts in the north to soaking-wet forests in the lake district and the extreme south.

Because of these diversities of environment, Chilean cuisine is highly varied. By and large, the country is a gastronomic heaven. Its basic culinary heritages are Indian and Spanish, but since the large cities, such as Santiago and Valparaiso, have numerous immigrant groups from European countries other than Spain all sorts of surprising creations may appear at one's table in restaurants and especially in private homes.

Every time I have visited Chile, I have been fascinated by the tremendous variety of seafood, always prepared ingeniously and tastefully. Clams and scallops, squid and octopuses, and an almost overwhelming range of fresh fish and crustaceans are available, and the Chileans know precisely how to prepare each species to perfection.

Chilean wines are world famous, but the fruits, of amazing diversity, should be better known. Several tasty cheeses are available, including some rather esoteric ones in the mountains, with quince paste often providing a perfect accompaniment. The finest paella I have ever had anywhere was in Valparaiso, a name, most aptly, meaning "vale of Paradise"; the finest rainbow trout of memory were caught near the most-active Volcán Osano.

Colombia

Colombia, a land of majestic towering snow-capped peaks, superb tropical beaches, orchids, and emeralds, is one of my favorite Latin American countries. On each visit I have found many new and delectable dishes to add to my roster of recipes, to re-create upon my return home.

The cuisines of Colombia differ widely. From the hot, coconut-fringed coastal cities, such as Cartagena and Santa Marta, to high chill Bogotá, the capital, the variations are simply amazing. I recollect with pleasure two very different picnics: one by a beach near Baranquilla, with coconuts, *escabeche de pescado*, and a pleasant green-corn casserole; the other by the impressive waterfall at Tequendama, catered by an elegant establishment in Bogotá, with cold roast stuffed chicken, crisp eggplant fritters, a marvelous array of crisp salads, and two delicious wines.

So many indigenous ingredients are available in Colombia that one seldom needs to repeat a menu. The Colombians are exceptionally inventive cooks, in small Andean towns as well as in the most posh tourist hotels.

Costa Rica

The name means "rich coast," and this small Central American country is indeed rich in a great many ways. Despite its dimensions, it offers the visitor such flamboyant spectacles as active volcanoes, a tremendous variety of orchids, splendid coastal jungles, and frigid, high-elevation "cloud forests."

The principal cities, San José and Cartago, have pleasant cosmopolitan restaurants, but it is in the countryside that one encounters truly indigenous *cocina costarriqueña.* Bananas and plantains are important crops here, largely for export, and also used in the preparation of many marvelous dishes. Costa Rican beef is good, and on the seacoasts an incredible diversity of marine species are to be had. All of these are prepared with a special touch that I find enchanting.

Such specialties as the fruits of the thorny *pejibaye* (peach palm) should be sampled. There are numerous ways of preparing and serving coconuts and indigenous fruits, some of which are extraordinary. In Costa Rica, I even drank an orchid-flower tea, designed to cure an attack of flu; the flavor of this Cattleya brew was bitter and not at all pleasant, but by the next morning I felt marvelous.

Costa Rica is largely Spanish in its heritage, with little Indian and almost no African influence. Paellas and *zarzuelas* and other characteristic Spanish dishes are much used, and they often include ingredients unique to Costa Rica.

Cuba

I have stayed in Cuba as both a visitor and a resident, and I consider it one of the most interesting of all the Caribbean islands. It is the largest of the Greater Antilles, measuring almost 700 miles from tip to tip. Its terrain is fascinating, from the palm-studded *mogotes,* or hummocks, of Pinar del Rio and the Isla de Pinos, to the high, chill, orchid-hung fern forests of the Sierra Maestra.

Cuba's culinary heritages are diverse. Basically Spanish, but with considerable influence from various African tribes, the island's cuisine today is not easily categorized, particularly in the large cities of Havana, Santiago, Camaguey, and Cienfuegos. Tropical crops—fruits and vegetables and nuts of all kinds—are indigenous or cultivated. Beef, pork, and other meats are of a high quality, and the coastal areas supply Cuba with rich and varied seafood.

The national dishes include *moros y cristianos* (a black beans and rice dish), spectacular morro crabs with piquant homemade *mayonesa,* and an extraordinary number of desserts and pastries that are not often found on the menus of other Latin American lands. Rum is certainly the national drink, although one also finds superb indigenous liqueurs, such as *crème de bananes.* Cuban coffee is of top caliber and very popular; so are *cafèzinhos,* a Brazilian fashion of serving strong black coffee in tiny cups, highly sweetened with the cane sugar that is so important to the Cuban economy. Spanish wines are also popular, including the effervescent *cidra,* a cider that is at once refreshing and singularly intoxicating.

Dominica

Dominica, a large and verdant Caribbean island, is technically part of the United Kingdom, one of the Lesser Antilles, the group extending from the Virgin Islands southwest to Aruba. In addition to the beauty of the island itself and the picturesque charm of its capital city, Roseau, Dominica offers the visitor a unique cuisine, which includes that of the Carib Indians. The last remaining members of this tribe, except for a small group in Trinidad, live in the rainy mountains of the interior of Dominica. They are descendants of cannibals and pugnacious even today, but they offer an interesting cuisine that makes a well-arranged trip to the mountains very rewarding.

These peaks are also the haunts of the crapaud, one of the culinary treasures of Dominica which is also found in Montserrat. The large legs of these frogs are either fried, or stewed in a frequently very peppery sauce, then served accompanied by hot rice and perhaps palm hearts from the woodlands.

Dominican Republic

Long known as Santo Domingo, this pleasant country forms the eastern half of the island of Hispaniola, of which Haiti occupies the western side. The Dominican Republic is thoroughly Spanish in all facets of its heritage, and here one can obtain some of the most memorable of Spanish–Latin American food. Spanish stews such as *cocido* are readily available, and Huevos Flamenco generally can be had for breakfast. Unusual seafood creations can be found in every seacoast city and town, including the capital, Santo Domingo.

In this tropical country many unusual fruits and vegetables help to make the cuisine pleasantly varied. There seem to be an inordinate number of exceptional cooks in the Dominican Republic, and their versions of a broiled-meat Carne Asada or a Pineapple Caramel Custard are simply delicious. In the large metropolis of Santo Domingo, one can find all sorts of ethnic dishes, with special emphasis on those of Spanish and Chinese origin.

At Lago de Enriquillo, in the far west, one can dine on

delicious fresh-caught fish, as well as rice casseroles the likes of which I have never encountered anywhere else in Latin America.

Ecuador

I have made many pleasant visits to this relatively small republic, and my most recent treks have combined botanical pursuits, specifically of orchids and bromeliads, with my culinary interests. In the cities, so-called continental cuisine largely prevails, but happily with a distinctively local touch. Quito, the capital, is a high-elevation city in which such culinary oddities as guinea pigs and purple potatoes are served, while at Guayaquil on the Pacific coast superb seafood of seemingly infinite variety is offered, often highly spiced and sometimes very peppery.

Exciting wild fruits and vegetables are used extensively, including the prickly big-leaved naranjilla and a couple of extremely rare palm fruits. On a visit to the Colorado Indians, when I had regained my composure after seeing their bowl haircuts and scarlet coloration—all over, even the hair—I partook of a meal consisting of a very peppery fish dish, roasted tapir, hard cassava bread, and a beer brewed from an assortment of wild vines, which afforded me my first hangover in fifteen years. Even without tapir and jungle beer, most visitors will enjoy sampling the cuisine, and Ecuador's lovely scenery provides a rewarding addition to any South American itinerary.

El Salvador

This smallest of the Central American republics is most picturesque, with its sometimes active volcanoes, splendid Pacific coastline, and attractive capital city, San Salvador—which incidentally has a number of delightful, well-stocked restaurants. Planes flying into San Salvador pass over a couple of volcanic crater lakes, one a rich green and the other a vivid blue, giving the traveler a startling but typical introduction to this remarkable land.

The Salvadoreños are exceptionally hospitable, ready to welcome visitors to their homes for luncheon or dinner. Some new-found friends arranged a memorable authentic feast of the country's cuisine for me when they discovered that I was interested in cookery and had written several books on the subject. We savored strange *percebes* brought from the coast by one of the group; a richly spiced seafood stew that contained about fifteen different species of edible marine creatures, from fish, shrimp, and lobster to octopus and local clams; yams in an orange-flavored sauce; a crisp green salad; boned chicken stuffed with ham and rice; and for dessert a native cheese and homemade guava paste.

I recommend El Salvador and hope that readers who visit this country will see Volcán Isalco, the "Beacon of the Pacific" (so called because of the regularity of its eruptions), in spectacular action.

French Antilles

It is perhaps not quite fair to place in one category all the islands of the French Antilles—Guadeloupe, Marie Galante, Martinique, and the French half of St. Martin (the other half is owned by the Dutch and called Sint Maarten)—but their cuisines are similar and very French, although the islands vary tremendously in physical appearance.

To take the smallest of the aggregation, the French or northern half of St. Martin has an outstanding tropical French cuisine, although I feel it is less distinguished than that in the larger French possessions farther south. Guadeloupe, Marie Galante, and Martinique (beyond the British island of Dominica) are wondrously French and wondrously tropical and scenic as well. Physically, Guadeloupe is almost split into two islands, the sections being called Grande Terre and Basse Terre. In all these French possessions, one finds onion soup made with Coconut Milk, superb rum drinks, and some of the finest seafood creations in the Lesser Antilles. The ingredients for the last mentioned include conchs, shrimp, langouste, and the roe of sea urchins. Lime juice frequently is added to these and other dishes with happy results, and casseroles are often made with cassava, calalu, and other tropical vegetables.

Martinique is probably best known for the disaster at St. Pierre, the town which in 1902 was destroyed by an explosion of heated gases from the volcano Mount Pelée. Today, however, it attracts visitors from all parts of the world, who delight in its scenic beauty and the fascinating cuisine that artfully combines a long French tradition with tropical largesse. In Martinique, tropical fruits, vegetables, and seafood are used to a greater extent than in the other islands of the French Antilles. The island has several splendid hotels which offer marvelous food, but it is in the less elegant guest houses that true Martinican cooking with all its intricacies can be found.

French Guiana

This, the easternmost of the countries on the north coast of South America previously known collectively as The Guianas, frequently is called Cayenne today, and logically so, for it is one of the world's largest suppliers of hot cayenne peppers, a fiery variant of the genus *Capsicum.* Some may remember it best for Devil's Island, the former French penal colony off its shore. Despite its hot climate, it is an intriguing land, and its cuisine offers much to the visitor.

As one would expect, French Guianese cooking is for the most part very peppery. Seafood is treated wonderfully in stews and chowders and soups. Cassava cakes, fried in oil, are often served with these. Frequently the cake batter includes minced onion and more hot peppers. I have enjoyed some relatively calm chicken and wild-game dishes, nicely spiced but without an excess of peppers, served with good wines imported from France. I recall with pleasure one of the finest bottles of Châteauneuf-du-Pape that I have ever found anywhere, and some delicate petits fours on the same menu.

Grenada

This is the "Nutmeg Island" and a most pleasant place it is. Nutmegs are just about the principal export from Grenada, and when the nuts are processed to remove the mace coating for separate treatment, the fragrance pervades the capital, St. George's, and many of the country towns as well. Good cooking is found everywhere on the island. A native specialty of note is a rice dish to which Grenadian cooks add just a tiny touch of freshly grated nutmeg during cooking and serve with butter and freshly snipped chives folded in at the last moment.

Grenada is one of the Lesser Antilles's most picturesque islands, in spite of its small size, or maybe because of it, and well worth exploring for its scenery and historic buildings and homes. The handsome capital town is particularly attractive when the poinciana trees are in full bloom.

Guatemala

This country is one of my personal favorites, with its towering volcanoes, magnificent lakes, such as Lake Atitlán, and, in its extensive Indian population, some of the most colorfully garbed people in all the Americas. Having spent a considerable amount of time exploring Guatemala, I can say that I never had a bad meal there, a statement that I cannot make about many countries—certainly not my own homeland. The food is varied and is usually best when one encounters native delicacies; however, in the capital, most restaurants purvey a sort of vague "continental" menu.

Corn figures prominently in the native cookery, and in the tropical interior one can be fed all sorts of esoterica, such as iguana, tapir, *tepescuintle,* and on occasion even roast snake. Coastal tropical towns offer marvelous seafood, often beautifully prepared and rather reminiscent of Mexican cooking. Around the splendid ruins at Tikal, however, the cuisine is Mayan, with such specialties as green-corn tortillas and fire-roasted wild turkey and deer, fiery-hot with chili peppers.

The Guatemalan people are tiny and look rather fragile, although they manage to stay alive in spite of sometimes shocking poverty. Even in the poorest small villages in the highlands one is at once made to feel welcome. These are the Guatemalans whom I enjoy the most; far too many city-dwellers seem to have adopted the manners of their visitors from other lands.

Guyana

Until recently Guyana was known as British Guiana, but today this marvelously diverse country is independent of Great Britain. Guyanese are very proud of all aspects of their country, including the capital city, Georgetown, and the myriad waterfalls that beautify the interior, the principal of these being Kaieteur on the Potaro River, one of the world's most majestic cascades.

Culturally, Guyana is wondrously mixed. Bush Negroes and Amerindians live in the interior, and large colonies of East Indians and other nationalities add culinary interest to the basically British heritage of the coast. In Georgetown, almost always in homes rather than in restaurants, I encountered some delectable and truly distinctive dishes, many of them not to be found anywhere else in the world. One of these is cassareep, a syrupy brew derived from grated cassava, which appears with some prominence as a seasoning in many Guyanese dishes. I did not find my introduction to cassareep overly pleasant, but I have come to enjoy it very much when it is properly used.

In coastal Guyana, marvelous seafood is available, but it is served less often in hotels and restaurants than in private homes. Coo-coo and *foo-foo* and various other delights of obvious African antecedents sometimes occur on the menu, invariably offering pleasant surprises.

Haiti

Haiti occupies the western part of the island of Hispaniola, with the Dominican Republic on the eastern side. Port-au-Prince is the capital and major city. The official language is French, but beginner's French will not serve you overly well, especially in the mountainous countryside where the lingua franca is a sort of African-French patois. In addition to being one of the most densely populated countries in Latin America, Haiti is among the poorest. In spite of its tragic history and its poverty, however, it is among my favorite countries in the Americas.

Haitian food is a fascinating amalgam of French *haute cuisine*, frequent and more than subtle touches of Africa, and indigenous tropical products from the sea and land. One may well encounter a spicy stew or *chaudre* of all of the splendors that the seacoast has to offer, or a delicate rice dish flavored with the unique Haitian black mushrooms, called *djon-djon*. Or, at a fête by a waterfall in the mountains, a picnic basket from one's hostelry contains a marvelously prepared cold *poulet sauté sec*, along with marinated artichokes, crusty French bread, and a bottle of exceptional French wine, properly chilled for the picnic.

Honduras

This seldom-visited republic in Central America should certainly be far better known, not only for its scenic coastal regions and the gloriously cool high pine forests in which spectacular orchids and bromeliads abound, but also for its varied regional cuisines.

The capital city, Tegucigalpa, offers a wide array of foods in its hotels and restaurants. Many of the specialties, artfully using the produce of the sea and rivers and the agricultural bounty of the land, reflect the Spanish heritage that still pervades this country, long known as Spanish Honduras. I have eaten—at one sitting—an elegant chilled gazpacho, followed by a luscious and varied paella (which I consider a difficult and controversial dish), a superb wild avocado salad with a piquant vinaigrette dressing, locally made hot crusty bread and sweet butter, and for dessert an almost overwhelming assemblage of Honduran fruits.

Scenically, Honduras offers a great deal, with its rather neglected pre-Columbian ruins, majestic forests and jungles, glorious beaches, and rocky seacoasts. The people are largely of Indian origin, hence almost automatically friendly and hospitable. Along the coast, if you can find someone who will prepare seacrab soup for you, please don't hesitate to be his guest. In the interior, as in neighboring Guatemala, the same applies to roast tapir or *tepescuintle* or iguana.

Jamaica

Christopher Columbus discovered the island of Jamaica on his second voyage to America, and I discovered it at a far later date. I am presently a resident of this intriguing island nation, and fortunately my work continues to take me to even the smallest hamlets of the country.

Jamaica's history is a complex one. First inhabited by Arawak Indians, subsequently occupied by the Spanish and English in turn, the island has a diverse heritage, as is so often the case with Latin American countries. Today the population is chiefly black, because of the early introduction of slaves from West Africa to work the extensive sugar plantations, but there are other ethnic groups, including Lebanese, Chinese, and Portuguese Jews, some of whose families have been there hundreds of years.

Naturally all these heritages have become involved in Jamaican cookery. The hot peppers beloved in Africa frequently figure prominently even in Chinese dishes. A gratifying number of reasonably authentic African recipes still appear, especially in the countryside—they are considered a bit old-fashioned in such cities as Kingston and Montego Bay.

Jamaica has a grand array of tropical vegetables and fruits, which during their seasons are found in abundance in the public markets. Much livestock is raised on the island, including poultry (chicken, duck, and turkey), cattle, goats, and pigs; even so, there are frequent shortages, when meats must be imported from abroad. The annual Independence Festival's Culinary Arts Competition was established several years ago to propagate an interest in local products and their use, and every August creations from all over the island appear for the judges to consider. From unusual appetizers and the hearty, spicy soups for which Jamaican cooks are famous to elegant, ornate desserts and homemade wines and liqueurs, this competition affords a superb survey of the island's cuisines.

Mexico

Mexican cookery is among the most complex and most delicious in the Western Hemisphere. It has thousands of years of culinary history. Because of the great size of the present nation and its climatic diversity, ranging from the sere northern states of Chihuahua and Baja California to tropical Oaxaca, Chipas, and the Yucatan peninsula, literally thousands of recipes are available today.

I very much enjoy Mexican cooking, unless too many of the myriad varieties of chili peppers appear in one dish, and even when several sorts of these are used, the adept addition of such ingredients as ground nuts, citrus juices, or even chocolate can pleasantly calm things down, even for my testy taster. Mexicans delight in using fresh ingredients, and as regards seafood, poultry, meat, fruits, and vegetables, the fresher the better. A visit to one of the large markets in the capital or in Guadalajara or Oaxaca is a rewarding experience; one encounters hitherto unknown edible items which, when properly prepared, are admirable contributions to the native cuisines.

The intricacies of the "corn kitchen" and the effective use of all the different *Capsicum* peppers make a fascinating study; my colleague, Elisabeth Lambert Ortiz, has covered these topics comprehensively in her definitive book, *The Complete Book of Mexican Cooking,* which I recommend most highly.

Much so-called Mexican cuisine in the United States, and even in lands farther south, has been bastardized, and to encounter the real thing on its home ground is indeed a thrill. If you have never had a chicken prepared in the true Yucatecan style, or turkey with a mole sauce in Puebla, or enchiladas as they should be made, you are certain to be delighted, and probably surprised as well.

Netherlands Antilles

The Netherlands Antilles include the tiny islands of Saba and St. Eustatius, Sint Maarten (the Dutch half of St. Martin), and Curaçao, Aruba, and Bonaire, off the north coast of Venezuela. These islands have scenery that varies from rather spectacular (Saba, for instance) to pleasantly subtle, and cuisines that successfully blend their three basic heritages—from Holland, Indonesia (formerly the Dutch East Indies), and tropical America.

One of the most marvelous versions of the rijstafel—the myriad-course Indonesian "rice table"—that I have ever eaten anywhere, even in Java, was served at a private home in Willemstad, the capital of Curaçao. In Sint Maarten, I found a splendid Caribbean seafood chowder, and at Bottom, the capital of Saba, lovely spicy Spekulaas cookies were served with strong, hot Dutch cocoa after a couple of sinus-clearing shots of *genever*, the extraordinary gin of the Netherlands, from a portly green bottle.

I doubt that I will ever master the linguistic intricacies of "papiamento," a language that one hears so often in the southerly Netherlands Antilles, any more than I will conquer the oddities of Dutch. But English is spoken everywhere on these islands, in addition to Portuguese, Spanish, French, and heaven only knows what else. In Aruba I took a taxi to see some rare cacti, and the rather unkempt driver spoke eight languages fluently.

The Netherlands Antilles fascinate me every time I visit any one of the islands—and they are all highly distinctive. I have only one serious complaint about these Dutch islands: because of the absolutely superb cookery, I always gain about five pounds on even the briefest of sojourns.

Nicaragua

This Central American republic is fantastically scenic, with myriad volcanoes (some still very active), gloriously cool cloud forests and fern forests, and beautiful beaches. The people, particularly outside the large cities, are hospitable and notably pleasant toward everyone. The food is, everywhere, sublime.

Like most of the Latin American lands, Nicaragua has a long Spanish history. However, it also has a considerable Indian population, and the Spanish and Indian cuisines have blended to create a remarkable native style of cooking. The rivers and large lakes afford a wide variety of fish (in Lago de Nicarague, one can catch tarpon and even man-eating sharks, the only fresh-water species in the world), and at such towns as Tipitapa, near Managua, one can have marvelous fresh fish cooked in pools of natural hot water and served with one of the volcanically hot pepper sauces that delight Nicaraguans.

In the high, cool mountains, at a hotel such as Santa Maria de Ostuma, a soup made with chayotes may precede roast wild pig, with Bizcocho de Crema for dessert. In the tall jungles of the province of Zelaya, I have relished roast paca served with freshly gathered hearts of palm and a most pleasant rice dish into which all sorts of native vegetables and even wild mushrooms were folded during the cooking, and with the meal a well-chilled bottle of delicious dry white Spanish wine.

The restaurants of Managua, Granada, and Corinto offer some splendid seafood esoterica, several species of which are unique to Nicaragua. American and "continental" cuisines are also available, but even the most elegant establishments offer such native delights as Nacatamales and Mondongo, and *queso de crema*, the perfectly delightful cheese from the district of Chinandega.

Panama

The Republic of Panama is an exceptionally scenic and diverse country, with a very tall, presumably extinct, giant volcano, El Burú, near the Costa Rican border and extensive swampy jungles toward the Colombian frontier in the province of Darién, where Balboa first glimpsed the Pacific Ocean. The offshore islands where the colorfully dressed San Blas Indians reside, and Taboga, where superlative fish and shellfish can be found, vie with such attractive spots as El Valle de Antón, where rare orchids cloak every citrus and guava tree.

The capital city, Panama, has ruins dating back several centuries. It also boasts modern hostelries and a grand assemblage of restaurants where both native and foreign cuisines can be enjoyed. Panamanian markets offer just about everything one might desire in the way of edibles: all varieties of seafood, good meats, both locally raised and imported, and tropical fruits and vegetables. The native cuisine includes unusual soups and stews, often made with bananas or plantains and the various tubers so frequently found on Latin American menus.

In Darién and Chiriquí provinces, one may encounter wild game, prepared tastefully, and find an opportunity to sample roasts of iguana, tapir, and even monkey.

Panama Canal Zone

Since so many residents of the Canal Zone come from the United States, the cuisine is a fascinating mixture of "American" and Panamanian. Hunting for game and fishing in the lakes that make up portions of the canal itself are favorite sports, and the results very frequently go into the pot at home, where they are afforded a special touch by the native cook.

Paraguay

Paraguay is a small, landlocked South American country that is scenically interesting, although much of it is swampland. It has only one major city, the capital Asunción, and there the cuisine is an artful combination of indigenous Guarani Indian, Spanish, and tropical American.

Asunción has a number of restaurants in which one may find authentic Paraguayan dishes, such as Zöo-Tosopy and the like, but I have found that the best food is to be had either in private homes or in the smaller towns. For example, in one town I encountered a superb stew made with palm hearts and a combination of beef and beef heart, all pleasantly spiced, served with boiled malanga and an exciting tomato and hot pepper sauce on the side; as a beverage, we drank clear rum reminiscent of Brazilian cachaça, rather startlingly served at room temperature in jelly glasses.

Paraguay is also known for maté, alias Paraguayan tea, made from the dried leaves of a species of holly tree, genus *Ilex.* One of the most widely drunk hot beverages in this country, as well as in Argentina, Uruguay, and much of southern Brazil, maté is usually served in a handsomely wrought gourd or other container and consumed through a special straining silver straw.

Peru

This large country varies climatically from incredibly dry desert regions to soaking-wet jungles and high Andean glaciers and paramos. I never tire of visiting Peru, whether making the exhausting trek to Macchu Pichu, exploring the torrid riverine jungles near Iquitos, or remaining in the capital city, Lima, to make sojourns into the neighboring countryside. In Lima, restaurants, hotels, and private homes offer highly sophisticated local and foreign cuisines, ranging from such special spicy appetizers as beef heart *anticuchos* to hearty stews made with corn and the myriad kinds of potatoes that are found in the spectacular markets and desserts that are either elegantly French or uniquely Peruvian.

Pisco, the brandy of Peru, is drunk everywhere in the country, and when one is in a chilly city such as Cuzco, it indeed warms one's cockles. Seafood is amazingly abundant in countless species, including many not to be seen elsewhere. It is available in all the coastal communities and, happily, in Lima and many other inland cities, where fresh-water fish caught in the rivers are also eaten.

In the high mountains, guinea pigs, *cui,* are a favorite meat, often served in a viciously hot pepper sauce, along with potatoes and some sort of corn. The several members of the llama family are also eaten on occasion, usually roasted and served with exceptionally peppery sauces on the side, along with chica, a rather insidious sort of beer brewed from crushed maize. Peru's cuisine is consistently interesting, unusual, and satisfying—I even learned to enjoy guinea pig and llama.

Puerto Rico

This sizable island of the Greater Antilles is politically part of the United States of America, but culturally and culinarily it remains very Latin. San Juan, the capital, has palatial skyscraper hotels as well as picturesque districts that date back several centuries. In many of the restaurants one is treated to authentic indigenous food, which includes an extraordinary number of specialties not to be encountered outside Puerto Rico.

Travelers who venture into the countryside to such delightful cities as Ponce and Mayagüez will encounter relics of the lengthy Spanish occupation of the island. They will also be treated to Spanish American food with distinctive tropical touches, such as meat-stuffed plantain circles called Piononos, and *asopaos* made with seafood, poultry, pork, or beef. One may have a pleasant repast at a very casual establishment on a magnificent coconut-fringed beach, or a picnic in the splendid, moist, tree-fern forests of El Yungue. Some of the most memorable menus I have enjoyed in the West Indies have been at elegant or modest private homes in Puerto Rico, where chilled Spanish *cidra* flowed and the cook and/or host or hostess created sheer enchantment in the kitchen.

St. Lucia & St. Vincent

Although both these Windward Islands are part of the United Kingdom, their ambience, scenery, and certainly cuisine are all so distinctive that I have chosen to discuss them in a separate entry. St. Lucia, the more northerly of the pair whose capital is Castries, is a splendid place, best known perhaps for the twin offshore towering cones of Gros Piton and Petit Piton. These are not far from the town of Soufrière, which takes its name from the nearby modest, though constantly erupting, volcano. Even though English is the official tongue, the common language is a patois French, similar to that spoken on Martinique and Guadeloupe. As one would anticipate, the cuisine is an amalgam of French and British heritages, with decided tropical flavors. Soups are hearty, often peppery, and French specialties such as *canard à l'orange* may well have been simmered with Coconut Milk, to afford that unique St. Lucian touch.

St. Vincent has a volcano, also called Soufrière, which has

had violent eruptions. It can readily be reached from the capital, Kingstown; for those fascinated by such eruptive mountains (as I am), it is eminently worth the trip. Interesting food is available in the hotels and a few of the restaurants, especially those in the countryside, and in private homes; the seafood is excellent and, again, has distinctive tropical touches. The interior of the island is mountainous, and often difficult of access, but its tropical woods are splendid, and a visit to them is very rewarding in spite of the difficulty.

Surinam

The large country of Surinam in the north of South America was formerly called Dutch Guiana and has just gained its independence from the Kingdom of the Netherlands.

It is an incredibly varied land, with huge rivers and handsome beaches and, in the interior toward the Brazilian frontier, spectacular mountains and jungles that have scarcely been explored. Paramaribo, the capital, is a thriving city, and in its hotels and restaurants, and especially in private homes, one can encounter just above everything edible imaginable. One will find Indonesian rijstafel, as well as such Dutch delights as Spekulaas cookies and *erwtensoep*, that hearty thick pea soup, which have been given a tropical touch by the addition of Coconut Milk to the cookies and minced hot chili peppers to the soup.

Though Surinam is essentially Dutch, it has a sizable East Indian population, and in the interior there are many villages of Bush Negroes, descendants of the African blacks who escaped from slavery; both groups retain their heritages to an extraordinary degree. A visit to a Bush Negro settlement is a fascinating experience, especially if one is invited to partake of the food, which combines distinctive West African recipes with South American ingredients.

Trinidad & Tobago

The large island of Trinidad and its smaller neighbor, Tobago, are now independent after having long been a part of the United Kingdom and before that, Spanish possessions. Both are tropical islands, offering all the scenic and culinary delights that are obtainable in such places. Tobago is far more modest in appearance and to me always seems a bit more British, not having the influence of the East Indians who form a large percentage of Trinidad's population. Tobago is the only place in the Western Hemisphere where I have enjoyed strong tea, cucumber sandwiches, and crumpets while sitting under coconut palms on a magnificent beach.

Trinidad has mountains, swamps, the famous asphalt Pitch Lake, and some of the most peppery food to be found anywhere. Carnival is a marvelous event, one for which virtually everyone works on costumes and dances and music for months in advance. Carnival food is special, and almost overwhelming in its variety. Everyone involved in the festivities invariably dances too much, eats too much, and drinks too much, and it is all a great deal of fun. Only Rio de Janeiro's *carnaval* can approximate Trinidad's festival, and thousands of visitors come from all over the world to participate.

Trinidadians make extensive use of different vegetables that are found in their markets, cooking them with ingenuity, and usually with more than a hint of curry seasonings and hot peppers. The seaside communities have superb fresh fish and shellfish, and the local cooks prepare these in pleasantly tropical style, frequently offering a selection of tasty fruits as dessert.

United States Virgin Islands

The islands known as the Virgins, belonging to the United States, are exceptionally attractive to tourists, who flock to them—St. Thomas and St. Croix in particular—in great numbers. Some of the islands and cays are small and rather desolate; others are large and scenic. The total population is only some eighty thousand, and from island to island the pleasant cuisines differ somewhat.

Seafood, of course, is the specialty everywhere, and marvelous dishes are offered, particularly on the two major islands and in St. John, where everything from appetizers of marinated octopus to a sort of stew, *cioppino*, can be encountered.

Since the soil of the island is generally not conducive to the cultivation of many crops or livestock, a great deal of food is imported. Consequently, the shops offer everything from spaghetti with meatballs to sukiyaki to Sancocho. The excellent tropical fruits that grow in these islands are often served, either fresh or in various beverages which are usually spiked with good local rum. Virgin Islands specialties include Akkra fritters and a local variation of calalu consisting of various kinds of wild "bush."

Uruguay

This relatively small country on the east coast of South America, with its marvelous capital city of Montevideo, offers a great deal to the visitor, especially the person interested in good food. Unlike many Latin American countries, Uruguay is not very thrilling scenically, save for its splendid beach-side cities, but in the cities and populous countryside one encounters much good and varied cuisine to make up for the lack of visual splendor.

Corn is widely grown and is often admirably combined with all kinds of meats, while seafood in infinite variety is offered along the coasts. During a botanical visit to a small town near Montevideo, I was offered a fascinating array of indigenous dishes, including a spicy seafood chowder, a corn and eggplant casserole, croquettes made with potatoes and minced pork, and an entire series of puddings, cakes, and other desserts. Peppery ground-meat-filled empanadas were served as appetizers along with exceptionally good Uruguayan beer, which I found to be more powerful than I had at first realized. Uruguay is ideal for a relaxing vacation during which one can sample and enjoy the different foods everywhere in the country.

Venezuela

Venezuela boasts the tallest free waterfall in the entire world, snow-capped mountains, superb beaches, one of the most sophisticated cities in the Western world, and utterly sublime, varied cooking.

Hallacas, intricately stuffed pastry turnovers akin to other empanadas and to the Nicaraguan Nacatamales, are the national dish, and despite the difficulties of their preparation, today they are served frequently, not just at Christmas time, as in the past. Venezuelan soups are exceptional and varied, prepared with many native ingredients including the diverse seafood of the coast and the distinctive tropical vegetables and fruits found at all elevations throughout the countryside.

Caracas, the capital, is a very large and modern metropolis, and its restaurants offer the cuisines of virtually every part of the globe, including Arabic, Chinese, old-time Spanish, and the *cocina auténtica* of the Venezuelans.

I have sampled the cooking throughout Venezuela. In the interior I have savored Sancochos and in the high mountains stews made with all kinds of ingredients and accompanied by superlative cold local beers. In Caracas I have been a guest at an elegant buffet which appeared to feature every imaginable delicacy, from imported Russian caviar and beef stroganoff to a coconut blancmange for dessert. In a jungle clearing on the Rio Orinoco my Amerindian hosts delighted me with peppery fish, fresh from the river, several rather strange, bushy vegetables that they had picked in the woodlands, and cassava cakes, all cooked over a rude charcoal fire and washed down with a frightening form of raw crystalline rum.

Appetizers

Appetizers, served either as sit-down preliminaries to be eaten with knife and fork or snacks eaten standing up, are prominent in Latin American cuisines. Some are rather elegant, while others are simplicity personified; they may precede a formidable multicourse menu or furnish the bulk of a much less ornate repast. In Peru and the Netherlands Antilles, there are diverse examples of skewered, broiled meats, notably *anticuchos* and Saté Bumbú. Throughout virtually the entire area, fritters, often spicy and typically served piping hot from the lard or oil, are made with all kinds of foods, from eggplant to sweet potatoes to taro leaves. Dried salt cod (Spanish *bacalao,* Portuguese *baculhau*) is made into numerous dishes, including Jamaica's stamp-and-go.

Spreads and dips, well flavored and again often spicy, are served with thin cassava wafers, bammies, lightly fried tortillas, crisp water crackers, or thinly sliced fresh toast. In Mexico, tiny meatballs appear as *Albondiguitas,* and small cubes of lean pork are roasted until crisp to form *carnitas.* There are also raw fish or shellfish creations ("cooked" by the action of the lime juice in which they are marinated), such as *ceviche* or Poisson Cru. Canapés and tiny tea sandwiches may be made with crisp watercress or seeded cucumber, covered with a shrimp or anchovy paste or perhaps homemade cream cheese and minced ripe olives or stuffed green olives.

AGUACATE CON SALSA CALIENTA
(Avocado in Heated Sauce)

One of my favorite ways of serving avocados, this dish is so unusual that I customarily offer it as a special course by itself before the entrée.

1 *tablespoon butter*
1½ *teaspoons tomato catsup*
1 *tablespoon warm water*
1 *tablespoon Worcestershire sauce*
1 *tablespoon cane vinegar or wine vinegar*
¼ *teaspoon salt*
½ *teaspoon dry mustard*
5 *whole cloves*
1 *tablespoon sugar*
3 *drops or more Tabasco sauce*
2 *medium ripe avocados*

In a saucepan, combine the butter, catsup, water, Worcestershire, vinegar, salt, mustard, cloves, sugar, and Tabasco. Heat until the mixture comes to a boil, stirring often. Lower heat at once, and simmer, uncovered, about 10 minutes.

Cut avocados in halves and discard pits; with a sharp knife make several cross-cuts about ½ inch deep in avocado flesh. Pour hot sauce into avocado halves, and serve at once. *Serves 4.*

GUACAMOLE
(Mexican Avocado Spread)

One of the best-known methods of serving avocado is guacamole, from Mexico. There are infinite variations, including the addition of crumbled fried bacon, diced tomatoes, and chopped hard-cooked eggs, but I prefer the following authentic recipe. Serve this excellent, exciting spread with beer or cocktails, or as a snack.

2 cups fork-mashed ripe avocado (prepared at the very last moment)
¼ cup fresh lime juice, or to taste
½ cup grated white onion
Salt to taste
¼ teaspoon or more freshly ground black pepper
Several dashes Tabasco sauce, or chopped seeded chili pepper to taste
¼ cup finely chopped pimiento (optional)
Crisp tortilla wedges or corn chips

Be sure that the avocado is a very good, smooth, ripe one. Combine all the other ingredients. Peel and mash the avocado at the last possible moment to avoid discoloration. Add the other ingredients and blend thoroughly. Serve with tortilla wedges or corn chips. *Serves 6.*

AKKRA
(Black-Eyed-Pea Fritters)

Akkra are small flavorful fritters, made with black-eyed peas and seasonings that seem to vary from cook to cook and fried in hot oil. Served either as appetizers or snacks, they are popular in many parts of the Caribbean. In Curaçao they are called *calas,* a name generally applied to rice fritters. Here is Elisabeth Lambert Ortiz's excellent recipe from Jamaica, where black-eyed peas are little known, since most Jamaicans prefer "red peas" (red kidney beans) to any other sort of legumes. Akkra and calas seem to be of African origin.

1 *cup dried black-eyed peas or soy beans*
2 *fresh red chili peppers, seeded and chopped*
2 *teaspoons salt*
Oil for frying

Soak the peas or soy beans overnight in cold water. Drain, rub off and discard the skins, cover peas again with cold water, and soak 2 to 3 hours longer. Drain and rinse.

Put peas or soy beans through a meat grinder, using the finest blade (or purée a little at a time in an electric blender). Grind the peppers. Add the salt and the ground peppers to the legumes and beat with a wooden spoon until mixture is light and fluffy and considerably increased in bulk.

Heat the oil in a heavy frying pan. Drop batter by tablespoonfuls into the oil and fry, turning once, until fritters are golden brown on both sides. Drain on paper towels. Serve hot, as an accompaniment to drinks. *Makes about 24 small fritters.*

Variation: I like to add about 1½ cups coarsely chopped onion, 2 large cloves garlic, minced, ½ to ¾ cup coarsely chopped green bell pepper, a large bay leaf, and ½ teaspoon basil to the peas while they cook. These seasonings add markedly to the flavor.

JAMAICAN CAVIAR

Doreen Kirkcaldy and I invented this "caviar" a number of years ago for a special "do" at Vale Royal, the home of the Minister of Finance and Planning, who was at the time Edward Seaga. Solomon Gundy, a sometimes fiery paste of salty fish, is available in most Jamaican food shops. The name is a variation of salmagundi, but the Jamaican ingredients are distinctive. Use the mixture in moderation, spread on crisp crackers, as canapés that are particularly good with well-chilled Red Stripe beer or Appleton rum cocktails.

4¼-ounce can Portuguese boneless, skinless sardines, packed in oil
Jamaican Solomon Gundy to taste
Pickapeppa or other hot pepper sauce to taste

Drain sardines, reserving the oil. Mash sardines with a fork (include a bit of the oil), until a smooth paste is obtained. Blend in a good amount of the Solomon Gundy and several dashes of Jamaican Pickapeppa sauce or other hot pepper sauce; mix well. Cover and refrigerate several hours to allow flavors to mellow. Remove from refrigerator 30 minutes before serving. *Serves about 6 to 8.*

COCONUT CHIPS

These are a favorite snack with beer and harder beverages in virtually all those parts of Latin America where coconuts grow. The chips should be served immediately after they are made, since they soon wilt and in the lowlands, where the coconut palms thrive, the humidity is usually high.

Crack open a dry coconut, drain off the liquid (reserve for another use), and remove the flesh. Peel off the brown outer skin and, using a sharp knife or vegetable peeler, cut the meat—from outside in—into very thin 2- by ½-inch strips. Place these on a lightly greased baking sheet and dry in a preheated 200° oven, often stirring gently so that all sides become lightly browned. Sprinkle with salt, if desired, while hot, and serve without delay. (Coconut chips are also available in cans.)

CASSAVA WAFER APPETIZERS

Cassava wafers, also known as Cassava Lace Cakes, are found in many parts of Latin America. These thin little cakes are sold in paper-wrapped, inexpensive packets; the thicker ones called bammies are usually homemade and seldom found in shops. The latter are usually fried until hot and crisp in oil or fat in which fish has been fried, so that they take on a pleasant flavor, one that I find most enticing when accompanied by some of the fish and cold beer.

Cassava wafers and bammies are made from *Manihot utilissima* (cassava root), which has been used in the Western Hemisphere for thousands of years and which, in some of its forms, contains enough hydrocyanic acid to kill off half the indigenous populace.

Here is a rather elegant appetizer made with cassava wafers.

Butter cassava wafers on their smooth sides and place on a hot griddle or in a skillet with a non-stick surface. When softened, use them to enclose small amounts of one or more of the following: grated sharp cheese seasoned with hot pepper sauce; crumbled bacon; chopped hard-cooked egg mixed with minced sweet green pepper; ground cooked ham seasoned with Worcestershire sauce; coarsely chopped cooked shrimp with minced scallion tops.

Arrange appetizers on a baking sheet and place under a preheated broiler until lightly toasted. Serve hot.

RUM CHICKEN BITES

These bites are justifiably popular in Puerto Rico and many of the nearby Virgin Islands, where they generally are served as hors d'oeuvres to accompany rum drinks. I also like them as an entrée for a light supper menu, perhaps with an avocado salad.

1 *large or 2 small frying chickens*
2 *tablespoons dark rum, or 3 tablespoons light rum*
2 *tablespoons soy sauce (preferably Japanese Kikkoman brand)*
½ *teaspoon sugar (omit if Kikkoman soy sauce is used)*
½ *teaspoon grated fresh ginger*
1 *cup flour*
2 *tablespoons cornstarch*
1 *large egg*
About ¾ cup water
Hot fat or oil for deep-frying

Using a sharp knife, carefully cut the chicken meat off the bones (including some of the skin, if desired, since it is very tasty). Reserve the remaining skin and remnants for use later in a hearty soup. Cut the meat into bite-sized (1-inch) chunks or cubes.

In a large bowl, combine the rum, soy sauce, sugar (if needed), and grated ginger. Add the chicken pieces, mix well, and set aside to marinate 1 hour.

In another bowl, combine the flour, cornstarch, egg, and enough water to make a thin batter.

Heat the fat or oil to 375°. Drain the marinated chicken pieces, dip them in the batter, and deep-fry, a few at a time, until nicely browned. Remove with a slotted spoon and drain on paper towels. Serve very hot. *Serves 6 to 8.*

AGUACATES RELLENOS
(Chicken-Stuffed Avocados)

These appear, with variations, in the cuisines of many Latin American countries. For the chicken I sometimes substitute shrimp or lobster, or a combination of the two, with pleasant results.

Fresh lemon or lime juice to taste
1 ***teaspoon or more salt***
1 ***teaspoon freshly ground white or black pepper***
4 ***tablespoons or more mayonnaise (preferably homemade)***
2 ***cups finely diced, well-seasoned cooked chicken (preferably white meat only)***
3 ***large ripe avocados***
1 ***cup finely shredded crisp lettuce***
3 ***tablespoons finely chopped ripe tomato***
1 ***to*** **2** ***tablespoons finely chopped green bell pepper***
2 ***tablespoons slivered black olives***
1 ***tablespoon mixed fresh parsley***
6 ***large lettuce leaves***

Chill all the ingredients except the salt and pepper. Make a dressing of the lemon or lime juice, salt, pepper, and mayonnaise. Stir in the chicken gently but well, and chill again, covered, until serving time.

When ready to serve, cut avocados in half, remove seeds, and brush flesh with a little additional lime or lemon juice to prevent discoloration. Gently stir shredded lettuce, tomato, and green pepper into the chicken mixture and fill the avocado halves. Sprinkle with slivered olives and minced parsley, and serve on lettuce leaves. *Serves 6.*

CURRIED EGGS À LA HODGSON

Curried eggs are popular in many English-speaking lands of Latin America, from the Bahamas and Jamaica southward. I was introduced to this particular version in the Hodgsons' lovely home overlooking San-San Bay in the parish of Portland, Jamaica, where I enjoyed their marvelous collection of Haitian paintings almost as much as the menu and the view. Rice and the customary curry condiments accompanied the main dish; dessert was an excellent Brie (a rarity in Jamaica) and water biscuits.

2 *cups grated dry coconut*
4 *cups cow's milk*
4 *tablespoons butter*
1 *cup finely chopped onion*
1 *small clove garlic, mashed*
½ *teaspoon thinly sliced fresh ginger*
2 *to* 3 *teaspoons imported curry powder (or homemade; see following recipe)*
3 *tablespoons flour*
1 *to* 2 *tablespoons fresh lime juice*
1 *cup currants*
Salt and freshly ground white pepper
12 *hard-cooked eggs, halved*
Hot freshly cooked white long-grain rice
Curry condiments: mango chutney, gingered banana chutney (see index), sliced cucumbers, and yogurt

Combine the grated coconut and the milk in a heavy saucepan and bring to a boil, stirring occasionally. Remove from heat and let stand 1 hour. Squeeze the coconut shreds and strain the liquid. Set aside.

In a large heavy skillet with a cover, melt the butter and sauté the onion, garlic, and ginger over medium heat, stirring until they soften. Thoroughly blend in the curry powder and flour and cook, stirring constantly, about 5 minutes. Gradually add the coconut-flavored milk and lime juice, stirring well after each addition. When thoroughly blended, simmer the sauce, stirring, until somewhat thickened; stir in the currants, salt, and pepper and simmer over low heat about 10 minutes. Add the egg halves, heat through, and correct seasonings. Serve hot with rice and curry condiments. *Serves 6.*

HOMEMADE CURRY POWDER

Commercially packaged curry powder is rarely used in the Eastern countries noted for their curry dishes. The components are usually added separately in varying amounts according to the recipe. While packaged powders of reasonably good quality, imported from India, can be bought in Near Eastern stores or good specialty stores, a better one can be prepared at home.

½ ***cup ground coriander***
¼ ***cup ground cumin***
1½ ***teaspoons each ground black pepper, ground turmeric, black mustard seed, chili powder, and salt***

Measure all ingredients into a jar, shake well, and store in a cool place.

ALBONDIGUITAS
(Tiny Mexican Meatballs)

Several years ago, when I was in Mexico on an orchid-seeking expedition, I was invited to address members of the Sociedad Mexicana de Orquidófilos in the capital. Throughout the world, collectors of orchids and other rare plants tend to share a sincere interest in good food, and my hosts were true gourmets. At a spectacular repast in the Pedregal prior to my lecture, one of the enticing items set before us was a huge elegant tray from Oaxaca displaying these unctuous tiny cocktail meatballs.

1 pound lean ground beef
1 cup cooked, drained, and minced spinach
¼ cup minced onion
¼ cup minced green bell pepper
¼ cup grated sharp cheese, such as Cheddar
½ to 1 small clove garlic, minced or mashed
1 large egg
1 teaspoon salt
½ teaspoon freshly ground black pepper
1 or 2 dashes hot pepper sauce
½ cup fine breadcrumbs
Salsa Fría (see index), heated (optional)

Thoroughly combine all ingredients except the breadcrumbs and Salsa Fría (if used), and chill, covered, for 1 hour. Form into firm balls about ¾ inch in diameter and roll in the breadcrumbs. Arrange balls on a heavily greased baking sheet or shallow pan, and bake in a preheated 375° to 400° oven about 20 to 30 minutes or until done to your taste, shaking and turning them so all sides are cooked. Serve on picks while still very hot in a warm, covered dish, with hot Salsa Fría on the side if desired. *Makes about 20 meatballs.*

POISSON CRU
(Raw "Lime-Cooked" Fish)

In *ceviche,* the most famous raw-fish creation of Latin America, the fish is literally "cooked" by marinating in lime juice. I enjoy ceviche very much, but I prefer this delicacy, which one may encounter in good restaurants and private homes in several parts of the Caribbean.

1½ pounds firm-fleshed fish, such as snapper or yellowtail, cut into ¼-inch dice
1 cup strained fresh lime juice
Hot pepper sauce to taste (usually about 6 drops)
2 tablespoons salt
3 to 3½ cups coarsely chopped ripe tomatoes
1 cup grated dry coconut
2 cups chilled shredded lettuce
Crisp crackers or crisp thin slices of toasted bread (unbuttered)

In a nonmetallic bowl, combine the diced fish with the lime juice, hot pepper sauce, salt, and ½ cup of the tomatoes. Cover tightly and refrigerate for 12 hours.

About 2 hours before serving, drain off the liquid, add the remaining tomatoes and the grated coconut, and mix well. Cover and refrigerate again.

About 15 minutes before serving, stir in the chilled shredded lettuce, mixing well. Drain and serve with crackers or toast. *Serves 4 to 6 generously.*

BABY SISTER'S APPETIZER SPREAD

Although I knew Baby Sister, who helped me in subtle fashion on previous books, in Southern Florida, this recipe, one of my favorite appetizer spreads, originated in Cuba.

1½ cups flaked cooked fresh tuna or 7-ounce can tuna packed in oil, or 2 cups finely chopped shelled shrimp or an equivalent amount of minced cooked salmon

2-ounce can anchovy fillets, drained and coarsely cut up

1 large hard-cooked egg, mashed

1 tablespoon minced fresh parsley

¼ teaspoon dry mustard

⅛ teaspoon oregano

1 or 2 dashes hot pepper sauce (preferably Tabasco)

1 tablespoon sweet pickle relish

1 tablespoon or more strained fresh lime juice

¼ cup bottled "French" dressing (the orange-colored kind that is not French at all)

Party rye or pumpernickel slices, sourdough bread, or crisp, lightly buttered soda crackers

Thoroughly combine all ingredients except the bread or crackers in a bowl, mashing them together lightly. Correct seasoning and chill, covered, for several hours. Spread on firm breads, such as rye, pumpernickel, or sourdough, or on crisp buttered soda crackers. *Serves 6 to 8.*

ESCABECHE DE CAMARONES
(Pickled Shrimp)

In this version, the shrimp are marinated in a piquant pickling mixture for at least 2 days.

1 cup peanut or soy oil
1 cup malt or cider vinegar
½ cup fresh lime juice
2 tablespoons sugar
5 bay leaves
1 teaspoon coarsely ground black pepper, or Tabasco sauce to taste
1 teaspoon dill seed
1 teaspoon celery seed
½ teaspoon tarragon
1 teaspoon dry mustard
¼ teaspoon cayenne pepper
3 pounds medium-sized fresh shrimp, cooked (see index), peeled, and deveined
8 medium onions, thinly sliced
Party rye or pumpernickel slices, or lightly buttered crisp crackers

In a heavy kettle, combine the oil, vinegar, lime juice, sugar, bay leaves, pepper or Tabasco sauce, dill and celery seed, tarragon, mustard, and cayenne pepper. Bring quickly to a boil, reduce heat, and simmer, covered, for 10 minutes. Add the shrimp and simmer for 3 minutes longer.

In a large casserole with a cover, arrange a layer of sliced onions, followed by a layer of shrimp; repeat until all onions and shrimp are used. Pour the hot marinade over all, being sure that shrimp and onions are well covered. Let cool, cover, and refrigerate at least 2 days. Serve, with the marinade, on the bread or crackers. *Serves 10 or more.*

Soups

Inventive cooks throughout Latin America pride themselves on their soups, chowders, and a myriad of other soupy dishes. The French have long had a reputation for being masters in the art of soup-making, but I think Latin Americans outdo them in many respects. The Spanish-speaking countries have hearty soups that are almost stews, usually including dried beans which have been slowly simmered with ham or pork or sausages, as well as an extraordinary diversity of herbs and spices. One can well make a meal from Sopa de Frijoles Negros, or Jamaican Red Pea Soup with Spinners.

Variations of seafood soups appear almost everywhere, some of these so thick and filled with edibles that they approach chowders in character. Clear, peppery fish teas from Barbados and Jamaica; turtle soup, with tropical vegetables added; Jamaican Pepperpot Soup—all are sheer delight. Coconut Soup is an interesting dish; Mexican Sopa de Ajo, made from a seemingly overwhelming number of garlic cloves, is subtle and superb; and the French Antilles version of onion soup has a special touch that makes it memorable.

The Latin Americans prepare both hot and chilled soups from almost every imaginable ingredient. Luscious purées of avocado are served either way, but the highly variable gazpacho is always offered at room temperature or well chilled, never hot. These soups are often sprinkled with minced garlic or parsley or scallion tops, adding tremendously to their appearance and flavor, and accompanied by freshly prepared croutons or toast fingers.

BAHAMIAN FISH CHOWDER

Latin American fish soups and chowders vary markedly in content, depending upon the seafood species available, but all, in my opinion, are absolutely splendid. Here is a most provocative recipe from the Bahamas.

4 *pounds snapper, grouper, or comparably flavorful fish, or an assortment of several species*
1½ *cups coarsely chopped celery (include some leafy tops)*
1½ *to* 2 *cups coarsely chopped onion*
1 *to* 2 *large cloves garlic, minced or mashed*
2 *large carrots, coarsely chopped*
¼ *cup minced fresh parsley*
2 *medium to large bay leaves*
2 *teaspoons salt*

½ teaspoon or more freshly ground black pepper
2 quarts water, or 1 quart water and 1 quart dry red wine
¼ pound salt pork or pig's tail, diced or chopped
1⅓ cups finely chopped onion
2 cups diced raw potatoes
½ cup butter
½ cup flour
Salt and freshly ground black pepper to taste
⅛ to ¼ teaspoon oregano
6 drops Tabasco sauce, or more
2 cups light cream

Clean the fish, reserving the bones and heads. Cut the flesh into sizable chunks, and reserve. In a large heavy kettle, place the fish bones and heads, the celery, coarsely chopped onion, garlic, carrots, parsley, bay leaves, 2 teaspoons salt, ½ teaspoon or more pepper, and water or water and wine. Bring to a boil, then lower heat and simmer, covered, about 20 minutes, stirring occasionally. Remove from heat and strain.

While the stock is simmering, sauté the diced salt pork or pig's tail in a large skillet until lightly browned. Add the finely chopped onion and cook until just tender but not brown. Add the strained stock and the diced potatoes and cook until potatoes are just tender, about 15 minutes.

In a small saucepan over low heat, make a roux by melting the butter and gradually stirring in the flour. Cook, stirring constantly, until thickened and very smooth. Add the roux to the chowder base in the skillet. Add the chunks of fish and cook, covered, until fish flakes easily. Add salt and pepper to taste, and the oregano, Tabasco sauce, and cream, and just heat through. Serve very hot in large bowls. *Serves 6 liberally.*

SOPA DE FRIJOLES NEGROS
(Black Bean Soup)

Though black beans and rice, under various names, are among the staple dishes in a great many parts of Latin America, black bean soup is a relative rarity. I can recollect only three occasions when I have been served it in this part of the world: once in an elegant Mexico City restaurant that prided itself on its "continental and French" cuisine; a second time in a private home in the town of Antigua, Guatemala, in the shadow of the destructive volcanoes Agua and Fuego; and the third time in a posh hotel in Rio de Janiero, where I suspect the potage came out of a can from the U.S.A.

The following recipe for a succulent homemade version justifies the considerable labor, lengthy simmering, and close attention to seasoning required. At my house it is accompanied by small chilled bowls of finely chopped onion, seeded wedges of juicy ripe limes, slivers of ripe avocado (cut at the last moment to avoid discoloration), and, if available, raw slivers of the Mexican and Guatemalan tuberous vegetable called *jicama* (also prepared at the last moment).

1 *pound dried black beans*
2 *quarts cold water*
2 *cups coarsely chopped onion*
½ *cup coarsely sliced scallions (include the green leafy tops)*
1 *cup coarsely chopped green bell pepper*
2 *large cloves garlic, minced or mashed*
1 *pound smoked ham, cubed, or ham hocks*
2 *medium-sized bay leaves, crumbled*
1 *tablespoon salt*
½ *teaspoon or more freshly ground black pepper*
¼ *teaspoon oregano or basil*
1 *or 2 dashes Tabasco sauce*
2 *teaspoons or more dry sherry or light or dark rum (optional)*

Accompaniments: finely chopped onion, lime wedges, sliced avocado, and, if available, slivered jicama, in chilled separate bowls

Pick over and rinse the beans. Place the beans and the cold water in a large heavy kettle. Cover, and bring quickly to a boil. Stir once, remove from the heat, and allow to stand, covered, for 1 hour. Return to the heat and cook, stirring occasionally and adding more water as needed, for 30 minutes. Add the onion, scallions, green pepper, garlic, the ham or pork hocks, bay leaves, salt, black pepper, oregano or basil, and Tabasco, and continue to cook, covered, over medium-low heat until beans are very tender—usually several hours. Press the soup through a fine sieve, correct seasoning, and allow to cool. Refrigerate for 12 hours or overnight, covered. To serve, reheat thoroughly over low heat, stir in dry sherry or rum to taste if desired, and serve with side containers of condiments. *Serves 8*

BOUILLON TROPICAL

Many Latin American soups are very hearty, but here is a lighter one, found with subtle variations in Argentina and Chile, where it often precedes seafood or roast beef or lamb chops.

2 ***tablespoons butter***
¼ ***cup finely chopped onion***
1 ***small clove garlic, minced***
5 ***cups strained rich beef stock***
3 ***cups canned tomato juice***
½ ***cup fresh orange juice***
½ ***small bay leaf***
1 ***whole allspice***
3 ***drops or more Tabasco sauce, or to taste***
Wafer-thin seeded orange slices (unpeeled)

Melt the butter in a skillet. Over moderately high heat sauté the onion and garlic, stirring constantly, until they soften. Transfer to a heavy saucepan and add the beef stock, tomato and orange juices, bay leaf, allspice, and Tabasco sauce. Bring to a boil, reduce heat, and simmer 15 minutes, stirring occasionally. Remove from heat and let stand at room temperature an hour or so. Remove and discard bay leaf and allspice, then reheat. Serve very hot, with orange slices floating on top. *Serves 6.*

CHUPÍN DE PESCADO A LA URUGUAYA
(Uruguayan Fish Soup)

This delectable seafood chowder makes admirable use of several of the myriad ocean species found off the coast of Uruguay.

1½ *pounds fish bones and heads*
5 *cups water*
4 *medium-sized bay leaves*
½ *to* 1 *teaspoon whole allspice*
3 *teaspoons or more salt*
¾ *cup olive oil*
3 *large onions, coarsely chopped*
2 *cups coarsely chopped celery*
1 *cup coarsely chopped green or red bell pepper*
3 *cloves garlic, minced or mashed*
2 *small hard-shell crabs, cracked*
1 *to* 1½ *pounds medium-sized shrimp, peeled and deveined*
1 *dozen mussels in their scrubbed shells*
1 *dozen clams in their scrubbed shells*
16-*ounce can Italian plum tomatoes (undrained)*
1 *pound sea bass, cut into thick pieces*
¼ *teaspoon or more sugar*

1 teaspoon freshly ground black pepper
¾ cup dry sherry

In a large heavy kettle or dutch oven, place the fish bones and heads, the water, bay leaves, allspice, and 1½ teaspoons of the salt. Bring to a boil, skimming off any scum that forms. Reduce the heat and simmer, uncovered, 30 minutes, stirring occasionally. Strain the stock, discarding bones, and set aside.

In the same kettle heat the oil and sauté the onions, celery, pepper, and garlic, stirring constantly, until the vegetables are tender but not browned. Add the crabs, shrimp, mussels, and clams to the vegetables and cook 5 minutes, stirring frequently. Break up the tomatoes with a fork and add to the kettle along with the sea bass, sugar, the remaining salt, the black pepper, and the reserved fish stock. Simmer 10 minutes, no longer. Add the sherry and bring to a boil. Serve *very* hot. *Serves 6 to 8 liberally.*

SOPA DE COCO
(Coconut Soup)

Here is a lovely, special soup from the Republic of Colombia, using Coconut Milk in a manner reminiscent of India. It has a subtlety that I find most refreshing.

2 large ripe coconuts, cracked
1 cup cow's milk, scalded
3 cups strained strong fish, beef, or poultry stock (fish stock is used most often in coastal Colombia)
2 egg yolks, well beaten
1 small red chili pepper, seeded and cut into pieces (optional)
Paprika to taste
Salt to taste

Grate the coconut meat and stir into the hot cow's milk. Let cool, then squeeze through cheesecloth or a linen napkin to extract all liquid. Add the stock, egg yolks, and red chili pepper, if desired (remove pepper in about 5 minutes).

To serve, reheat gently, sprinkle with paprika and salt to taste, and accompany with strips of toast or tortillas. *Serves 4 to 6.*

SOPA DE AJO
(Garlic Soup)

Variations of garlic soup can be found in many countries, including Italy, Spain, and Mexico. I first encountered this recipe in Hermosillo, Mexico, during an orchidological trek; it is not nearly as garlicky as one would anticipate.

10 *large cloves garlic*
½ *teaspoon flour*
3 *tablespoons butter, or* 2 *tablespoons butter and* 1 *tablespoon olive oil*
1 *quart strained rich beef or chicken stock*
Salt and freshly ground white or black pepper to taste
4 *large eggs*
2 *tablespoons finely crumbled white cheese, such as goats' milk cheese or Romano*
1 *tablespoon chopped fresh parsley*
Salsa Fría *(see index)*

Peel garlic cloves and mash very fine; mix with the ½ teaspoon of flour. In a heavy pot, melt the butter or oil and butter, and sauté the garlic, stirring, until it is soft and commences to brown. Add the stock, salt, and pepper, and mix well. Bring to a boil and cook, covered, over medium heat, 15 minutes. If desired, strain soup. Keep soup hot.

Gently slip the eggs into the hot soup, one at a time, and poach, basting with the soup. Remove the eggs with a slotted spoon and place one in each serving bowl. Add very hot soup and sprinkle cheese and parsley over top. Serve immediately, with Salsa Fría as a condiment. *Serves 4.*

GAZPACHO

Gazpacho originated in Spain as a sort of on-the-spot lunch dish, made with available materials. These often included dry crusty bread, olives, and very bountiful quantities of Spanish olive oil, and sometimes very little else. This chilled soup has in recent years become "sophisticated" and now is served in fancy restaurants all over the world, usually puréed, so that the final creation has little character and sometimes even less flavor. I very much prefer the following version, found, with variations, throughout Latin America.

1 *cup peeled cucumber, sliced wafer-thin*
¼ *cup finely chopped onion*
1 *or* 2 *large cloves garlic, minced or mashed*
½ *cup finely chopped green bell pepper*
½ *cup coarsely chopped watercress leaves (optional, but very nice)*
2 *to* 2½ *cups coarsely chopped ripe tomatoes*
1 *to* 1½ *cups water*
2 *tablespoons or more olive oil*
2 *tablespoons or more wine vinegar or malt vinegar*
Salt and freshly ground black pepper to taste
½ *teaspoon paprika*
Tabasco sauce to taste

Thoroughly but gently combine all ingredients. Cover and chill 12 hours, then serve in chilled bowls. *Serves 4 liberally.*

SOUPE À L'OIGNON
(Island Onion Soup)

Perhaps it is logical to find onion soup in those Caribbean islands with French antecedents, but it is also logical to find that it has a subtle difference in a tropical setting. This version comes from Martinique and Guadaloupe.

2 *tablespoons butter*
2 *tablespoons olive oil*
2 *pounds onions, sliced wafer-thin*
1 *to* 2 *tablespoons sugar*
1 *teaspoon or more salt*
2 *tablespoons flour, or slightly more*
6 *cups strained rich fish, chicken, or beef stock (fish or chicken stock is often used in the French Antilles)*
½ *to* 1 *cup rich Coconut Cream (see index)*
Crisply toasted, buttered French bread slices

In a deep heavy pot, heat the butter and oil until rather hot. Add the sliced onions, sprinkle with sugar, and cook until limp and browned. Add the salt and stir in the flour. Stir in the stock and simmer, uncovered, until soup is done, about 35 minutes.

Toward the end of the cooking time, reduce heat, gently stir in the Coconut Cream, and simmer about 5 minutes. Correct seasoning, and serve soup very hot, placing a slice of French bread in each bowl or coconut half-shell if desired, and ladling the soup over it. *Serves about 6.*

CREAM OF PEANUT SOUP

There are many different kinds of peanut soup in Latin American cuisines. This creamy potage is especially pleasant and a little heartier than most of its relations.

- 2 *cups roasted, shelled peanuts*
- 2 *tablespoons cornstarch*
- 3 *cups milk*
- 3 *cups hot strained rich chicken stock*
- 2 *tablespoons grated or minced onion*
- 1 *tablespoon slivered green bell pepper*
- 2 *teaspoons salt*
- *Tabasco or other hot pepper sauce, in moderation*
- 1 *cup shredded or finely chopped well-seasoned cooked chicken*

Put the peanuts through a food grinder, using a fine blade, or whirl briefly in a blender. Set aside. In a large heavy pot with a cover, blend the cornstarch with the milk, stirring until smooth. Gradually add the hot chicken stock, crushed peanuts, onion, green pepper, salt, and a touch of Tabasco or hot pepper sauce (more can be added at the table). Bring to a boil, cover, and cook over medium heat 5 minutes. Beat with a rotary or electric beater 1 minute, then stir in the chicken, reheat quickly, and serve very hot. *Serves 6.*

JAMAICAN PEPPERPOT SOUP

In Guyana and the more southerly islands of the West Indies, Pepperpot is a hearty stew made with the cassava essence known as cassareep. But in Jamaica, the green leafy vegetable called calalu is used as the major coloring and flavoring agent in this rather spicy soup, which appears on virtually every restaurant menu and frequently in private homes. Every good Jamaican cook has her or his own version of this attractive and tasty soup. Here is one often served at my home.

1 *large bunch (about* 1 *pound) fresh calalu*
1 *large pig's tail and/or* ½ *pound diced salt beef or salt pork*
1½ *to* 2 *cups coarsely chopped onion*
1 *large clove garlic, minced*
1 *large sprig fresh thyme, or about* ½ *teaspoon dried thyme*
1 *chili pepper, seeded and chopped, or hot pepper sauce to taste*
2 *quarts water*
½ *pound or more yams, peeled and sliced or diced*
½ *pound dasheen, peeled and sliced or diced*
Salt and freshly ground black pepper to taste
1 *dozen small okras, sliced, or* 1 *package frozen okra, thawed and sliced*
1 *tablespoon butter or cooking oil*
½ *cup chopped cooked shrimp (see index) (optional)*
1 *cup Coconut Milk (see index) (optional)*

Remove the tender leaves from the stems of the calalu and shred; chop the tender stem tips. Set these aside.

In a large heavy pot with a cover, place the meat along with the onion, garlic, thyme, chili pepper or sauce, and water. Simmer, covered, 1 hour. Add the reserved calalu and the yams, dasheen, salt and black pepper, and cook, covered, until meat and vegetables are tender. If desired, pick out the bones of the pig's tail and rub the soup through a sieve or whirl briefly in a blender. (I prefer the soup rather lumpy and textured.)

Meanwhile, in a small skillet, sauté the okra in butter, turning as needed, until lightly browned. Add to soup, along with the shrimp and/or Coconut Milk, if desired. Heat through, correct seasonings, and serve very hot. *Serves 6 liberally.*

OLIVE'S RED PEA SOUP WITH SPINNERS
(Red Kidney Bean Soup with Dumplings)

Red peas are known in most places as red kidney beans, or *frijoles colorados*, but the name red peas is used in most of the English-speaking islands of the Caribbean. For a popular and exceptionally hearty Jamaican soup that contains these red peas, here, quoted verbatim, is Mrs. Olive Whyte's recipe as it is cooked in the kitchen of Mr. and Mrs. John Hearne of Stony Hill: "Measure about a pint of peas. Wash it properly and then add it to about a quart of cold water. Then you put it to boil with your beef bones or whatever meat you want to use such as salt beef or pig's tail. Leave to boil for about two hours or more because the peas might be tough. The water will be drying out before it is being cooked but you can gently add some more cold water. Let the peas cook until they are soft. Then you crushed the peas with a fork or through the blender. When finish, put it in a strainer with some of the liquid so you can be able to get it going through the strainer very easily. Bring it back to boil. Then if you want to, you add yam, sweet potatoes, coco, and so on. A few Spinners or dumplin's add to it would make it more tasteful. Then you add your skellion and thyme and a little pepper and don't forget salt."

1 pound (about 2 cups) dried red beans (frijoles colorados, red kidney beans, California pink beans, or chili beans)
2 quarts water
¼ pound salt pork or salt beef, diced, or 1 large pig's tail, diced or chopped, or a few beef bones
2 cups chopped scallions (include the green tops), or 1 cup chopped small onions
¼ cup chopped celery (include leafy tops)
2 to 3 tablespoons finely chopped fresh parsley
½ teaspoon dried thyme, or 2 sprigs fresh thyme
1 chili pepper, seeded and chopped, or hot pepper sauce to taste
Salt and freshly ground black pepper to taste
Spinners (see following recipe)

Pick over the beans and place them in a large heavy kettle with a cover. Add salted water to cover, bring to a boil, stir once, then remove from heat and allow to stand 1 hour. Add meat (I prefer a combination of salt pork and pig's tail), scallions or onions, celery, parsley, thyme, and chili pepper or hot pepper sauce. Cover kettle and simmer until beans are very tender, usually about 2½ hours. Mix the batter for the Spinners while soup is cooking.

Put the soup through a food mill or purée lightly in blender—the soup should retain some texture. Season with salt and black pepper. Drop the Spinners onto the soup and cook, covered, until the Spinners are done, about 15 minutes. Serve soup, with about 5 Spinners to a serving, while very hot. *Serves 6.*

SPINNERS
(Dumplings)

1 cup flour (increase to 1¼ cups if cornmeal is not used)
¼ cup cornmeal (optional, but very nice)

1 teaspoon granulated or light brown sugar (optional)
1 teaspoon salt
½ teaspoon freshly ground black pepper
2 tablespoons butter, softened
Water

Sift the dry ingredients together, then rub butter into them until mixture becomes crumbly. Add enough water to make a rather stiff dough. Form into neat balls or torpedo shapes about half the size of a walnut. Cook as in preceding recipe. *Makes about 30 small dumplings.*

CHILEAN SHRIMP STEW

When I first encountered this dish some years ago in Valparaiso, Chile, that splendid seaside city near Santiago, I was unable to obtain the precise ingredients. I have since remade the stew with notable success on many occasions. Chilean shrimp, scallops, crabs, and oysters are all subtly different from North American species, but judicious substitutions can be made for almost comparable results. I like to serve the stew with crisp, oven-hot unsalted soda crackers.

2 cups dry white wine (preferably Chilean)
3 cups bottled clam juice
½ to ¾ cup minced onion
2 tablespoons minced fresh parsley (include some stems)
2 pounds fresh shrimp, peeled, deveined, and quartered
½ pound scallops, cut into quarters if very large
½ pound crabmeat, picked over
½ teaspoon freshly ground white pepper, or a dash or more hot pepper sauce
1 dozen shelled oysters, left whole or halved
¼ cup or more butter

In a heavy kettle with a cover, combine the wine, clam juice, onion, and parsley. Bring to a boil, then reduce heat and simmer, covered, 10 minutes. Add shrimp, scallops, and crabmeat. Cover again and simmer 10 minutes. Add the white pepper or hot pepper sauce, oysters, and butter, and heat gently 5 minutes. Serve very hot. *Serves 6 to 8.*

SOPA SERGIPE
(Brazilian Sweet-Potato Soup)

One can make this soup as "hot" as desired, for in certain authentic variations it is very spicy indeed. Personally, I like it better not quite as piquant as it often is in its homeland. In Brazil, especially in the northern states, sweet potatoes are exceptionally popular.

3 *tablespoons butter or dendê (palm oil, generally used in Brazil)*
1 *pound small sweet potatoes, peeled and diced*
¾ *cup diced celery (optional)*
⅓ *to* ½ *cup diced green bell pepper*
¾ *to* 1 *cup diced onion*
5 *cups well-seasoned rich chicken stock*
1 *teaspoon tapioca*
½ *cup coarsely chopped roasted peanuts*
1 *cup Coconut Cream (see index)*
⅛ *teaspoon freshly grated nutmeg*
Salt to taste
Chopped seeded chili pepper or Tabasco sauce to taste (be gentle here)

Melt the butter or heat the oil in a large heavy pot, and sauté the sweet potatoes, celery (if used), green pepper, and onion, stirring often, until just soft. Add the chicken stock, blending well. Bring to a simmer and cook about 10 minutes, stirring often. (If desired, at this point whirl hot soup in a blender or force through a sieve.) Add the tapioca and cook over low heat until tapioca is almost tender. Add the peanuts, Coconut Cream, nutmeg, salt, and chili pepper or Tabasco and heat through (do not allow to boil). Serve hot, correcting the seasonings if necessary. *Serves 6 to 8.*

SOPA DE LEGUMBRES
(Hearty Vegetable Soup)

This is just about the best and heartiest vegetable soup I know and one that appears, with variations, subtle or otherwise, in many parts of Latin America. The addition of Cornmeal Dumplings is optional, but they add a pleasant touch. This soup makes an excellent supper entrée, accompanied by a green salad, with ice cream or sherbet for dessert.

1 large meaty beef, lamb, pork, or ham bone
Water
Chicken bones (optional)
1 pound tomatoes, peeled if desired and coarsely diced
1 pound fresh spinach or other greens, coarsely chopped
1 cup diced potatoes
1 cup diagonally sliced green beans
½ cup sliced scraped carrot
½ cup coarsely chopped peeled turnip
½ cup coarsely chopped celery (include some leaves)
½ cup coarsely chopped green bell pepper
½ cup chopped mushroom caps or stems, sautéed in a bit of butter
½ cup sliced scallions (include the green tops)
½ cup coarsely chopped onion
1 clove garlic, minced or mashed
Salt and freshly ground black pepper to taste
Chopped seeded chili pepper, or Tabasco sauce, to taste (optional)

Herbs of your choice—oregano, basil, thyme, and/or marjoram—in moderation
Cornmeal Dumplings (optional; see following recipe)

Place soup bone in a pot, and add water to cover. Cover pot and bring water to a boil, skimming off and discarding any scum which rises. The chicken bones can be added at this juncture if desired; do not use an entire chicken for this recipe. Add all the vegetables and more water as needed, and cook over low heat until the vegetables are as tender as you prefer. (Other kinds of vegetables may be added or substituted.) During cooking, add salt, pepper, chili pepper or Tabasco sauce if desired, and herb or herbs of your choice.

While soup is cooking, mix the batter for the Cornmeal Dumplings, if they are to be used. Fifteen minutes before the end of cooking time (do not overcook soup), drop the dumpling batter by tablespoonfuls into the simmering soup. Cover the pot tightly and simmer soup until dumplings are done, about 15 minutes. Remove dumplings immediately. Serve the soup piping hot in commodious bowls, with several dumplings per serving. *Serves 6 to 8.*

CORNMEAL DUMPLINGS

2 *eggs*
½ *cup milk*
1 *cup cornmeal*
¼ *cup flour*
1 *teaspoon baking powder*
½ *teaspoon salt*
1 *tablespoon melted butter*

Combine the eggs and milk in a bowl and beat. Sift together the dry ingredients and add to the eggs. Stir in the melted butter. Cook as in preceding recipe. *Makes 12 or more dumplings.*

Grains & Pasta

Rice and corn are the most important grains in the American tropics, appearing almost everywhere. Both long-grain and short-grain rice are usually available, and imported wild rice —another genus of the grass family, and fiendishly expensive here—can be found occasionally. Rice, usually the long-grain form, is served as a normal starch, though plain and sweet potatoes, malanga, and other tuberous vegetables are also found on the menu.

Rice appears as a thickening agent in soups, chilled in unusual salads, and used in sumptuous desserts and crisp fried appetizers. Arroz con Pollo is among the most famous Latin American dishes, with Paella perhaps a close second. Peppery rice fritters, sometimes with shredded salt codfish folded in, are favorites.

Macaroni, spaghetti, and other forms of pasta, although usually associated with Italian or Oriental cuisines, are found in most Latin lands. Almost everyone has learned to enjoy varieties of pasta, and there are huge colonies of persons of Italian and Chinese ancestry in many parts of Latin America. In Jamaica, one can acquire freshly made Chinese noodles, useful in so many ways, as well as a wide range of pasta, either manufactured locally or imported from Trinidad. Many fine restaurants also prepare their own fresh pasta, for the procedure involved is not at all difficult. I often make green tagliatelle or lasagna noodles, using puréed calalu or the leaves of bok-choi for the coloring and flavoring ingredient.

CUBAN RICE AMBOS MUNDOS STYLE

In times past, many of us who visited Cuba often put up, when in Havana, at the Hotel Ambos Mundos on Calle Obispo, in the old part of the city. Señor Manuel Asper made everyone from Ernest Hemingway to more obscure guests feel very much at home and in the rooftop restaurant presented all sorts of unusual culinary pleasantries. This popular rice dish was served occasionally for luncheon, with fried ripe plantain sections, a salad of shredded lettuce and ripe avocado slices, and plenty of beer. Almost invariably I had guava paste with rather crumbly cream cheese for dessert, followed by a tiny cup of very rich, sweet Cuban coffee.

4 ***to*** **6** ***thin slices sirloin or other good-quality lean beef, each about ¼ inch thick and weighing*** **10** ***ounces***

Juice of one or two large ripe limes

1 ***or*** **2** ***dashes Tabasco or other hot pepper sauce (optional)***

3 ***to*** **4** ***tablespoons olive oil (preferably Spanish)***

¾ ***cup thinly sliced onions, separated into rings***

1 ***or*** **2** ***medium cloves garlic, minced or mashed***

½ cup slivered green bell pepper

1 cup finely chopped peeled ripe tomato

Salt and freshly ground black pepper to taste

2 to 3 tablespoons lard or olive oil

4 to 6 cups hot, freshly cooked, white long-grain rice

4 to 6 large eggs, fried

2 tablespoons minced fresh parsley

If necessary, pound each slice of beef briefly with a meat mallet to tenderize. Place on a plate and sprinkle with lime juice and with Tabasco or other hot pepper sauce if desired. Marinate at room temperature for about 2 hours, turning twice.

Meanwhile, heat the 3 to 4 tablespoons olive oil in a skillet over medium heat and cook the onion rings, garlic, green pepper, and tomato until soft. Season with salt and black pepper and keep warm.

Drain the marinated beef slices and dry. In another skillet heat the 2 to 3 tablespoons lard or olive oil; when very hot, quickly sauté the meat, turning only once with kitchen tongs or two forks. Spoon about 1 cup of the hot rice on each plate. Arrange meat slices on the rice, spoon on some of the vegetables, and top each serving with a fried egg. Sprinkle with parsley and serve at once. *Serves 4 to 6.*

CACEROLA CUBANA DE ARROZ Y CALABAZA
(Cuban Rice, Calabaza, and Sausage Casserole)

Calabaza is the distinctive "West Indian pumpkin," about which I waxed enthusiastic in my vegetable cookbook. In English-speaking Latin lands it is called "pumpkin" or "punkin," but it is an entirely different vegetable from the North American pie pumpkin. I enjoy it prepared in many different fashions, but especially in this very hearty Cuban dish, which is also found, with subtle variations, in many other parts of Latin America. The Spanish-type sausages are obligatory to the success of the recipe, as is true calabaza.

- **1 *tablespoon lard***
- **1½ *cups thickly sliced chorizo, butifarra, or longaniza sausage***
- **½ *cup coarsely chopped onion***
- **1 *or* 2 *small cloves garlic, minced or mashed***
- **⅓ *cup coarsely chopped green bell pepper***
- **⅓ *cup coarsely chopped scallions (include the green tops)***
- **2 *cups white long-grain rice***
- **3 *or more cups hot rich chicken stock***
- **2 *cups peeled and cubed calabaza, cooked* al dente**
- **1½ *cups cubed cooked chicken***
- ***Salt and freshly ground black pepper to taste***
- ***Saffron, or achiote or bija powder, to taste***
- **3 *large firm ripe bananas, thickly sliced, browned in butter, and kept warm***

In a large heavy skillet with a cover, melt the lard and fry the sausage slices until well browned; remove with a slotted spoon and drain on paper towels. Using the same lard, sauté the onion, garlic, green pepper, and scallions, stirring, until soft. Add the rice and cook for about 3 minutes, stirring often. Return the sausage slices to the skillet, add the chicken stock, mix well, cover, and cook over very low heat, stirring occasionally, until the rice is just tender. Add more stock if rice absorbs liquid too quickly.

Stir in the calabaza, chicken, salt and pepper, and the saffron or the achiote or bija powder, and heat through. The rice mixture should be rather dry but never overcooked. Top each portion with several slices of browned ripe banana and serve very hot. *Serves 6.*

RICE CALALU

Calalu means different things in different parts of Latin America. In most of the English-speaking areas, it is a leafy green, also called Chinese spinach or *bhaji*. It is most often used in a hearty soup, although also chopped and cooked with such seasonings as pig's tail, salt pork, and even salt cod. In this unusually tasty calalu recipe from Guyana salt beef can be used.

½ pound salt beef, soaked in cold water to remove excess salt, or ½ pound pig's tail
1 large bunch fresh calalu
¾ cup coarsely chopped white onion
2 medium or large cloves garlic, minced or mashed
2 tablespoons butter or a combination of oil and butter
6 small okras, thinly sliced
1½ cups white long-grain rice
3 cups Coconut Milk (see index)
Salt and freshly ground black or white pepper to taste

Cut salt beef or pig's tail into bite-sized pieces and cook in water to cover until tender. Drain, reserving some of the stock to cook with the rice, if desired. Wash and coarsely chop the leaves and small stems of calalu and drain well.

In a heavy pot with a cover, sauté onion and garlic in butter or oil and butter over medium heat until almost tender. Add okra slices, and cook them, stirring often, until tender. Add salt beef or pig's tail, the rice and Coconut Milk, salt and pepper, and, if desired, the reserved meat stock, unless it is too salty. Cover pot and cook until rice is tender, about 20 minutes. Stir in calalu just to heat through and soften, and serve very hot, correcting the seasoning if needed. *Serves 4 to 6 liberally.*

ARROZ CON CAMARONES
(Rice with Shrimp)

There are countless subtle variations of rice dishes in combination with shrimp or other seafood. Here is an especially pleasant and easy one from the Dominican Republic, which I enjoy with a rather standardized menu that includes a salad of chopped lettuce and wafer-thin slices of cucumbers, dressed with olive oil and lime juice; hot crusty garlic bread; and for dessert, cubes of cream cheese and guava paste.

1 ***cup white long-grain rice***
2 ***tablespoons olive oil or other cooking oil***
½ ***cup coarsely chopped onion***
1 ***large clove garlic, minced or mashed***
½ ***cup or more coarsely chopped green or red bell pepper***
1¾ ***cups shrimp stock or other fish stock or canned clam juice***
1 ***pound medium-sized fresh shrimp, peeled and deveined***
1½ ***teaspoons salt, or to taste***
½ ***teaspoon oregano or basil***
1 ***seeded chili pepper, left whole or coarsely chopped***
Seeded lime wedges for garnish (optional)

Wash the rice thoroughly, removing any discolored grains. Drain and pat completely dry with paper towels; set aside.

Heat the oil in a skillet and sauté onion and garlic; when onion is brown, remove garlic. Add the rice to the oil and onion, together with the green or red pepper. Mix thoroughly and cook for a few minutes, being careful not to brown the rice. Add the stock or clam juice, cover, and simmer over low heat 15 minutes. Stir in the shrimp, making sure that they reach the bottom of the pan. Add the salt, oregano or basil, and chili pepper, cover, and simmer over low heat until rice is fluffy and shrimp are just tender but not overcooked.

Serve very hot, garnished with wedges of seeded limes if desired. *Serves 4.*

RIZ AU DJON-DJON
(Haitian Rice with Black Mushrooms)

This recipe calls for the little black mushrooms that grow only in Haiti. Since these are rarely available outside that country, you may substitute dried black mushrooms. The rice in the original dish turns blackish.

1 *cup coarsely chopped Haitian black mushrooms, or about* 4 *to* 6 *dried black mushrooms, coarsely chopped*
2½ *cups hot water*
1 *teaspoon butter*
2 *teaspoons olive oil*
½ *pound diced lean pork*
2 *tablespoons finely chopped scallions (include the green tops)*
1 *small clove garlic, mashed*
Salt to taste
Chopped seeded chili pepper, or hot pepper sauce, to taste
1 *cup white long-grain rice*

In a bowl, blanch the Haitian black mushrooms or dried mushrooms in the hot water until the liquid turns dark in color.

Melt the butter in a heavy saucepan with a cover, add the olive oil, and sauté the pork, scallions, and garlic, stirring often, until well browned. Add salt and chili pepper or hot pepper sauce and mix well. Add the mushrooms and their liquid, bring to a boil, and stir in the rice. Cover and cook over low heat, stirring once or twice, until rice is tender and liquid largely absorbed, about 20 minutes. Correct seasoning and serve very hot. *Serves 4 to 6.*

GINGER-COCONUT RICE

This interestingly flavored rice is popular in a great many West Indian islands and other parts of Latin America, with subtle and not too subtle variants occurring almost everywhere. It is served with curries, roast meats such as lamb or pork, and especially chicken dishes.

¼ cup butter
1 large onion, thinly sliced
1 teaspoon fresh ginger, or ½ teaspoon ground dried ginger
1½ cups white long-grain rice
2¼ cups well-seasoned rich chicken stock
⅔ cup freshly grated dry coconut
2 tablespoons minced fresh parsley

In a large heavy saucepan with a cover, melt the butter, add the onion and ginger, and sauté until onion is soft, stirring occasionally. Add the rice, stir through, and continue to cook over medium heat until rice becomes translucent. Stir in the stock, cover pan, and simmer over low heat 10 minutes. Stir in the coconut and continue to cook until rice is tender, about 10 more minutes, stirring in parsley toward end of cooking. Serve at once. *Serves 6.*

FRIED CHINESE NOODLES, TROPICAL STYLE

The Chinese colonies are extensive in many parts of Latin America, and in them one can encouter luscious dishes in which local specialties are introduced into the Oriental cuisines. Fried Chinese Noodles are popular in Jamaica, Trinidad, and elsewhere.

2 quarts lightly salted water
½ pound dried Chinese noodles
4 tablespoons peanut oil
1 cup minced cooked ham or roast pork
½ cup finely sliced scallions (include the green tops)
¼ cup or more lengthwise-sliced onions
1 cup finely sliced celery or bok-choi cut on the diagonal (include some leafy tops)
1 cup strained rich beef or chicken stock
1 teaspoon cornstarch
¼ cup water
1 large egg
2 teaspoons or more soy sauce
Hot pepper sauce to taste (optional)

Bring two quarts of salted water to a boil, add noodles, and cook until just *al dente*. Drain and rinse under cold running water. Cover drained noodles and chill until ready to use.

To prepare the sauce, heat 2 tablespoons of the peanut oil over high heat in a wok or sizable skillet with a cover. Add the ham or pork, scallions, onions, and celery or bok-choi and quickly stir-fry until the vegetables are slightly cooked but still crisp. Add the stock, mix thoroughly, cover, and heat through.

In a bowl, combine the cornstarch with ¼ cup water, and blend in the egg, beating well. Add the soy sauce and hot pepper sauce (if used), and pour the mixture into a skillet. Simmer uncovered, stirring often but carefully, until sauce thickens.

Meanwhile, in another skillet or wok, heat the remaining 2 tablespoons peanut oil and stir-fry the chilled boiled noodles until lightly browned but not crisp. Arrange noodles on a heated serving platter, pour over the ham or pork sauce, and serve immediately. *Serves 4.*

PAELLA

There must be dozens of different "authentic" versions of paella, a marvelous medley of ingredients—generally seafood, chicken, and rice—that technically should be prepared in a special wide shallow pan, the *paellero*. The making of a superb paella is not something to be taken lightly in Latin America, but here is a basic but comprehensive set of instructions.

1 *dozen small clams in their shells*
1 *quart mussels in their shells (optional)*
1 *teaspoon oregano*
2 *teaspoons salt*
¼ *teaspoon freshly ground black pepper*
1 *large clove garlic, mashed or minced*
6 *tablespoons olive oil*
1 *teaspoon wine vinegar*
1 *2-pound chicken, cut into pieces*
2 *tablespoons butter*
¾ *cup cooked ham in julienne slices*
1 *or* 2 *chorizo sausages thinly sliced*
1½ *tablespoons finely chopped salt pork*
1 *cup coarsely chopped onion*
½ *to* ¾ *cup coarsely chopped green bell pepper*
1 *teaspoon chopped cilantro (fresh coriander), or* ⅛ *teaspoon ground coriander*
1 *teaspoon or more drained capers*
2 *cups peeled and coarsely chopped ripe tomatoes*
2¼ *cups white long-grain rice*
3 *cups boiling fish stock or chicken stock*
1 *cup dry white wine*
¼ *teaspoon powdered saffron, or* ½ *teaspoon achiote or bija*
2 *to* 3 *cups cooked lobster meat, in large chunks*
2 *pounds medium-sized shrimp, cooked (see index), peeled, and deveined*

2 cups drained canned tiny peas (petits pois)
1 cup halved cooked artichoke hearts
6½-ounce can pimientos, drained and cut into thin slices

Scrub the clams and, if you are using them, scrub the mussels and remove their beards. Set aside.

In a bowl combine the oregano, salt, pepper, garlic, 2 tablespoons of the olive oil, and the vinegar and mix well; rub this into the chicken. Heat the remaining 4 tablespoons of olive oil and the butter in a paellero or a large heavy skillet with a cover and brown the chicken pieces lightly over medium heat, turning with tongs when needed. Add the ham, chorizos, salt pork, onion, green pepper, cilantro or ground coriander, capers, and tomatoes. Mix well, cover, and cook about 15 minutes, stirring once. Add the rice, boiling stock, wine, and saffron or achiote or bija, and mix gently but thoroughly. Cover and cook over medium heat until rice is tender, about 20 minutes. Add the lobster meat, shrimp, peas, and artichoke hearts, cover, and heat through.

Meanwhile, in a covered kettle, steam the clams and the mussels (if used) in seasoned water until their shells open, then drain. Arrange these on top of the ingredients in the paellero or skillet, along with the pimiento slices, and serve directly from the pan, being certain that each person gets samples of everything involved. *Serves 6 to 8 liberally.*

SALSA ITALIANA BUENOS AIRES
(Pasta Sauce Buenos Aires)

Pasta frequently appears on good tropical tables, popular types being old-time elbow macaroni with sharp Cheddar cheese, cannelloni, or thin spaghetti with this sumptuous sauce. I have adapted and expanded the recipe, encountered in Buenos Aires, where a great many people of Italian ancestry live.

1 pound thick lean bacon, diced
¼ cup coarsely chopped fresh parsley
½ to ¾ cup coarsely chopped peeled ripe tomatoes
¼ teaspoon dried basil, or to taste
Salt and freshly ground black pepper to taste
¾ cup butter
1 pound fresh mushrooms, diced
2 large eggs
2 tablespoons or more freshly grated Parmesan, Romano, or pecorino cheese
Hot spaghetti or other pasta, cooked al dente
Additional freshly grated hard cheese, for the table

In a sizable skillet with a cover, cook the bacon over medium heat, stirring often, until pieces are almost crisp. Drain off all but one tablespoon fat, and reserve bacon. To this skillet add the parsley, tomatoes, basil, salt, and black pepper. Cover and simmer over reduced heat about 15 minutes, stirring once or twice.

Meanwhile, in another small skillet, melt ¼ cup of the butter, and sauté the mushrooms, stirring often, until lightly browned. When the mixture in the large skillet has cooked, add to it the mushrooms, their butter, the reserved bacon, and the remaining ½ cup butter; mix thoroughly.

In a bowl, combine the eggs, barely stirring, with about 2 tablespoons grated Parmesan or other hard cheese. Add this to the mixture in the skillet, stirring over low heat until eggs just start to set. Remove from heat at once, and pour the sauce over the hot pasta at the table, offering additional freshly grated cheese on the side. *Serves 4 to 6.*

Fish & Shellfish

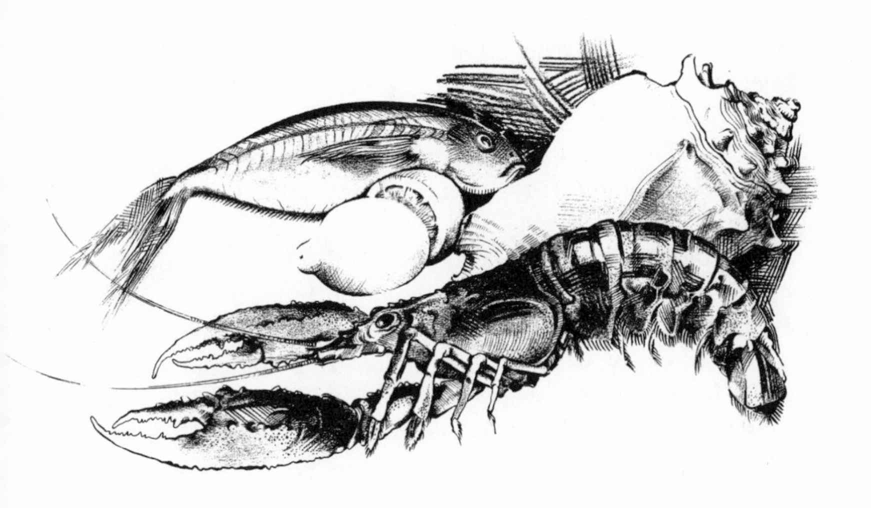

The islands and all Latin American countries that have coastlines offer the gastronomically inclined paradisiacal delights in infinite variety. Each island or country has its own favorite species, typically prepared in a fashion characteristic of the place.

Marine seafood is used in recipes ranging from appetizers to main courses, not neglecting a marvelous series of soups, chowders, and stews, these often spicy and peppery. We find such hearty dishes as Brazil's Vatapá, and fish tea from Jamaica, Barbados, and Antigua. There are thick bisques made with lobster or shrimp, all superlative, especially if the roasted shells of the crustacean have been pulverized and added to the broth along with the chopped flesh.

Scallops, oysters, abalones, and squid and octopuses (known in Jamaica by the charming name of Sea Puss) all figure in Latin American cuisine. In Nicaragua and Costa Rica there are esoteric species, such as the ugly blackish *percebes;* when one recovers from the initial shock of its appearance, one will find it luscious flavored with a few drops of lime juice and a dash of Tabasco sauce.

I have no idea how many species of fish are to be found in the Atlantic, Caribbean, or Pacific, but the total count must run into the hundreds. Many kinds are smoked, others are relegated exclusively to soups and chowders, and still others are fried, baked, or broiled (if sufficiently large, with a savory stuffing) and basted during cooking with lime juice or olive oil or butter (or a combination) until the flesh flakes easily.

One of the most memorable broiled fish I ever ate anywhere in the world was at a friend's home in Stony Hill, Jamaica; a large kingfish, stuffed with a piquant rice mixture, was basted liberally with a combination of butter and olive oil while being cooked over a bed of hot charcoal. I have prepared at my own home a conch chowder with all sorts of additions, being careful to put in the minced, lime-marinated mollusks at the very last minute, just to heat through—otherwise they are as tough as automobile tires.

Jamaica has some two hundred named rivers and sizable streams. Some of my friends on this island on occasion bring me grand supplies of little *jongas,* a distinctive species of crawfish found in the Negro River and its tributaries in the parish of St. Thomas. These are either poached until they are a rich, red color or, with tremendous, tedious labor, made into a thick bisque. In the chill streams of the parish of Portland, there is a rather nasty-appearing blackish mollusk known as *bussu,* which, when cooked with very hot Jamaican peppers, onions, and garlic, affords one a splendid and distinctive soup. Almost every other Latin American island or country is also blessed with habitats for fresh-water fish and shellfish and has comparable delights, from rainbow trout to clams.

BACALAO A LA VIZCAINA
(Biscayan Salt Cod)

Dried salted cod, called *bacalao* in Spanish and *bacalhau* in Portuguese, is one of the staple delights in many parts of Latin America. This version of a flavorful salt fish dish is found in Cuba and many islands and mainland countries southward. It tastes infinitely better if prepared in advance, refrigerated well covered overnight, and reheated the next day. I enjoy serving it with boiled potatoes, a basil-touched salad, and a suitable wine.

2 *pounds dried salt cod*
3 *tablespoons olive oil*
1½ *to* 2 *cups finely chopped onion*
4 *medium to large cloves garlic, minced*
Chopped seeded chili pepper, or Tabasco sauce, to taste
1 *cup minced or grated raw potato*
2 *cups or more finely chopped ripe tomato, peeled and seeded if desired*
½ *cup finely chopped green bell pepper*
1 *bay leaf, torn into pieces*
Salt and freshly ground black pepper to taste

Soak salt cod overnight in cold water to cover. The next day, discard water and replace with fresh cold water to cover; soak fish again until they become pliable, then drain.

Place the fish in a large heavy container, cover with fresh cold water, and bring to a boil, then remove from heat. Reserving the stock, cut the fish into small serving pieces, removing all bones.

Heat the oil in a casserole, and slowly fry the onion and garlic, stirring, until lightly browned. Add the chili peppers or Tabasco, then place the minced potato over this mixture.

Press the tomato through a fine sieve onto the potato, and sprinkle with chopped green pepper. Arrange the fish on top and add some of the reserved stock, the bay leaf, and salt and pepper. Simmer over very low heat, stirring occasionally, until the fish is very tender and the sauce is thickened and somewhat reduced. If necessary, add a bit more stock. *Serves 6.*

PESCADO ASADO CON ARROZ
(Baked Fish with Rice Stuffing)

This is a marvelous way to prepare firm-fleshed fish such as red snapper or mangrove snapper. If any stuffing is left over, bake it alongside the fish in a separate casserole dish, perhaps basting it with some of the fish juices. Be careful not to overcook the fish. The original recipe came from the Caribbean coast of Costa Rica.

3- or 4-pound cleaned whole red snapper or mangrove snapper, or comparable firm-fleshed fish
Salt and freshly ground black pepper
2 tablespoons butter
3 tablespoons or more minced onion
2 tablespoons minced green bell pepper
3 cups freshly cooked white long-grain rice
3 tablespoons coarsely chopped ripe tomato
2 to 3 tablespoons slivered Brazil nuts or cashews toasted in butter
2 to 3 tablespoons melted butter
Minced fresh parsley
Seeded lime or lemon wedges

Rinse the cleaned fish and pat dry with paper towels. Lightly sprinkle inside and out with salt and pepper and set aside.

To make the stuffing, melt the 2 tablespoons butter in a sizable skillet and sauté the onion and green pepper, stirring often, until just softened. Stir in the cooked rice, tomato, and nuts. Mix gently but well, then loosely stuff the fish, closing the cavity with skewers or kitchen twine. Place the stuffed fish in a large, shallow, buttered baking dish, brush liberally with the melted butter, and bake in a preheated 350° oven, basting frequently with the juices. The fish is done when it flakes easily if touched with a toothpick or fork.

Place the fish on a heated platter, sprinkle with parsley, and garnish with lime or lemon wedges. *Serves 4.*

BAKED MACKEREL, CORA'S STYLE

This baked fresh Spanish mackerel dish, served on several of the Leeward Islands, is highly recommended. It seems best when accompanied by buttered boiled potatoes with lots of seasoning and minced fresh parsley, a cabbage slaw with a rather piquant dressing, heated crusty bread, and a dry white wine. Dessert can be homemade tropical-fruit ice or sherbet.

1 *teaspoon salt*
½ *teaspoon freshly ground black pepper*
⅓ *cup flour*
1 3-*pound mackerel, cleaned and split*
3 *tablespoons olive oil or a combination of olive oil and other cooking oil*
3 *cups diced ripe tomatoes*
3 *cups sliced scallions (include the green tops)*
1 *medium or large clove garlic, minced or mashed*
1 *teaspoon light brown or granulated sugar*
½ *cup dry white wine*

Combine the salt, pepper, and flour and lightly dust the split fish. Heat the oil in a skillet and quickly brown the mackerel halves on both sides, turning with care. Place the fish, skin side down, in a shallow baking pan with a cover. Sprinkle with the tomatoes, scallions, garlic, and sugar. Pour the wine around the fish, cover, and bake in a preheated 350° oven, basting occasionally, for about 12 minutes. Remove the fish and arrange it on a platter; serve the sauce in a separate bowl. *Serves 4 to 6.*

SALMON TROPICALE

I first found this spectacular dish at a posh hostelry in Guyana, where canned salmon was used to excellent advantage (fresh salmon are of course not available). I have since made it on several occasions for special guests, all of whom enjoyed it tremendously. So did the cook, namely me.

4 *whole coconuts*
1½ *tablespoons butter*
½ *cup finely chopped onion*
1 *medium clove garlic, minced or mashed*
¼ *teaspoon freshly ground black pepper*
Hot pepper sauce to taste
1 *to* 2 *teaspoons curry powder, preferably homemade (see index)*
6 *tablespoons flour*
16*-ounce can prime salmon, drained and picked over (reserve liquid)*
2½ *cups coconut water*
4 *tablespoons chopped mango chutney*
½ *teaspoon or more salt*
1 *to* 1½ *tablespoons lime juice*
¾ *cup diced and peeled partially ripe papaya*
Flour and water, for a paste
Cooked white long-grain rice, served hot
Accompaniments: mango chutney, chopped seeded cucumber, and chopped salted peanuts

Carefully saw off the tops of the coconuts, drain coconuts, and reserve the liquid. Remove the coconut meat from the tops of the nuts, leaving meat in the bottoms and reserving both the top and bottom shells. Grate the coconut meat and toast it in a 200° oven, stirring often, until nicely browned; set aside.

In a large skillet with a cover, melt the butter and sauté the onion and garlic until just soft. Add the black pepper, pepper sauce, and curry powder. Cook 5 minutes, stirring often, then sprinkle in the flour and blend. Add the liquid from the salmon can and 2½ cups of the reserved coconut water. Cook, stirring often, until the sauce is smooth and thickened.

Flake the salmon into the sauce, then add the chutney, salt, lime juice, and papaya. Spoon this mixture into the coconut shells, replace the tops, and seal with a paste made of flour and water—be generous with the paste. Carefully arrange filled coconuts upright in a sizable baking dish. To stabilize them, set them in the baking dish in metal rings such as flan rings or empty tuna fish cans from which you have removed the bottoms as well as the tops. Pour cold water around them to a depth of 1 inch, and bake in a preheated 350° oven 1 hour. Allow your guests to crack off the coconut tops at the table. Serve the rice separately, over which the filling can be spooned, and accompaniments of mango chutney, chopped seeded cucumber, chopped salted peanuts, and the reserved toasted coconut. *Serves 4.*

HUACHINANGO A LA VERACRUZANA
(Red Snapper Veracruz Style)

Very fresh fish can be prepared tastefully in a great many ways. One of my favorite Latin American *pescado* recipes is this Mexican classic, which I first encountered on its home grounds many years ago in the picturesque coastal city of Veracruz. It is an elegant, delectable creation, for which I quote Elisabeth Lambert Ortiz's recipe.

6 large red-snapper fillets
Flour
Salt and freshly ground black pepper to taste
½ cup olive oil
1 medium or large onion, finely chopped
1 medium or large clove garlic, minced
2 cups tomato purée
⅛ teaspoon ground cinnamon
⅛ teaspoon ground cloves
3 canned* jalapeño *chili peppers, seeded and cut into strips
Juice of ½ lemon or lime
½ teaspoon sugar
12 small new potatoes, cooked and peeled
Butter
3 slices white bread, cut into triangles
½ cup pimiento-stuffed green olives, halved

Dust the fillets lightly with flour that has been seasoned with salt and pepper. Heat ¼ cup of the oil in a large skillet and sauté fish on both sides until golden and easily flaked; set aside and keep warm.

Add the remaining oil, onion, and garlic to a skillet and fry until onion is translucent but not brown. Add the tomato purée, cinnamon, and cloves and cook, stirring, about 5 minutes; add the chilies, lemon or lime juice, sugar, and salt and pepper to taste, and bring to a boil. Reduce heat, add the cooked potatoes and fish, and just heat through (do not cook). Meanwhile, melt a little butter in a skillet; when hot, sauté bread triangles until light brown.

To serve, cover the bottom of a hot platter with the sauce. Arrange the fish, surround with the potatoes, and garnish with the olives and fried bread. *Serves 6.*

BAHAMIAN CONCH FRITTERS

Conchs (pronounced "konks") are common in many Latin American lands and on relatively frequent occasions figure prominently in their cuisines. In the Bahamas, in particular, fried conchs and conch fritters, stews, and salads are sometimes served more than once daily. Baby conchs, although not always available, are infinitely more tender than mature ones. The muscle of the conch is the edible portion, and this can be very durable indeed. Tenderizing is usually done by pounding with the side of a heavy plate or a kitchen mallet, and then perhaps marinating in lime juice. This recipe comes from the Bahamas.

***6** conchs, preferably young ones*
***1** cup finely chopped onion*
***½** cup coarsely chopped peeled tomato*
***2** cloves garlic, minced or mashed*
***½** green bell pepper, coarsely chopped*
***1** teaspoon salt*
***1** cup coarse cracker crumbs*
***¼** cup chopped fresh parsley*
***3** eggs, separated*
***4** tablespoons butter or a combination of oil and butter*
Tartar sauce, or ½ cup melted butter, mixed with 1 tablespoon fresh lemon or lime juice
Tabasco sauce or other hot pepper sauce to taste (optional, but typical)

Finely grind or mince the conchs and combine them with the onion, tomato, garlic, green pepper, salt, cracker crumbs, and parsley. Beat the egg yolks slightly; beat the whites in another bowl until stiff; fold whites into yolks. Add to the conch mixture.

Heat the butter or combination of oil and butter in a

skillet and drop in the batter by spoonfuls. Fry, turning once, until well browned on both sides, and serve with Tartar Sauce or lemon or lime butter; and with Tabasco or other hot pepper sauce if desired. *Serves 6 to 8.*

LOBSTER ACAPULCO

This is a favorite dish on the western coast of Mexico, and its fame has spread throughout most parts of the American tropics. It is a delectable creation and remarkably easy to prepare.

2 or 3 medium-sized lobsters, or 6 to 8 small ("chicken") lobsters, cooked until tender in a well-seasoned stock

2 tablespoons each of butter and olive oil, or ¼ cup olive oil

1 large clove garlic, minced or mashed

2 large green chili peppers, seeded and coarsely chopped

¾ cup olive oil

¼ cup fresh lime juice

1 or 2 dashes hot pepper sauce

1 teaspoon salt

1 cup or slightly more wafer-thin slices small Bermuda or sweet onion, chilled

2 large oranges, thinly sliced, seeded, and chilled

Cut the lobster meat into bite-sized pieces and set aside. In a large skillet, heat the butter and olive oil together (preferred) or heat the ¼ cup olive oil, and sauté the lobster with the garlic, turning often. Remove with a slotted spoon to a bowl, and combine with the chili peppers, ¾ cup olive oil, lime juice, hot pepper sauce, and salt. Cover and chill at least one hour.

Serve garnished with onion and orange slices. *Serves 6 to 8.*

AGGIE'S CURRIED LOBSTER SOUFFLÉ

One of Jamaica's most glorious private homes is situated beyond Port Maria, in the parish of St. Mary, and there I have had the privilege of staying on a number of memorable occasions. I shall never forget the evening when, with an incredible full moon looming over the gardens, my hostess served this elegant soufflé. As the entrée, it was accompanied by crisp, hot East Indian *pappadums,* so light that mine actually floated off the table in a soft tropical breeze!

1 *cup milk*
¼ *cup freshly grated dry coconut*
½ *teaspoon light brown sugar*
4 *tablespoons butter*
¼ *cup grated onion*
¼*-inch piece fresh ginger, finely chopped*
1 *small clove garlic, mashed*
1½ *teaspoons curry powder, preferably homemade (see index)*
3 *tablespoons flour*
4 *egg yolks, well beaten*
1 *cup well-drained canned tiny peas (petits pois)*
1 *cup shredded cooked, well-seasoned lobster*
4 *egg whites, beaten until stiff with salt and freshly ground white pepper to taste*

Combine the milk with the grated coconut and brown sugar in a saucepan and bring just to a boil. Remove from heat immediately, stir well, and allow to stand 1 hour.

Melt the butter in a skillet and briefly sauté the onion over medium heat. Add the ginger and garlic and continue to cook, stirring constantly, until onion becomes soft. Stir in the curry powder, then gradually add the milk-coconut mixture, and cook over low heat, stirring often, about 10 minutes. Reserve ⅓ cup or more of the milk-coconut mixture and blend with the flour to make a smooth, thin paste; stir this into the sauce and continue to cook, stirring constantly, 5 minutes.

In another saucepan, over low heat, heat the egg yolks and very gradually add the sauce, stirring briskly to prevent yolks from cooking too quickly. Alternately stir in the peas and lobster meat, mixing thoroughly. Fold in the stiffly beaten egg whites and pour the mixture into a buttered 1½-quart soufflé dish or 6 buttered individual soufflé dishes or ramekins. Bake in a preheated 375° oven, about 40 minutes for the large soufflé, 25 to 30 minutes for the individual ones. Serve immediately, accompanied by hot crisp-fried Indian *pappadums,* if you have them. *Serves 6.*

COQUILLES À LA PAUL
(Scallops, Paul's Style)

A number of varieties of scallops occur throughout most parts of Latin America and also frequently appear on menus, either raw with just a dash of lemon or lime juice and a touch of hot sauce, or cooked lightly in stews or in other delightful creations. Here is a perfectly marvelous version of scallops which I encountered many years ago in French Guiana. It was served in handsome big scallop shells, which oddly enough had been imported from the Philippines. Paul, who was the chef, was from Brazil.

2 *pounds fresh sea scallops, rinsed in cold water and drained*
1½ *cups dry white wine*
3 *whole black peppercorns*
½ *small bay leaf*
2 *teaspoons ground toasted cashews*
⅓ *cup boiling water*
6 *tablespoons butter*
⅓ *cup finely chopped onion*

½ teaspoon curry powder, homemade if possible (see index)
2 tablespoons flour
2 teaspoons tomato purée
1 cup Coconut Milk (see index)
2 teaspoons fresh lime juice
3 tablespoons heavy cream
Salt and freshly ground black pepper to taste
Minced fresh parsley
Seeded lime wedges
Hot pepper sauce

Place scallops (cut into halves, if desired) in a heavy saucepan with the wine, peppercorns, and bay leaf. Bring to a boil and poach 3 to 5 minutes, depending upon the size of the scallops. Remove pan from heat and let scallops cool in the liquid. Meanwhile, place the cashews in a small bowl, cover with the boiling water, mixing thoroughly, and allow to stand, stirring occasionally, 15 minutes.

Melt the butter in a sizable skillet and sauté the onion over medium heat until soft, stirring often. Stir in the curry powder and cook for a minute, then gradually blend in the flour, cooking and stirring for an additional minute or so, until well blended. Combine the tomato purée with the Coconut Milk and carefully blend in, a little at a time, stirring and cooking after each addition. Gradually add the nut-water mixture in tiny amounts, stirring well after each addition. Stir in the lime juice, then the cream, and, over lowest heat, simmer, stirring, until a smooth, flavorful sauce is obtained.

Add the scallops, season with salt and pepper, stir and spoon into scallop shells. Sprinkle with parsley, and serve hot, with lime wedges; offer hot pepper sauce on the side. *Serves 4.*

ALEX'S BASIC RECIPE FOR COOKING SHRIMP

Here is one of my favorite methods for cooking shrimp. I developed it to eliminate the sometimes strong iodine taste that some of these crustaceans possess when improperly prepared.

1 *quart water*
5 or 6 *whole cloves*
1 *tablespoon salt*
½ *teaspoon freshly ground black pepper*
½ *teaspoon oregano*
3 *tablespoons malt or cider vinegar*
1 *pound fresh shrimp*

Put the water into a large saucepan with a cover, along with the cloves, salt, pepper, oregano, and vinegar, and bring to a rolling boil, covered. Add the shrimp and return to a boil. Reduce heat so water barely simmers, cover, and simmer 2 to 5 minutes—never longer. Remove from heat. Drain and rinse the shrimp immediately under cold running water. Remove the shells, and then the black back veins, if desired—they are gritty but it is really not necessary to take them out. Use in the recipes for shrimp dishes. Be very careful not to overcook.

CHARCOAL-GRILLED SHRIMP

When roasted over charcoal on a brazier or old-fashioned coal pot, shrimp take on a superlative flavor and texture not otherwise obtainable. This delightful recipe, easy and exceptionally tasty, is popular in varied forms in most Latin American countries. I like to serve the shrimp with plenty of hot fluffy rice or a mushroom risotto and a big tossed green salad. Plenty of cold beer is the perfect beverage with this meal.

1 cup unsweetened pineapple juice
⅓ cup soy sauce
3 tablespoons honey, or to taste
1 tablespoon butter
½ teaspoon, more or less to taste, slivered fresh ginger or ground dried ginger
1½ tablespoons cornstarch
2 pounds medium or jumbo fresh shrimp, peeled and deveined

Mix ¾ cup of the pineapple juice, the soy sauce, honey, butter, and ginger in a saucepan; bring to a boil. Blend the cornstarch into the remaining pineapple juice and stir into the sauce. Remove from heat and let cool slightly. Pour the sauce over the shrimp, making sure that all are coated with the marinade; cover and refrigerate 1 to 2 hours.

Place shrimp on skewers and broil over medium-hot charcoal, 8 to 10 minutes, turning to brown evenly; if desired, brush with the marinade. Do not overcook, and serve while very hot. *Serves about 6 liberally.*

INDONESIAN SHRIMP PATTIES

These distinctive patties originated in Indonesia but have been happily adopted, complete with their special dip, in the cuisines of the Netherlands Antilles and Surinam. Lobster can be used instead of shrimp.

1 pound medium-sized shrimp
¼ cup finely chopped scallions (include the green tops)
1 large egg, slightly beaten
2 tablespoons flour
½ cup peanut or soy oil
Javanese Dip (see following recipe)

Following the directions on page 88, cook the shrimp until barely done. Drain thoroughly, let cool, and peel off shells, and chop shrimp fine. Add the scallions, egg, and flour, mixing well, and form into flat cakes about 1¼ inches or slightly more in diameter.

Heat the oil until very hot and sauté the shrimp cakes until just lightly brown on both sides; drain on paper towels. Serve at once with Javanese Dip, along with beer, or as an appetizer with cocktails. *Serves 4 to 6.*

JAVANESE DIP

1 *cup fish stock (Japanese* **dashi-konbu,** *a mixture of seaweed and grated dried bonita fish flakes, makes an excellent stock)*

3 *tablespoons dry sherry or sake*

3 *tablespoons or less soy sauce (preferably Japanese Kikkoman)*

½ *teaspoon shredded fresh ginger or ¼ teaspoon ground dried ginger*

1 *teaspoon finely chopped scallion tops*

In a saucepan bring to a boil the stock, sherry or sake, and soy sauce. While still hot, pour it over tiny pinches of fresh or dried ginger and scallion tops in small individual dipping dishes. Keep the unused dip warm until needed. *Makes enough for 6 servings.*

EMPADINHAS DE CAMARÃO
(*Shrimp Turnovers*)

In various parts of Latin America, these little pastries are variously known as *empanadas, empanaditas,* turnovers, or patties, as well as by other regional names. The pastry is filled with a variety of foods, such as peppery minced vegetables, mixtures of vegetables and ground meat or seafood, and exceedingly hot spicy meat, ground or chopped. They are highly popular; for thousands of persons, many of them school children, on such islands as Jamaica, meat patties and a soft drink or crushed ice flavored with sweet fruit syrup form the normal luncheon fare. The pastry is often tinted with bija powder or yellow food coloring, sometimes to a rather startling degree. These shrimp-filled empadinhas are from Brazil.

Enough of your favorite pastry to make* 12 3-*inch turnovers
1½ *to* 2 *tablespoons olive oil or a combination of oil and butter*
¾ *cup finely chopped onion*
1 *large clove garlic, mashed or minced*
1½ *cups peeled, coarsely chopped ripe tomatoes*
1 *pound medium-sized fresh shrimp, cooked (see index) and minced*
Dash or more hot pepper sauce
Salt and freshly ground black pepper to taste
2 *tablespoons finely chopped stuffed or pitted green olives*
2 *tablespoons finely chopped fresh parsley*
1 *egg yolk, beaten lightly*

Prepare the pastry, roll out to a thickness of about ⅛-inch on a lightly floured board, and cut out twelve circles about 6 inches in diameter.

Heat the oil or oil-butter combination in a sizable skillet with a cover, and sauté onion and garlic, stirring until soft. Add the tomatoes, minced shrimp, hot pepper sauce, salt, and black pepper. Simmer, covered, for a couple of minutes, then stir in the olives and parsley. Correct the seasoning (this filling should be rather piquant) and divide mixture evenly among the pastry circles, spooning it just off the center of each. Fold over turnovers, brush edges with cold water, and pinch tightly together. Place empadinhas on a baking sheet and brush tops with beaten egg yolk. Bake in a preheated 400° oven until pastry is nicely browned and crusty, approximately 20 minutes. Empadinhas ideally should be served directly from the baking sheets while very hot. *Serves 6.*

TRINIDAD SHRIMP CURRY

There doubtless are as many variations of shrimp and lobster curries as there are islands and countries in Latin America. Each ethnic group has its own special way with these crustaceans. Here, from Trinidad, is a fine example of a good authentic East Indian shrimp curry. Serve it with plenty of hot steamed rice, and perhaps with iced beer for a hot-day picnic.

2 ***pounds medium-sized fresh shrimp***
3 ***tablespoons fresh lime juice***
3 ***tablespoons butter***
3 ***tablespoons cooking oil***
2 ***large onions, sliced***
4 ***tomatoes, peeled and chopped***
2 ***medium to large bay leaves (crushed in a mortar if desired)***

1 teaspoon turmeric
1 teaspoon coriander
1 teaspoon cumin
½ teaspoon black mustard seed
1 teaspoon freshly ground black pepper, or Tabasco sauce to taste
½ to 1 teaspoon salt
2 cups water
Hot fluffy white long-grain rice
Pimientos, cut into strips, for garnish

Boil the shrimp according to the directions on page 88. When just pink in color, drain and let cool, then remove the shells and the back veins. Sprinkle with lime juice and set aside.

Heat the butter and oil in a skillet and sauté the onions and tomatoes along with the bay leaves, turmeric, coriander, cumin, mustard seed, pepper or Tabasco sauce, and salt. Cover and simmer over low heat 10 minutes. Add the shrimp and the 2 cups water, cover, and simmer about 30 minutes. Serve garnished with strips of pimiento, atop of or alongside plenty of hot, fluffy rice. *Serves 4 liberally.*

VATAPÁ
(Brazilian Shrimp and Cornmeal)

There are a great many recipes for this traditional Brazilian dish, but here is one of which I am especially fond. This is a very hearty culinary delight, one perhaps to be accompanied only by a crisp lettuce salad and a bottle of the excellent Brazilian beer, Brahma Chopps.

2 tablespoons dendê (palm oil) or olive oil
1½ cups finely chopped onion
1 medium or large clove garlic, minced or mashed
Chopped seeded chili peppers to taste
4 cups water
2 teaspoons salt
1 bay leaf
1½ pounds medium-sized fresh shrimp, shelled and deveined
1 pound snapper, cod, or halibut, boned and cut into 3-inch chunks
1½ to 1¾ cups Coconut Milk (see index)
½ pound dried shrimp, finely chopped (available in Latin and Japanese grocery stores)
2 cups finely ground roasted peanuts
½ cup yellow cornmeal
¼ cup butter, softened
Salt and freshly ground black pepper to taste

In a sizable heavy kettle or pot, heat the oil and sauté the onion, garlic, and chili peppers 10 minutes, stirring often. Add the water, salt, and bay leaf, bring to a boil, and add the fresh shrimp and the fish. Cook over low heat 10 minutes. With a slotted spoon recover the shrimp and fish and reserve; strain the stock and reserve.

Combine the Coconut Milk with the dried shrimp and peanuts in a medium-sized saucepan, bring to a boil, and simmer over low heat 15 minutes, stirring often. Strain; reserve shrimp. Combine the reserved stock with the peanut–Coconut Milk mixture, bring to a boil, and stir in the cornmeal. Simmer 30 minutes over low heat, stirring frequently.

Blend in the butter and the reserved shrimp and fish, season with salt and black pepper, and serve very hot in deep bowls. *Serves 6 to 8.*

MARISCOS CON FRUTAS
(Argentine Fruited Seafood)

In Argentina, where fruits in overwhelming array abound, inventive cooks have devised a series of marvelous dishes combining fruit with diverse meats. At first glance, the roster of ingredients may seem rather odd, but rest assured that our Argentine friends know very well what they are about.

2 medium-sized lobsters (about 1½ pounds each) cooked
1 cup white long-grain rice
7 tablespoons butter
Ground saffron, or achiote or bija, to taste
2½ cups boiling strained rich chicken stock
1 pound medium-sized fresh shrimp, cooked (see index), peeled, and deveined (cut lengthwise into halves, if desired)
¾ pound picked-over, flaked, cooked crabmeat
3 tablespoons finely chopped onion
½ teaspoon or less minced garlic
2 tablespoons finely chopped green bell pepper
1 tablespoon or more flour
1½ cups milk
Salt to taste
1 or 2 dashes Tabasco or other hot pepper sauce
¼ cup slivered pimientos
½ cup drained canned tiny peas (petits pois)
3 oranges, peeled, thinly sliced, and seeded
1 or 2 large ripe avocados, peeled and at last moment thinly sliced
2 grapefruit, peeled and carefully sectioned
Seeded lime or lemon wedges

Remove meat from lobsters, cut into neat cubes or slices, and set aside.

In a saucepan with a tight lid, combine the rice, 3 tablespoons of the butter, the saffron or achiote or bija, and the boiling chicken stock. Mix thoroughly, bring to a quick boil, then cover and simmer over reduced heat until rice is tender and liquid absorbed (about 20 minutes).

Meanwhile, in a heavy saucepan with a cover, melt the remaining 4 tablespoons of butter, add the lobster, shrimp, crabmeat, onion, garlic, and green pepper, and gently sauté, stirring, for a few minutes. Sprinkle with the flour, mix thoroughly, then gradually add the milk, stirring after each addition and cooking until sauce is somewhat thickened. Cover and simmer 5 minutes, then add the salt and Tabasco sauce. Remove from heat and keep warm.

When the rice is done, very gently stir in the pimientos and peas. Press the hot rice mixture into 8 custard cups or timbale molds, then quickly but carefully unmold them around the margin of a heated large serving platter, ideally an unadorned white one.

Quickly reheat the seafood mixture (don't boil) and turn it into the center of the platter. Arrange the orange and avocado slices, grapefruit sections, and lime or lemon wedges around the platter, and serve at once. *Serves 8.*

ZARZUELA ISLA DE PINOS
(Isle of Pines Shellfish Stew)

In the Spanish language, *zarzuela* generally means a particularly Spanish form of light opera. But culinarily, a zarzuela is a wonderful medley of seafood in a sort of stew, and is singularly refreshing. One encounters this dish from Cuba southward, with divergences all along the way. This is an especially tasty version from the Isla de Pinos, off the south Cuban coast, which I ate with enjoyment whenever it was available. The original recipe from Spain calls for mussels in their shells. But a long time ago I decided that these shellfish, despite their pleasantries, require too much work and too much worry about season and edibility (often dubious) and, except for ornament, do not add much to a dish. Hence I have substituted canned minced clams here.

¼ cup olive oil (preferably Spanish)
1 cup or more finely chopped onion
1 large clove garlic, minced or mashed
1 large green bell pepper, coarsely chopped
2 pounds ripe fresh tomatoes, peeled if desired and coarsely chopped, or a 17-ounce can Italian plum tomatoes (undrained)
½ cup finely ground almonds (optional, but typical)
2 teaspoons salt
½ teaspoon freshly ground black pepper
1 large bay leaf, crumbled
⅛ teaspoon powdered saffron, or ¼ teaspoon ground annatto or bija
1 cup dry white or red wine (I prefer the latter)
1 to 2 tablespoons fresh lime or lemon juice
10 ½-ounce can minced clams, undrained
1 pound medium-sized fresh shrimp, shelled and deveined, left whole or cut into bite-sized pieces
½ pound sea scallops, cut into halves if large
1½ pounds fresh or frozen lobster meat, cooked and cut into bite-sized pieces

In a heavy kettle or pot with a cover, heat the olive oil and over medium heat cook the onion, garlic, and green pepper until tender, usually about 5 minutes. Add the tomatoes and their liquid, the almonds (if used), salt, black pepper, bay leaf, and saffron, annatto, or bija. Blend in wine and lime or lemon juice and cook uncovered over high heat until the amount of liquid is reduced by about half. Add the clams and their liquid, the shrimp, scallops, and lobster, and cover and cook until shrimp are tender, about 5 to 8 minutes (do not overcook). Correct seasoning, and serve very hot. *Serves 8 to 10.*

CRAPAUDS
(Fried Frogs' Legs)

The cool, wet mountain forests of Dominica and Montserrat are the habitat of the giant bullfrogs known as crapauds. Also called "mountain chickens," they are fried, stewed, or used in a sort of spicy soup, all admirable delicacies.

½ cup grated onion
2 to 3 medium cloves garlic, minced or mashed
½ teaspoon ground cloves
1 teaspoon or more salt
½ teaspoon freshly ground black pepper
1 tablespoon cider vinegar
6 pairs fresh crapauds' legs (if you are where they can be found), or 12 pairs fresh medium-sized frogs' legs, split in half
1 cup olive oil or combination of olive and vegetable oil
1 cup flour
Seeded lime wedges

Combine the onion, garlic, ground cloves, salt, pepper, and vinegar in a bowl. Add the frogs' legs and marinate one hour or more, turning often.

Heat the oil in a heavy skillet. Dry the frogs' legs on paper towels, then dredge with the flour. Fry a few at a time, about 5 minutes on each side. Drain on paper towels and serve hot, with lime wedges. *Serves 6.*

Poultry & Eggs

In Latin America there are abundant supplies of chicken, duck, and turkey (the last occurs as a wild bird in Mexico and Guatemala), as well as guinea hen, pigeon, and dove. There are also a considerable number of wild species of fowl, some of which are rather odd in flavor and appearance, such as the coot, some of the wild ducks, and smaller birds, such as parrots.

Chicken is certainly the favorite fowl, being prepared in every island and mainland country in a marvelous variety of fashions, such as the *pibil* of Yucatan, Belize's Escabeche de Pollo, and the widespread Arroz con Pollo, with dozens of regional variations, all delectable. Duck is stuffed with coconut, served in the French fashion with orange slices, and braised with rice and olives in a hearty dish. Turkey is anointed with the extraordinary Mexican Mole Sauce to form a culinary spectacular, or is roasted over charcoal, with a peppery stuffing baked separately. Guinea hens, pigeons, and doves are broiled or stuffed and usually served with side sauces, and the wild birds—even parrots—can be rather good when broiled over a wood fire or a bed of charcoal and basted with a buttery sauce.

Soups and stews are made from all these birds. Hearty chicken and duck soups with dumplings or other accouterments appear in the cuisines of many Caribbean islands as well as other parts of Latin America, requiring few additions to make a most satisfactory supper menu. The rich Brazilian chicken soup, *canja,* in particular, should be sampled by everyone. Arroz con Pollo and the stewlike *asopaos* of Puerto Rico and the Virgin Islands use chicken admirably, and the variants are well worth study by the good cook. Some are peppery, others are colored with saffron or achiote or bija, and yet others are seasoned with oregano or cilantro.

ENCHILADAS DE POLLO
(Chicken Enchiladas)

Though Costa Rica lies some distance from Mexico and its intricate "corn kitchens," tortillas frequently appear at tables in San José and Cartago and other cities and towns. Tico (Costa Rican) cookery is often rather peppery. These enchiladas, often served in Costa Rica, are delectable creations.

½ to ¾ cup finely chopped seasoned cooked chicken

½ cup finely chopped pitted or stuffed Spanish green olives

½ cup seeded or seedless raisins, plumped in boiling water and drained

12 freshly made or softened tortillas

2 large eggs, beaten lightly

½ cup lard

2 tablespoons olive oil or a combination of olive and other cooking oil

1 cup finely chopped onion

½ cup finely chopped green bell pepper

2 cups coarsely chopped ripe, peeled tomatoes

Chopped seeded red chili peppers, or hot pepper sauce, to taste

Salt and freshly ground black pepper to taste

Shredded sharp cheese

Minced small white onion or finely sliced green scallion tops

Shredded crisp lettuce

Thoroughly but gently combine the chicken, olives, and raisins in a bowl. Dip the tortillas into the beaten eggs. Divide the chicken mixture evenly among the tortillas, spooning a little down the center of each one, then roll up. Heat the lard in a skillet; when hot, fry stuffed tortillas quickly. Set aside.

In another skillet, heat the oil and sauté the onion and green pepper, about 8 minutes, stirring. Add the tomatoes, cover, and continue to cook over low heat, stirring once or twice, until all vegetables are soft and well blended. Add the chili peppers or hot pepper sauce, blend, and simmer a few minutes. Add salt and black pepper. Pour this sauce over the stuffed tortillas and sprinkle with cheese and minced onion or sliced scallion tops. Arrange the shredded lettuce around the tortillas and serve hot. *Serves 6.*

POLLO SAN SALVADOR
(Chicken Salvadoreño Style)

Chicken, turkey, and various wild fowls, often cooked with cilantro, figure prominently in the cuisine of El Salvador. Friends in the capital city served this main dish on my last visit, together with fried ripe plantains, a marvelous local version of Caesar salad with home-grown romaine lettuce, crusty potato pancakes, and for dessert a selection of indigenous fruits of the season with a special cheese from the volcanic highlands.

2 *tablespoons butter*
2 *tablespoons olive oil (preferably Spanish)*
4 *large onions, thinly sliced lengthwise*
3 *tablespoons tomato paste*
2 *teaspoons Worcestershire sauce*
1 *or* 2 *dashes hot pepper sauce*
½ *cup dry red wine*
1 *tablespoon minced cilantro (fresh coriander), or ¼ teaspoon ground coriander*
2 2½*-pound chickens, halved, well-seasoned, broiled over charcoal, and served hot*

In a heavy skillet over medium heat, melt the butter, add the oil, and sauté the onions until soft and golden. Blend the Worcestershire and hot pepper sauces with the red wine, and stir into the onions, along with the tomato paste and cilantro. Simmer until flavors are nicely blended, then add the hot, freshly broiled chicken halves. Serve with white or sweet potatoes, yams, cassava, or rice. *Serves 4 liberally.*

ARROZ CON POLLO CATALINA
(Catalina's Chicken and Rice)

Every country in the American tropics has its own version of Arroz con Pollo and virtually every inventive cook adds special touches to this famous dish. Here is my friend Catalina's version, which she serves with a big tossed green salad, heated crusty Cuban or French bread, and nicely chilled dry wine or rosé wine, and fresh fruit of the season as dessert.

½ cup olive oil (preferably Spanish) or a combination of olive oil and other cooking oil
1 to 1½ cups coarsely chopped onion
2 medium cloves garlic, minced or mashed
¾ cup coarsely chopped green bell pepper
1 3-pound chicken, cut into serving pieces
1½ cups coarsely chopped ripe tomatoes
1 quart rich chicken stock
About 2 teaspoons salt, or to taste
Freshly ground black pepper to taste
1 small to medium bay leaf
⅛ teaspoon powdered saffron, or ¼ teaspoon achiote or bija
1 to 2 drops yellow food coloring (optional)
2 cups white long-grain rice
½ to ¾ cup drained canned tiny peas
1 hard-cooked egg, thinly sliced
4 to 8 drained canned asparagus stalks
2 tablespoons minced fresh parsley
2 large pimientos, thinly sliced

In a large heavy ovenproof container on top of the stove, heat the oil and sauté the onion, garlic, and green pepper, stirring often, until soft; remove vegetables with a slotted spoon and reserve. Add the chicken pieces to the oil, brown well, then return the cooked vegetables to the pan, along with the tomatoes, chicken stock, salt, black pepper, and bay leaf. Bring to a boil, then stir in the saffron or achiote or bija, the food coloring if desired, and the rice. Cover and bake in a preheated 350° oven until rice is tender, about 20 minutes, stirring gently once or twice to mix all ingredients. Remove cover, and garnish with the peas, sliced egg, asparagus, parsley, and pimientos; just heat through, and serve at once, directly from the container. *Serves 4.*

POLLO CON ACEITUNAS
(Chicken with Spanish Green Olives)

This is a classic and absolutely delectable dish often encountered in Latin America. The finest version I ever had was at the elegant Nejapa Country Club in Managua, Nicaragua, a city whose cuisine alone made the trip to this marvelously scenic land worthwhile. It is typically served with rice, a salad of thinly sliced tomatoes and shredded lettuce with a piquant oil-and-vinegar dressing, and a custard flan as dessert.

¼ cup olive oil
3 tablespoons butter
2 frying chickens, cut into serving pieces
1 cup diced baked ham (½-inch cubes)
1 cup dry white vermouth
¾ cup small pitted green Spanish olives
1½ teaspoons paprika
Salt and freshly ground black pepper to taste

In a large skillet with a cover, combine the olive oil and butter over medium heat and sauté the chicken pieces, without crowding, turning often until very well browned. Remove with tongs and keep warm. Add ham dice to the skillet and sauté until lightly browned; remove with a slotted spoon and keep warm with the chicken. Pour the vermouth into the skillet over high heat and scrape up all bits of meat; cook, stirring, until vermouth is reduced by half. Return the chicken and ham to the skillet and add the green olives, paprika, salt, and pepper. Cover and cook over low heat until chicken is tender, about 20 minutes. Serve hot. *Serves 4.*

JAMAICAN FRICASSEED CHICKEN

A superb Jamaican version of the ever-popular fricassee. Serve with hot fluffy rice, a big tossed green vinaigrette-dressed salad, and heated crusty bread.

3½ pound chicken, cut into serving pieces
Salt and freshly ground black pepper
1½ cups coarsely chopped onion
1 medium or large clove garlic, sliced
2 tablespoons butter
2 tablespoons or less olive oil or other cooking oil
½ to ¾ cup coarsely chopped green bell pepper
1¾ cups hot water
½ teaspoon grated fresh ginger
1 whole hot pepper, Annaheim, cayenne, or other species, unbroken (optional)
3 tablespoons tomato catsup
2 tablespoons good soy sauce

Season chicken pieces with salt, black pepper, onion, and garlic, and keep in a covered container for 2 hours. Remove onion and garlic and reserve. Heat the butter and oil and brown the chicken, turning as needed with tongs or two forks. Add the reserved onion and garlic along with the green pepper and cook about 5 minutes, stirring constantly. Add hot water, ginger, hot pepper, catsup, and soy sauce, and simmer, covered, until chicken is tender, about 30 minutes. If necessary, add a little more water. Correct seasoning and serve hot. *Serves 6.*

ESCABECHE DE POLLO
(Bolivian Pickled Chicken)

Travelers in Latin America quickly become familiar with the widespread and popular *escabeche de pescado*, an often volcanically hot pickled fish creation. This dish, made with chicken, is found much less frequently, although it appears in the cuisines of Mexico, Belize, and Bolivia. This Bolivian version is delicious served with boiled potatoes and fried ripe plaintain sprinkled with a dash of lime juice.

1 *large chicken, cut into pieces*
2 *large onions, thinly sliced*
3 *carrots, pared and cut into quarters*
1 *green bell pepper, sliced*
½ *cup olive oil*
1 *cup malt or wine vinegar*
Salt and freshly ground black pepper to taste
1 *large bay leaf, crumbled*
¼ *teaspoon ground allspice*

Combine all ingredients in a pot with a cover and cook over low heat until chicken is tender. Correct seasoning, and let cool before serving. *Serves 4.*

PATO BRASILEIRO
(Brazilian Duck)

Duck is one of the more popular birds in Latin America. Although I very much relish duck with orange sauce in the French style, I prefer the following Brazilian treatment. Since there is not much meat on the average duck after cooking, for this rather extravagant creation I serve one duck for every two guests.

2 dressed ducklings or ducks
¼ cup strained fresh lime juice
3 teaspoons salt
1¼ teaspoons freshly ground black pepper
1½ cups coarsely grated dry coconut
½ cup finely chopped green scallion tops
2 small to medium bay leaves
¼ cup light rum
3 cups strained fresh orange juice
2 tablespoons grated orange peel (no white)
4 firm ripe bananas, cut into 1-inch pieces
2 tablespoons flour
3 tablespoons warm water or dry red wine
¼ cup finely chopped Brazil nuts
¼ cup Curaçao liqueur
1 cup cubed well-chilled currant or Antidesma jelly (optional, but very nice)

Rinse ducks and dry them with paper towels. Sprinkle with the lime juice and rub in the salt and pepper. Mix the grated coconut, scallion tops, bay leaves, and rum, and lightly stuff cavities of ducks. Roast in preheated 425° oven 20 minutes; drain off fat. Mix orange juice and peel and pour over ducks, then continue roasting until ducks are done to taste, usually about 50 minutes longer. About 10 minutes before end of roasting time, add the banana chunks to the pan.

Remove ducks and bananas from the pan and arrange on a large, heated serving platter. Skim fat from pan and discard. Mix the flour and warm water or wine together into a paste and stir into the pan juices. Over high heat on top of the stove, cook the mixture, stirring constantly, until it boils. Reduce heat, blend in Brazil nuts and Curaçao, and simmer, stirring constantly, about 5 minutes. Pour the gravy into a serving dish, and keep hot.

Carve the ducks and serve with the banana chunks. Serve the hot gravy and the chilled jelly cubes (if used) in separate containers. *Serves 4 liberally.*

PATO CON PAPAYA
(Duck with Papaya)

This marvelous recipe for duck cooked with papayas is found in several versions in various parts of Latin America, from Cuba (where papaya is known as *fruta bomba*) and Puerto Rico (where it is called *lechosa*) southward. I enjoy it with a risotto into which sautéed bits of mushrooms have been blended, a salad of crisp watercress with a piquant oil-lemon juice dressing, hot crusty bread, and fresh fruit and cheese for dessert.

2 *ducklings or ducks*
2 *small green but mature papayas*
2 *tablespoons olive oil*
1½ *to* 2 *cups thinly sliced onion*
1 *medium clove garlic, minced or mashed*
1 *small bay leaf, crumbled*
1 *teaspoon salt*
½ *teaspoon freshly ground black pepper*
2 *tablespoons flour*
1 *cup rich duck or chicken stock or water*

Cut ducklings into serving-sized pieces, rinse, and pat dry. Peel the papayas, cut in half, scoop out seeds (you may wish to use the seeds in a salad dressing), and cut flesh into thick chunks. Heat the oil in a large heavy skillet or a dutch oven with a cover and sauté the onion and garlic with the bay leaf, stirring often, until the onion softens and starts to brown. Remove vegetables with a slotted spoon, discarding pieces of bay leaf.

Thoroughly brown the pieces of duckling in the oil, turning often, and sprinkle with salt and pepper. Remove duck and keep warm. Drain off all but about 2 tablespoons of the fat, thoroughly blend in the flour, and gradually blend in the stock or water. Simmer, stirring often, a few minutes, then return onion, garlic, and duckling pieces to the pan. Mix with the sauce, cover, and simmer gently until duck is tender, about 45 minutes. About 20 minutes before end of cooking time, add the papaya pieces, mix, re-cover, and continue to simmer. Do not overcook—the papaya should be rather firm. Correct seasoning and serve very hot. *Serves 4.*

PAVO RELLENO DOS BOCAS
(Stuffed Turkey Dos Bocas)

Many years ago I visited Dos Bocas, the elegant hill home of Señora Hermelia Casas de Almeida outside of Santiago de Cuba, where all the niceties of Cuban hospitality made themselves known, even including a personal waiter in white gloves for each guest at luncheon. The *pièce de résistance* at one such luncheon was this extraordinary boned ham-stuffed turkey. When I tried to make the dish myself, I found that although the results were marvelously tasty, the labor involved was almost too much. Have you ever tried to bone a turkey?

12- to 15-pound turkey, boned but intact
2 cups or more fresh lime juice
Oregano to taste
Salt and freshly ground black pepper to taste
10 to 12 cups ½-inch crisp croutons
2 pounds lean ham, well seasoned, baked, and coarsely ground
1½ cups chopped plumped raisins
⅓ cup finely chopped pimiento-stuffed olives
⅓ cup finely chopped sour pickles
⅓ cup finely chopped pistachios or walnuts
3 tablespoons butter
2 cups finely chopped onion
2 large cloves garlic, minced or mashed
1½ to 2 cups Coconut Milk (see index)
1 cup water
2 cups dry white wine

Rinse the boned turkey and rub it thoroughly inside and out with the lime juice. Sprinkle rather liberally with oregano, salt, and black pepper.

In a large bowl, mix the croutons, ham, raisins, olives, pickles, and nuts. Heat the butter and sauté onion and garlic, stirring, until soft. Add to the crouton mixture and stir gently until well mixed. Stir in the Coconut Milk. When ready to roast the turkey, stuff with the mixture and truss or sew the cavities.

Put the water and wine in a roasting pan. Place stuffed turkey on a rack in the pan and roast in a preheated 350° oven until bird is tender and done to taste, usually about 1¾ hours or slightly longer. Baste every 15 minutes or so with pan drippings. Remove turkey from oven, allow to stand 15 minutes, then carve with a very sharp knife. *Serves 12.*

MOLE DE GUAJOLOTE
(Mole Sauce for Turkey)

According to legend, the nuns at a convent in Puebla, a lovely old city in Mexico, were once informed that they would soon receive a visit from a most important personage of the church. They must feed this dignitary, but their stocks were low, so they gathered together all that they had at hand, killed their only turkey, and served this extraordinary dish to the honored visitor. The good nuns certainly had a grand number of ingredients at their disposal! This is Elena Zelayeta's recipe, and she hopes that you will have access to a Mexican shop to acquire all the authentic ingredients.

15 *mulato chilies*
15 *ancho chilies*
5 *pasilla chilies*

2 tablespoons mixed seeds from chilies
⅓ cup blanched almonds
⅓ cup peanuts
⅓ cup calabaza seeds or pumpkins seeds
1 tortilla, fried crisp
1 French roll, cut in half and fried crisp
2 tablespoons sesame seeds
1 2-inch piece stick cinnamon
3 whole cloves
6 whole black peppercorns
2 cloves garlic, peeled
10-ounce can tomatillos
3 tomatoes, peeled
2 ounces Mexican chocolate
2 quarts chicken broth
½ cup lard
1 teaspoon sugar
Salt to taste
1 turkey, roasted and cut into serving pieces
1½ tablespoons toasted sesame seeds (optional)

Wash and dry the chilies. (They are all different flavors and colors and can be found at Mexican food stores, where you will find many of the other ingredients called for.) Toast the chilies lightly in an ungreased skillet, remove the seeds, and soak the chilies in hot water to cover, until tender. Toast chili seeds with almonds, peanuts, and pumpkin seeds.

Purée in a blender or put through a food grinder all the above ingredients, together with the tortilla, French roll, the 2 tablespoons of the sesame seeds, the cinnamon, cloves, black peppercorns, garlic, tomatillos, tomatoes, and chocolate. Add one quart of the broth to the puréed or ground mixture, mix well, and strain.

Heat the lard, add strained sauce, sugar, and salt. Cook, stirring often, until sauce is thick. Add the remaining broth and the turkey pieces and heat through. If desired, before serving, sprinkle with the toasted sesame seeds. *Serves 10 to 12.*

CASTRIES STUFFING

I first had this sumptuous stuffing in guinea fowl in a private home at Castries, the capital of the island of St. Lucia. Knowing my fascination with volcanoes, my hosts had taken me to see Soufrière, and upon our weary return, we were served the stuffed guineas with a risotto, a tomato and cucumber salad with a vinaigrette dressing, and an elegant array of fresh fruits and cheese.

2½ cups tiny crisp croutons
2 cups mashed ripe banana
1 tablespoon fresh lime juice
2 teaspoons grated lime peel (without any white)
1 tablespoon dark rum
½ teaspoon or more salt
Freshly ground black pepper to taste
Hot pepper sauce to taste

Thoroughly combine all ingredients and use at once to stuff poultry, such as guinea fowl, duck, pigeon, dove, or chicken. Or bake the stuffing separately, basting occasionally with the juices from the seasoned fowl. *Makes about 4 cups.*

HUEVOS FLAMENCO
(Eggs Flamenco)

On festive occasions, and many occasions which are not so festive, Huevos Flamenco are offered by good Latin cooks from Cuba southward. The recipe presumably originated in Spain, but happily it has been adopted in the American tropics. This dish is often served with a lettuce and tomato or avocado salad, heated crusty bread, and a beverage, which may be tea or coffee or wine.

***1** tablespoon butter*
***1** tablespoon olive oil*
***½** to **¾** cup finely chopped onion*
***1** small clove garlic, minced or mashed*
***1½** cups diced baked ham, or **½** pound chorizo sausages, thinly sliced*
***½** cup rich chicken stock*
***½** to **¾** cup coarsely chopped ripe tomato*
***2** teaspoons minced fresh parsley*
***½** teaspoon salt*
***¼** teaspoon freshly ground black pepper*
***¼** cup diced pimientos*
***8** large eggs*
***1** cup drained canned tiny peas*
***8** or more fresh asparagus spears, boiled (or the same amount of drained canned asparagus spears)*

Heat the butter and oil in a skillet and sauté the onion and garlic until just tender. Add the ham or chorizos, the chicken stock, tomato, parsley, salt, and pepper. Cover and simmer over very low heat, stirring occasionally, 15 minutes or longer; the sauce should be nicely blended and flavorful.

Add the pimientos and divide the sauce among 4 individual ovenproof casseroles or ramekins. Break 2 eggs into each casserole and arrange tiny peas and asparagus spears around them, settling these down into the sauce. Bake in a preheated 350° oven until the eggs set, and serve immediately. *Serves 4.*

Meats

All kinds of meats are available in Latin America. Beef and pork are probably the most prominent, since cattle and pigs are raised extensively in many localities, but lamb, mutton, goat, and many far more esoteric species, including tapir, monkey, iguana, snake, even tepescuintle, guinea pig, and llama, are found in regional cookery.

Organ meats, frequently known by the British name of "offal," abound in the English-speaking areas and include everything from tripe and kidneys to liver and brains. I have come to enjoy these "variety meats" far more than I did when I resided in the United States; today in my home in Jamaica I frequently prepare calf's liver (which in the past I could never abide), whenever good supplies are available, as well as the skewered broiled Peruvian anticuchos, made from bits of beef heart.

Stews and hearty souplike mixtures featuring meats are exceptionally popular. Some of these tremendously involved medleys have a wide range of meats and vegetables added during cooking. Meat dishes are often served with rice, white potatoes, sweet potatoes, or one of the more exotic tropical starchy vegetables, plus a salad, perhaps some crusty heated bread, and a dessert.

Many different seasonings are used by Latin American cooks. Some of these, such as the juice of ripe limes or lemons or even sour (Seville) oranges, or vinegars in variety, not only season but also tenderize rather durable meats. In some regions, meats are so scarce (or the populace is so poor) that they are used solely as a seasoning ingredient, being added to starchy dishes only in very small amounts.

Ground or finely minced meats, in particular beef and pork, are made into a wide variety of sausages, especially in the Spanish- and Portuguese-speaking lands, where such delights as chorizo, linguica, butifarra, and longaniza are to be found. Meat-filled pastries, from Jamaican patties to Venezuelan hallacas are exceedingly popular, as are meat loaves, often elaborate like the famous Matambre which is found in many South American countries.

BIFE A FRIGIDEIRA
(Portuguese Beefsteak)

This favorite way of preparing steak in Brazil is Portuguese in origin. Serve it with boiled potatoes, dressed with butter and plenty of minced parsley, a crisp green salad, and a pleasant bottle of wine, perhaps from the southern part of Brazil. *Frigideira* has nothing to do with a refrigerator; in Portuguese it means a frying pan, the utensil in which the steak is cooked.

¼ *cup butter*
1 *medium clove garlic, mashed*
½ *small bay leaf*
1 *small or medium-sized beefsteak of your choice*
Salt and freshly ground black pepper
2 *tablespoons dry white wine*
1 *tablespoon wine vinegar*
1 *thin slice smoked ham, heated*
1 *teaspoon minced fresh parsley*

In a heavy skillet, melt the butter and sauté the garlic and bay leaf briefly. Lightly season the steak with salt and pepper, then quickly sear on both sides, cooking to desired degree of doneness. Remove steak to a heated serving platter. Add the wine and vinegar to the skillet, increase heat, and reduce the sauce to about half, scraping up all bits of browned meat. Top the steak with the heated ham slice, pour the sauce over it, sprinkle with parsley, and serve immediately. *Serves 1.*

CARNE ASADA
(Argentine Broiled Beef)

The Argentine asado consists of meat from the pampas, broiled over hot coals and served with spicy sauces and a minimum of other accouterments. Maté, chilled beer, or one of the excellent Argentinian wines is customarily served as a beverage, and dessert is an assortment of regional cheeses and luscious fruits of many varieties.

1 5-*pound piece beef short ribs*
Salt and freshly ground black pepper to taste
1 *to* 2 *cups coarsely chopped onion*
1 *or* 2 *large cloves garlic, minced*
¾ *cup coarsely chopped green bell pepper*
2 *cups peeled and coarsely chopped ripe tomatoes*
2 *tablespoons minced fresh parsley*
3 *tablespoons olive oil*
2 *tablespoons wine or cider vinegar*

Season beef ribs with salt and black pepper to taste, being rather liberal, and arrange over hot coals (wood coals rather than charcoal are often used for a genuine asado). Broil, turning as needed, to desired degree of doneness, usually about 60 to 80 minutes.

Meanwhile, in a saucepan, cook the onion, garlic, green pepper, tomatoes, parsley, olive oil, and vinegar over medium heat, stirring often, until thickened and well flavored. If desired, brush this sauce over the meat toward the end of the broiling; otherwise serve separately while hot. *Serves 4 liberally.*

CARNE ESPAÑOLA EN SALSA NEGRA
(Spanish Beef in Black Sauce)

This robust casserole, slowly simmered and with some rather unusual ingredients, is Spanish in origin but appears in Latin American countries from Cuba to Argentina. It is one of my favorites to serve around Christmas time, when the palate wearies of turkey and duck and goose.

2 tablespoons olive oil
2 cups thinly sliced onions
1 small clove garlic, minced or mashed
2 pounds lean stewing beef, cut into ½-inch cubes
2 teaspoons salt
¼ teaspoon freshly ground black pepper
2 tablespoons fresh lime juice
2 tablespoons halved raisins
2 cups hot rich beef stock, or 1 cup stock and 1 cup dry red wine
2 cups thinly sliced potatoes
½ cup sliced pitted black olives
1 teaspoon drained capers

In a heavy container with a cover, heat the oil and sauté the onions and garlic, stirring often, until they start to brown; remove with a slotted spoon and reserve. Add the cubed meat, sprinkle with salt and pepper, and brown thoroughly on all sides. Add the lime juice, raisins, and stock or stock and wine. Cover and simmer until beef is tender, about 50 minutes, stirring occasionally. Add the potatoes, olives, and capers, cover container again, and simmer until potatoes are tender. Correct the seasoning and serve hot, with plenty of the sauce. *Serves 4 to 6.*

CARNE MOLIDA VENEZOLANA
(Venezuelan Meat Loaf)

In several of the English-speaking countries and islands, meat loaves are known as beef loaves, even though they may contain more ground pork than beef. They are usually very heavily touched with hot peppers. On the other hand, in Spanish-speaking Venezuela this much calmer version is found.

1½ pounds lean ground beef
¾ cup fresh firm breadcrumbs (preferably made from French bread)
2 large eggs, beaten
½ cup freshly grated Swiss or comparable cheese
Salt and freshly ground black pepper to taste
5 tablespoons olive oil
2 cups finely chopped onion
1 small or medium clove garlic, minced or mashed
2 tablespoons finely chopped green bell pepper
¼ teaspoon thyme
¼ teaspoon basil or oregano
¼ cup finely chopped fresh parsley (include some stems)
2½ cups coarsely chopped peeled ripe tomatoes

In a large bowl, place the beef, breadcrumbs, eggs, cheese, and rather liberal amounts of salt and pepper. Heat 2 tablespoons of the oil in a skillet and sauté ½ cup of the onions, the garlic, and the green pepper, stirring often, until soft. Add to the ingredients in the bowl, and mix thoroughly but gently—excess handling can make the meat loaf tough. Shape into a loaf with your hands and place in a shallow baking dish.

Add the remaining 3 tablespoons olive oil to the skillet, and in this sauté the remaining 1½ cups onion until soft. Blend in the thyme, basil or oregano, parsley, and tomatoes and simmer, covered, adding salt and pepper to taste. When a flavorful mixture is obtained, spoon around the meat loaf. Bake in preheated 375° oven, basting often with the sauce, until meat is done, usually about 1 hour. Serve hot or warm, sliced. *Serves 4 to 6.*

CHURRASCO
(Barbecued Steak)

In this great specialty of Argentina, Uruguay, and parts of southern Brazil, the steaks are typically cooked on special leaning grids over a wood fire that has burnt down to vivid coals; charcoal can also be used.

2 *cups finely chopped scallions, or* 1½ *cups finely chopped white onion*
1 *cup plus* 2 *tablespoons butter*
½ *teaspoon or slightly more crumbled rosemary or oregano, or a combination of both*
1½ *teaspoons salt*
1 *tablespoon freshly ground black pepper*
1 *cup dry white wine*
½ *cup wine vinegar or cider vinegar*
7-*pound sirloin steak, or* 2 3½- *to* 4-*pound steaks, about* 3 *inches thick*

To make the sauce, sauté the scallions or onions in 1 cup of the butter, stirring often. Add the rosemary and/or oregano, salt, pepper, wine, and vinegar. Bring to a boil, lower heat, and simmer, 5 minutes, stirring. Correct seasoning and add the remaining butter.

Broil the steak over a hot bed of charcoal until done to taste: rare, about 30 minutes; medium, 40 minutes; well done, 60 minutes or slightly more. Test doneness by cutting steak open in the middle with a sharp knife. Pour the sauce over the meat for serving. *Serves 6.*

CHILI CON CARNE, ALEX'S STYLE

Rather than get into arguments over the origins of chili con carne (whether Mexico or Texas or California), or over its variants (which are legion), I prefer to offer my favorite recipe for the dish. Ideally, it should be preceded by a well-seasoned avocado guacamole surrounded by pieces of crisp tortillas; accompanied by rice, cornbread into which slivered onion, green pepper, and sharp Cheddar or jack cheese have been folded prior to baking, a raw spinach and mushroom salad with vinaigrette dressing; and for dessert fresh fruit or a fruit sherbet. Beer is the perfect beverage.

3 ***tablespoons olive oil or other cooking oil***
1½ ***pounds good stewing beef, cut into neat ½-inch cubes***
1½ ***to* 2** ***cups coarsely chopped onion***
2 ***medium cloves garlic, minced or mashed***
¾ ***cup coarsely chopped green bell pepper***
2 ***tablespoons or more chili powder***
1½ ***teaspoons crumbled oregano***
½ ***to* 1** ***teaspoon ground cumin (optional)***
1 ***or* 2** ***dashes Tabasco or other hot pepper sauce***
10½*-ounce can beef consommé (undiluted), or* 1¼ ***cups rich freshly made beef stock***
16*-ounce can Italian plum tomatoes (undrained)*
2 ***to* 3** ***tablespoons tomato paste***
1½ ***teaspoons salt***
1 ***pound dried red kidney beans, cooked until tender, and well seasoned***
4 ***to* 6** ***cups hot freshly cooked white long-grain rice***

In a dutch oven or other large heavy container with a cover, heat the oil over rather high heat, and quickly brown the beef cubes on all sides, turning often. Remove with a slotted spoon and keep warm. Add the onion, garlic, and green pepper, and cook over somewhat reduced heat, stirring often, until vegetables are soft but not browned. Stir in chili powder (some forms are much "hotter" than others), oregano, cumin (if desired), and Tabasco or hot pepper sauce. Add next the beef consommé or stock and tomatoes (break these up). Thoroughly blend in tomato paste as needed. Add the salt, mix well, cover container, and simmer about 15 minutes. Return the beef cubes, mix thoroughly, and continue to simmer, still covered, over low heat, until meat is very tender, adding a bit more beef consommé or stock if needed—the chili should be rather soupy. Add the red beans, along with some of their cooking liquid if desired; mix, cover, and simmer for 30 minutes, until very hot. Correct the seasoning, and serve chili in big deep soup plates or bowls, preferably atop hot fluffy rice—or alongside it, if you wish to be a purist. *Serves 4 to 6.*

Variation: This succulent recipe can also be made with lean pork or chunks of chicken; the latter will not need the lengthy cooking of the beef or pork.

FEIJOADA COMPLETA
(Brazil's National Dish)

The national dish of Brazil is a marvelous medley of many ingredients. Its production is time-consuming, and outside Brazil some of the special ingredients are hard to find. However, *carne seca,* which is essential to the authenticity and success of the recipe, is now available in specialty shops in large cities all over the United States, as well as in most of the Latin American countries. This recipe comes from my book on vegetable cookery, where it is featured under Black Beans.

1 pound carne seca (sun-dried salted beef)
4 cups feijoes (dried black beans)
1 small smoked beef tongue
1 pound lingüiça *(Portuguese sausages)*
½ pound lean bacon, in 1 piece
2 meaty pig's feet
1 pound lean stewing beef, in 2 pieces
2 tablespoons lard
2 cups coarsely chopped onion
2 or 3 medium cloves garlic, minced or mashed
⅓ cup rather coarsely chopped parsley
2 teaspoons or more salt
½ teaspoon or more freshly ground black pepper
Farofa (see following recipe)
1½ pounds collards or kale (or 3 packages of the frozen variety)
4 large oranges (unpeeled), thinly sliced and seeded
Hot steamed or boiled white long-grain rice

Soak the carne seca in water to cover in the refrigerator overnight. The next day, pick over and rinse the beans. Place them in a large heavy kettle, cover with cold water, cover container, and bring to a boil. Remove from heat and allow to stand, covered, 1 hour. Over medium heat, still covered, bring beans to a boil and then simmer.

While the beans cook, soak the beef tongue in water 30 minutes, drain, and parboil in fresh water until skin can be removed. Drain the carne seca and cut into 1-inch cubes. Rinse sausages and drain. Place these meats, along with the bacon, pig's feet, and stewing beef, in another large heavy kettle with a cover, add water just to cover, and simmer, covered, over very low heat until all meats are tender but not overcooked.

In a skillet, melt the lard and sauté the onion and garlic until onion is soft, adding the parsley toward the end of the cooking time.

Season the cooked beans (make sure they are tender) with the salt and pepper (or follow the recipe for Haitian Black Beans [see index]). Add about 1 cup cooked beans to the skillet and mash them thoroughly with a fork. Turn contents of skillet into the bean kettle and add the meats and most of their liquid—carefully, since the mixture should not be too soupy. Cover the kettle and simmer 20 minutes or so to blend the flavors.

To serve, remove meats, slice, and arrange on a large heated platter; traditionally, the tongue is in the middle, the smoked meats at one end, the fresh at the other. Pour the undrained beans into a large bowl and serve with a ladle. Offer a side bowl of farofa.

Boil or steam the collards or kale until tender and serve in another bowl, arranging orange slices atop. Each guest takes a large scoop of hot rice, tops it with beans plus some of the liquor, obtains a sampling of every sort of meat and of collards, takes an orange slice, and sprinkles the entire array with farofa to taste. *Serves 6 to 10 liberally.*

FAROFA
(Toasted Cassava Flour)

Farofa is used with an extraordinary array of dishes. In Brazil it is made by spreading about 1 pound of the flour—there called *farinha de mandioca*—in a shallow pan, which is placed in a slow oven. The flour is stirred often, until it takes on a delicate tan color, or perhaps a darker brown, depending on personal predilection. It can then be sprinkled over various dishes, from Feijoada Completa to simpler soups, vegetables, and meats; it imparts a delicious flavor.

CARNE CON JENJIBRE
(Ginger Beef)

This flavorful dish is found in several cuisines within Latin America, usually prepared with fresh ginger rather than powdered ginger. The fresh root is an irregular, nubbly object, with much more potency than the powdered product. I like this dish served with hot, fluffy rice, fried ripe bananas or plantains, and sliced tomatoes with a vinaigrette dressing. Caramel flan makes a well-nigh perfect finale to the menu.

4-pound piece of beef, as for a pot roast
½ to ¾ teaspoon grated fresh ginger
¾ to 1 teaspoon turmeric
2 teaspoons or more salt
2 to 3 tablespoons lard or combination of butter and oil
1 cup coarsely chopped onion
2 medium garlic cloves, minced or mashed
2 cups peeled and coarsely chopped ripe tomatoes
1 cup rich beef stock
Tabasco sauce, or chopped seeded chili peppers, to taste (optional, but typical)

Sprinkle beef with ginger, turmeric, and salt, and rub seasoning into the meat on all sides with your fingers. In a kettle with a cover, heat the lard or butter and oil and brown beef on all sides over rather high heat. Remove the meat and place the onion, garlic, tomatoes, beef stock, and Tabasco sauce or chopped chili peppers (if used) on the bottom of the kettle, and replace the seasoned beef on top. Simmer, covered, over low heat until the beef is tender and done to your taste, usually about 2½ to 3 hours. Remove from heat and allow to stand about 20 minutes before carving. If desired, purée the cooked vegetables and make them into a gravy to be served with the beef. *Serves 6.*

ANGUILLA KEBABS

These kebabs from Anguilla in the British West Indies are akin to Indonesian barbecued meat and can be varied in any fashion that takes the cook's fancy. I very much enjoy this version.

½ *cup unsweetened pineapple juice*
¼ *cup distilled white vinegar*
2 *tablespoons molasses*
2 *teaspoons salt*
Freshly ground black pepper to taste
2 *pounds beef sirloin, cut in* 1½*-inch cubes or strips*
12 *small white onions, peeled*
2 *quarts boiling water*
12 *cherry or plum tomatoes, peeled if desired*
2 *medium green or red bell peppers, seeded and cut into* 1½*-inch squares*
12 1*-inch cubes fresh or canned pineapple*

Combine the pineapple juice, vinegar, molasses, salt, and several grinds of black pepper. Add the beef and marinate at room temperature 1 hour. Drain, reserving the marinade to use for basting.

Meanwhile, drop the whole onions into the boiling water and simmer 5 minutes. Drain well. Thread the beef (if cut into strips, double up the pieces), the onions, tomatoes, pepper strips, and pineapple cubes alternately on four 12- to 14-inch metal, bamboo, or wooden skewers. Brush liberally with the reserved marinade.

Using either a charcoal grill or an oven broiler, cook the kebabs 4 inches from the heat, basting liberally with the marinade and turning every 3 minutes or so until the beef is cooked to desired degree of doneness. Serve accompanied by plain boiled rice, or rice into which toasted nuts, such as peanuts or cashews, and perhaps finely chopped green scallion tops have been folded during the cooking. Pour any remaining marinade over the kebabs as they are presented at the table. *Serves 6 to 8.*

KESHY YENA
(Cheese Stuffed with Beef)

Keshy Yena—the name is obviously a corruption of Spanish *queso lleno* (stuffed cheese)—is one of the classic dishes of the Netherlands Antilles. Various kinds of cheeses can be used for this basic recipe, which can be made in a ramekin, scallop dish, or other such utensil. In any form, it is sheer delight to the palate. Accompany with coleslaw and a light dessert.

1 ***cup unsalted butter***
½ ***cup chopped onion***
1½ ***pounds lean ground beef***
¾ ***cup chopped green or red bell pepper***
1 ***chili pepper, seeded and, if desired, chopped, or a dash of sambal or Tabasco or other hot pepper sauce***
½ ***cup sliced mushrooms, sautéed in butter if desired***
2 ***tablespoons brandy or rum, heated***
1 ***large ripe tomato, peeled and coarsely chopped***
2 ***hard-cooked eggs, coarsely chopped***
¼ ***cup seedless raisins or currants***
¼ ***cup pitted black olives or stuffed green olives, coarsely chopped***
¼ ***cup finely chopped gherkins or dill pickles or sweet pickle relish***
1 ***tablespoon tomato catsup***
½ ***cup Brown Sauce (see following recipe)***
Salt and freshly ground black or white pepper to taste
4-***pound whole Edam cheese (unpeeled)***

Heat the butter in a heavy skillet and sauté the onion until golden brown. Add the ground beef and sauté lightly. Add the bell pepper, chili pepper or hot pepper sauce, and mushrooms and sauté 5 minutes longer, stirring often and taking care that mixture does not burn. Pour the brandy (or rum) over the mixture and ignite, stirring until flame dies. Add the tomato, eggs, raisins or currants, olives, pickles, catsup, and Brown Sauce, season with salt and pepper, and gently simmer 5 minutes, stirring occasionally.

Meanwhile, remove the red casing from the cheese if desired, and cut off a "lid." Hollow out the lid and the bottom of the shell, cover them with cold water, and soak 1 hour. Drain and wipe dry. Grate the scooped-out cheese and add 1 cup to the meat mixture, reserving the remaining grated cheese for another use (spreads, dips, or toppings for casseroles). Pack the mixture into the cheese shell, replace the lid, and bake in a buttered casserole in a preheated 350° oven 30 minutes. Do not overcook or the cheese will become tough instead of soft and bubbly. Slide the cheese out of the casserole onto a heated serving dish, cut into neat wedges, and serve immediately. *Serves 6 to 8.*

BROWN SAUCE

3 tablespoons unsalted butter
3 tablespoons flour
1½ cups rich beef stock
2 teaspoons tomato purée
¼ teaspoon salt
¼ teaspoon freshly ground black pepper

Melt the butter in a saucepan over medium heat and add the flour. Stir well with a wire whisk or spoon until the roux is golden but not brown. Slowly add, ½ cup at a time, the beef stock. After the sauce begins to thicken, add the tomato purée and season with salt and pepper. *Makes about 2 cups.*

NACATAMALES
(Nicaraguan Tamales)

Nicaraguan cuisine is little known outside that spectacular land. The national version of tamales requires a bit of time and effort, but when served very hot with rice, re-fried red beans, and sautéed ripe plantains, they are magnificent fare.

3 cups white cornmeal
1 quart cold water
1 quart boiling water
6 tablespoons butter
5 teaspoons salt
2 large eggs, beaten well
4 cups diced raw lean beef
3 cups diced raw lean pork
3 cups diced raw chicken
3 small cloves garlic, minced or mashed
2 cups drained canned chick peas, coarsely chopped
⅓ cup olive oil
3 cups coarsely chopped ripe tomatoes
1 cup coarsely chopped green bell pepper
3 cups coarsely chopped onion
½ teaspoon ground dried chili pepper
½ cup finely chopped fresh parsley
4 tablespoons cider vinegar
2 teaspoons sugar
3 teaspoons capers, coarsely chopped if desired
¾ cup halved seedless raisins
¾ cup stuffed green olives, thinly sliced
⅓ cup crumbled fried bacon
2 cups cooked fresh corn kernels
1 cup drained tiny green peas
⅓ cup diced pimientos
Banana leaves, about 8 by 15 inches in size*

Combine the cornmeal with a little cold water, then add this to a saucepan containing the 1 quart rapidly boiling water, stirring constantly. Add the butter and 2 teaspoons of the salt. Remove from heat and stir in the eggs until a smooth dough results. Reserve.

Meanwhile, in a large saucepan combine the beef, pork, chicken, the remaining cold water, the garlic, and the chick peas. Bring to a quick boil, then reduce heat and cook, stirring occasionally, until meats are tender. Drain well.

In a large skillet with a cover, heat the oil and add the tomatoes, green pepper, onion, chili pepper, parsley, the remaining 3 teaspoons of salt, the vinegar, sugar, and cooked meats. Cover and cook over low heat 15 minutes, stirring occasionally. Remove from heat and gently stir in the capers, raisins, olives, bacon, corn, peas, and pimientos.

Blanch the banana leaves in boiling water, and drain partially. Spread about 4 tablespoons of the dough mixture on the center of each banana frond, patting out to a thin layer. Place about 2 to 3 tablespoons of the meat-vegetable mixture on one side of the flattened dough, and roll the dough up carefully and tightly, sealing edges as thoroughly as possible with a little warm water or more dough, if needed. Fold the banana leaves around the Nacatamales and tie them securely with kitchen string or banana trash. Place in a large pot in salted water to cover, and simmer over very low heat, covered, about 1 hour. Serve Nacatamales in their banana-leaf packets, hot or at room temperature, and open at the table. *Serves 8 to 10.*

* If you are far from the banana plantations, you can substitute corn husks for banana leaves, following the wrapping directions for Humitas (see Index). You may have to make smaller Nacatamales.

PASTEL DE CHOCLO
(Chilean Meat Pie)

This famous Chilean meat pie with a filling of canned cream-style corn is often served with boiled, parsley-sprinkled potatoes and a large salad of crisp greens with vinaigrette dressing.

2 *cups finely chopped or ground roast beef or lamb*
¾ *cup finely chopped onion*
10 *stuffed green olives or pitted black olives, minced or ground*
2 *hard-cooked eggs, minced or ground*
½ *to* ¾ *teaspoon oregano*
¾ *teaspoon salt*
1 *or* 2 *dashes of hot pepper sauce*
¼ *cup rich beef stock*
17*-ounce can cream-style corn, or* 2 *cups cooked fresh corn*
2 *large eggs, beaten well*
Freshly ground black pepper to taste

Mix together the meat, onion, olives, and hard-cooked eggs. Blend in the oregano, ½ teaspoon of the salt, the hot pepper sauce, and the stock. In another bowl, combine the corn, beaten eggs, the remaining ¼ teaspoon salt, and the black pepper, mixing well. Line the bottom and sides of a well-greased 9-inch pie plate with the meat mixture, patting firmly into place up to the rim. Fill with the corn mixture. Bake in a preheated 375° oven 45 minutes. Increase heat to 400° and bake until well browned on top, about 15 minutes. Remove from oven, let cool 10 minutes, and cut into six wedges to serve. *Serves 6.*

MATAMBRE
(Stuffed Beef Roll)

Matambre (literally, "kill hunger") is characteristic of Argentina, but I have encountered this luscious beef roll in many other parts of Latin America, frequently under different names. I heartily recommend it for picnics, luncheons, or suppers.

2½-pound flank steak
2 teaspoons salt
1 teaspoon freshly ground black pepper
½ teaspoon ground thyme or oregano
¼ cup finely chopped fresh parsley (include some stems)
¼ cup wine vinegar
½ pound spinach, calalu, or bok-choi leaves, or other greens rather neutral in flavor
1½ cups fresh breadcrumbs (from French bread)
3 tablespoons cow's milk or Coconut Milk (see index)
½ cup fresh green peas
4 slices bacon, cut into tiny dice and fried until crisp
4 medium to large carrots, cooked until firm-tender and cut lengthwise into julienne strips
4 hard-cooked eggs, quartered lengthwise
2 cups strained rich beef stock
1 cup water or dry red wine

Place steak in a glass bowl or other non-metallic container. Sprinkle with 1 teaspoon of the salt, ½ teaspoon of the pepper, the thyme or oregano, parsley, and vinegar. Cover and marinate in the refrigerator 12 hours. Then drain.

Spread the spinach or other vegetable leaves (no stems, please) over the steak. Combine the breadcrumbs with the milk, peas, bacon, and remaining salt and pepper and spread this filling over the spinach leaves. Arrange julienne pieces of carrot and egg quarters on top. Roll up the steak the long way tightly and carefully. Tie with pieces of kitchen twine about 1 inch apart and two additional pieces of twine lengthwise. Place in a large ovenproof dish and add the beef broth and water or wine. Cover and place in a preheated 375° oven. Bake until meat is tender, usually about 1½ hours. Remove from oven, and allow to stand 10 minutes or so. Cut off strings and with a sharp knife cut into neat ¼-inch slices. Serve hot, moistened with the pan juices. Or, as I prefer, chill, cut in thin slices, and serve cold. *Serves 6.*

STUFFED BEEF ROLLS
(Brazilian Rouladen or Argentine Bracciole)

These may not seem typically Latin fare, but I have encountered them on several occasions. I like these served with plenty of minced fresh parsley, riced or creamed potatoes, and a crisp tossed green salad with vinaigrette dressing. Commence the menu with canapés of sardines mashed with Cheddar cheese, spread on crisp crackers or thin toast, then run under a preheated broiler. The finale could be mango pie or a tropical ice or ice cream, perhaps coconut.

1½ *pounds beef, top round or sirloin, cut into* 4 *large slices, each about* ¼ *inch thick*
2 *tablespoons olive oil or other cooking oil*
2 *tablespoons butter*
¾ *cup finely chopped onion*
2 *large cloves garlic, minced or mashed*
2 *tablespoons finely chopped green bell pepper*
2 *large hard-cooked eggs, coarsely mashed*
3 *medium-sized dill pickles or other pickles, finely chopped*

⅓ cup or more finely diced lean bacon
1 tablespoon or more prepared mustard
¼ to ½ teaspoon mixed herbs, such as parsley, chives, tarragon, and thyme
Pinch of oregano or basil
Salt and freshly ground black pepper
Tabasco sauce, or chopped seeded chili pepper, to taste (optional, but authentic)
11-ounce can condensed beef consommé (or 1½ cups freshly made rich beef stock)
1 cup dry red wine
Flour (optional)

Using a kitchen mallet or the edge of a sturdy kitchen plate, pound the beef slices thoroughly to tenderize. Cut each slice in half, crosswise, and set aside.

In a large heavy skillet with a cover, heat the oil and butter and cook the onion, garlic, and green pepper until soft, stirring often. Remove vegetables with a slotted spoon and reserve. In a large bowl, thoroughly combine the pickles, bacon, mustard, herb mixture, oregano or basil, salt, pepper, and Tabasco or chili pepper if used. Spread the beef slices with 2 liberal teaspoons or more of the filling, and firmly roll them up, tying with string to keep stuffing inside. In the same skillet over medium heat thoroughly brown the beef rolls, 3 or so at a time, turning them with great care so stuffing does not fall out. As each is done, remove with a slotted spoon and keep warm. Combine the consommé stock and red wine, add to the skillet, and cook for a few minutes, stirring often to pick up all particles of meat. Return onion mixture to the pan, mix thoroughly, then add the beef rolls. Simmer, covered, until rolls are tender, usually about 30 minutes, carefully turning the rolls often. When beef rolls are done, put them on heated plates, and remove strings. If desired, thicken the sauce by gradually blending in a bit of flour. Serve sauce over the beef rolls. *Serves 4.*

ROPA VIEJA
("Old Clothes")

As the name suggests, the meat in this dish, when fully prepared and shredded, indeed resembles old clothes. The recipe probably originated in Spain and appears especially in Cuba. Some versions of this hearty, delicious dish are rather on the fiery side. This one is taken from Elisabeth Lambert Ortiz's *The Complete Book of Caribbean Cooking.*

2½-*pound flank steak*
1 *carrot, scraped and sliced*
1 *turnip, peeled and cubed*
1 *leek, chopped*
2 *tablespoons olive oil*
1 *large onion, finely chopped*
1 *clove garlic, chopped*
1 *green bell pepper, chopped*
1 *fresh red or green chili pepper, seeded and chopped*
2 *large tomatoes, peeled and chopped (about* 2 *cups)*
1 *bay leaf*
⅛ *teaspoon ground cinnamon*
⅛ *teaspoon ground cloves*
Salt and freshly ground black pepper
2 *pimientos, chopped*
1 *tablespoon capers (optional)*
Breadcrumbs (optional)
Triangles of fried bread, for garnish

Put the steak, carrot, turnip, and leek in a pot, add water to cover, and simmer gently until meat is tender, about 1½ hours. Allow the meat to become cool enough to handle, then shred it until it resembles the name of the recipe—ragged old clothes. Reserve the stock.

Heat the oil in a large heavy frying pan and sauté the onion, garlic, bell pepper, and chili pepper until the onion is tender but not browned. Add the tomatoes, bay leaf, cinnamon, cloves, salt, and black pepper, and simmer until the sauce is thick and the flavors are well blended. Stir in 2 cups of the reserved stock, the shredded meat, and the pimientos, and simmer about 5 minutes longer. Add the capers, if desired. The sauce, which should be abundant, may be thickened with breadcrumbs. Serve garnished with triangles of fried bread. *Serves 6.*

SATÉ BUMBÚ
(Spicy Barbecued Meat)

Much of the food of the Netherlands Antilles is distinctly spicy-hot. This is due in large part to the Indonesian influence, which is reflected in the almost daily use of a wide variety of volcanic sambal peppers. Here is a good hot Dutch West Indian culinary delight, one of the delightful *satés* which are exceptionally popular in this part of the globe.

4 small white onions
2 cloves garlic
¼ teaspoon cayenne pepper, or several dashes Tabasco sauce
1 tablespoon dark brown sugar
1 teaspoon fresh lime juice
1½ teaspoons curry powder, or to taste
½ teaspoon whole cloves
½ teaspoon grated fresh ginger
3 tablespoons warm water
3 tablespoons soy sauce
1½ pounds beefsteak, cut into neat 1-inch cubes
Peanut Saté Sauce (see following recipe)

Grind together onions and garlic, using the fine blade of a food mill. Place in a bowl along with the cayenne pepper or Tabasco sauce, the brown sugar, lime juice, curry powder, cloves, and ginger, then blend in the water and soy sauce. Add the meat cubes, toss, and marinate in refrigerator 6 hours.

Reserving the marinade, arrange meat on skewers and broil 3 inches from heat 15 to 20 minutes. Brush with the marinade and turn often. Serve with Peanut Saté Sauce. *Serves 6.*

PEANUT SATÉ SAUCE

2 ***tablespoons olive oil***
2 ***tablespoons grated onion***
1 ***tablespoon dark brown sugar***
1 ***teaspoon or more fresh lime juice***
⅛ ***teaspoon salt***
¼ ***cup peanut butter***
1 ***cup Coconut Milk (see index)***

Lightly heat the olive oil and cook the onion 5 minutes (do not brown). Add the brown sugar, lime juice, salt, and peanut butter, blending well. Add the Coconut Milk gradually, stirring, and cook until sauce is thickened and smooth. Serve with satés or other meats. *Makes about* 1½ *cups.*

AFRICAN CABBAGE BALLS

Found especially in Latin lands with a strong African heritage, these are fiery-hot but interesting as an entrée for lunch or supper.

2 tablespoons peanut oil plus ½ cup
1 cup minced onion
⅓ cup minced green bell pepper
⅓ cup minced peeled tomato
3 cups very finely shredded firm cabbage (remove coarse ribs and cores and save for a vegetable soup)
½ pound calf's liver, minced or put through a food chopper (use coarse blade)
2 cups cooked white long-grain rice
¾ teaspoon salt
½ teaspoon freshly ground black pepper
Tanzanian Hot Sauce (see following recipe)

Heat 2 tablespoons of the oil in a large skillet over rather high heat, and sauté the onion and green pepper, stirring constantly, until they are slightly browned. Stir in the tomato and cook a moment or so longer. Remove the skillet from the heat and stir in the cabbage, liver, rice, salt, and black pepper, mixing thoroughly. Allow to cool slightly, then form into compact balls about 1 inch in diameter. Heat the remaining ½ cup oil in the skillet and fry the balls a few at a time, turning as needed with a slotted spoon, until very brown and rather crisp on all sides. Serve hot, with Tanzanian Hot Sauce on the side, into which the Cabbage Balls can be dunked to taste. *Serves 6.*

TANZANIAN HOT SAUCE

1 cup minced green bell pepper
2 cups peeled and coarsely chopped ripe tomatoes
½ cup finely chopped onion
1 or 2 medium cloves garlic, minced or mashed
Tabasco or other hot pepper sauce to taste
1 to 2 tablespoons minced fresh parsley
1 teaspoon salt

Thoroughly combine all the ingredients and allow to mellow at room temperature for several hours. Any leftover sauce can be strained and either refrigerated or frozen, to use later as an excellent addition, in small quantities, to soups, stews, and the like. *Makes a scant 4 cups.*

ZÖO-TOSOPY
(Ground-Beef Stew)

The cuisine of Paraguay features a considerable number of dishes of Guarani Indian origin, some of which are surprising. The pureblood native population has been reduced through intermarriage, but such culinary creations as Zöotosopy survive.

1 pound coarsely ground or finely chopped beef
6 cups cold water
½ cup dendê or other vegetable oil
2 large onions, coarsely chopped
2 large tomatoes, peeled and coarsely chopped
2 green bananas, sliced crosswise into large chunks
¼ cup white long-grain rice
1 teaspoon or more salt
Several dashes Tabasco or other hot pepper sauce, or to taste

In a large heavy pot, mix the beef with the water, cover, and simmer over low heat.

Separately, heat the oil in a skillet and fry the onions, tomatoes, and green bananas until the vegetables are slightly soft. Combine the vegetables with the beef in the pot and add the rice, salt, and hot pepper sauce. Simmer, covered, until rice is just tender, about 20 minutes. Serve very hot in bowls. *Serves 4 liberally.*

GRENADIAN LAMB STEW

This interesting dish incorporates lamb (which in most parts of Latin America is usually imported), unripe green bananas, and sweet potatoes. I first encountered it at a friend's home in the island of Grenada.

2 *pounds boneless lamb, cut into* 1-*inch pieces*
1½ *cups coarsely chopped onion*
1 *large clove garlic, minced*
1½ *cups coarsely chopped ripe tomatoes*
½ *teaspoon oregano*
½ *teaspoon freshly grated nutmeg*
2 *thin slices fresh ginger*
½ *cup rich, strong, freshly brewed hot coffee*
½ *cup hot water*
8 *small to medium-sized sweet potatoes, peeled and cut into bite-sized pieces*
12 *or more small to medium-sized carrots, scraped and cut into bite-sized pieces*
3 *green bananas, cut into bite-sized pieces*
Salt and freshly ground black pepper to taste

In a large ovenproof casserole with a cover, arrange lamb pieces and sprinkle with the onion, garlic, and tomatoes. Thoroughly mix the oregano, nutmeg, ginger, coffee, and hot water, and pour over the vegetables and lamb. Cover and bake without stirring in a preheated 400° oven until lamb is almost tender, about 1 hour. Stir in the sweet potatoes, carrots, and bananas and add a little more hot water if necessary. Cover and continue to bake until lamb and vegetables are tender, usually about 30 minutes longer. Correct seasoning with salt and pepper, and serve very hot in large bowls. *Serves 6.*

LAMB-STUFFED PEPPERS

Red or green bell peppers, as distinct from hot varieties, often figure in Latin American menus stuffed with meat and/or other vegetables. This recipe, made with lamb, is from Aruba and Curaçao; an all-vegetable recipe from Brazil appears on page 163.

6 large green or red bell peppers
1½ pounds ground lean lamb
1 cup white long-grain rice, freshly cooked until just tender, light, and fluffy
Salt and black pepper to taste
½ cup finely chopped chives or green scallion tops
¼ cup coarsely chopped pine nuts or cashews
½ cup coarsely grated Edam cheese
Creole, tomato, or mushroom sauce

Parboil the peppers about 15 minutes, then drain. Combine the lamb, rice, salt, black pepper, chives or scallion tops, pine nuts or cashews, and a bit of the cheese; stuff the peppers with this mixture. Divide the remaining cheese over the peppers, as a topping, and bake in a preheated 350° oven for approximately 30 minutes, or until topping is melted or crusty, as you prefer, and the peppers are tender. (The filling should be suitably cooked by this time.)

Serve hot or cool as a festive luncheon item. A creole or tomato sauce can be served with this dish, or one containing sautéed mushrooms. *Serves 6.*

AJÍ DE CARNE
(Bolivian Peppery Pork)

Bolivians delight in peppery dishes; this one is typically served with potatoes or rice, and for dessert sweet pastries or fresh fruit.

¼ cup olive oil
2½ cups coarsely chopped onion
2 or 3 large cloves garlic, minced or mashed
2 pounds lean boneless pork, cut into ¾-inch cubes
2 cups coarsely chopped peeled ripe tomatoes
Chopped, seeded red chili pepper to taste
¼ teaspoon ground cinnamon
⅛ teaspoon ground cloves
Salt to taste
¼ teaspoon saffron, or achiote or bija to taste
1½ cups strained rich chicken stock
3 medium-sized potatoes, peeled and quartered
2 green bananas, cut into thick slices
3 tablespoons heavy dairy cream or Coconut Cream (see index)
1 tablespoon molasses
¼ cup finely chopped peanuts, cashews, or Brazil nuts

In a large heavy pot with a cover, heat the olive oil and sauté the onion and garlic over medium heat, stirring, until soft. Add the pork, and brown thoroughly. Add the tomatoes, chili pepper, cinnamon, cloves, salt, saffron, or achiote or bija, and stock, and simmer over low heat, covered, about 30 minutes. Add the potatoes and bananas, cover, and simmer 20 minutes longer. Add the heavy dairy cream or Coconut Cream, molasses, and nuts. Mix through, re-cover, and simmer, covered, until pork and vegetables are tender. *Serves 6.*

ROAST SUCKLING PIG WITH SEASONED RICE STUFFING

Roast pig is very popular in most parts of Latin America for feast days and other special events. The basic method of cooking is the same everywhere, but the stuffing varies considerably. Oftentimes it is an old-fashioned bread-cube stuffing, much like that used for chickens, but also popular is this seasoned rice stuffing, which I enjoy very much. The stuffing always must be placed in the cleaned, dried cavity just prior to roasting the pig, never earlier, to avoid possible food poisoning.

3 ***to*** **4** ***tablespoons butter***
1 ***cup coarsely chopped onion***
1 ***to*** **2** ***medium to large cloves garlic, minced or mashed***
1 ***cup coarsely sliced celery (include some leafy tops)***
3 ***cups freshly cooked white long-grain rice***
¼ ***teaspoon ground thyme***
½ ***teaspoon or more salt***
Freshly ground black pepper to taste
Apple juice to taste (other juices, such as papaya, may be substituted)
10-***pound prepared and cleaned suckling pig***
1 ***whole apple, orange, or banana***

In a skillet, melt the butter and sauté the onion, garlic, and celery for 5 minutes over medium heat, stirring constantly. Combine with the rice, thyme, salt, pepper, and sufficient apple juice to moisten. Just prior to roasting, stuff cavity of pig, and close with skewers or kitchen twine. Place a piece of wood in the pig's mouth to hold it open, and cover the ears and tail with aluminum foil to prevent burning. Roast on a baking sheet or in a large pan in a preheated 325°

oven until pig is done, usually about 4 hours, basting frequently with pan juices.

To serve, remove the piece of wood from the mouth and insert a whole apple, orange, banana, or other fruit for adornment. *Serves 10 or more.*

PUERCO ASADO AL ESTILO CUBANO
(Cuban Roast Pork)

This method of cooking roast pork is common in many parts of Latin America. I find it marvelously flavorful, either piping-hot from the oven or chilled and thinly sliced for a light supper entrée. The hot roast is especially good with rice, fried ripe plantains garnished with lime wedges, black beans and rice, and caramel flan.

4- to 5-pound lean roast of pork, loin, leg, or shoulder
⅓ to ½ cup fresh lime juice
3 or more large cloves garlic, minced or mashed
1 to 1½ teaspoons oregano
Salt and freshly ground black pepper

Sprinkle entire pork roast with some of the lime juice, and rub in the garlic, oregano, salt, and black pepper. In a preheated 500° oven, sear the roast 15 minutes, then reduce heat to 350°. Baste frequently with remaining lime juice, and roast about 2 hours or until rather well done. Remove from oven and allow to stand 15 minutes before carving. *Serves 4 liberally.*

PORK CHOPS APPLETON

Appleton is the name of the town in the parish of St. Elizabeth, Jamaica, where the most popular Jamaican rum is produced. Pork in all its forms takes very well to rum, as this recipe from my *Rum Cookbook* will quickly disclose. I like to serve these chops with hot fluffy rice and a big crisp cabbage slaw.

2 tablespoons butter
8 lean pork chops, cut about ½ inch thick
½ cup finely chopped onion
¼ cup finely chopped green bell pepper
¼ cup finely chopped ripe tomato, peeled if desired
¼ cup coarsely chopped fresh ripe pineapple or drained canned chunks
Salt and freshly ground black pepper to taste
2 jiggers light or dark Jamaica rum

In a heavy skillet with a cover, melt the butter and brown the chops on both sides, turning with tongs. Remove the chops and keep warm in a 200° oven. Add the onion, green pepper, tomato, and pineapple to the skillet, and cook, covered about 15 minutes, stirring occasionally.

Return the chops to the skillet, season to taste with salt and pepper, and cook, covered, until meat is tender, approximately 30 to 40 minutes.

Warm the rum, pour over the pork chops, and ignite. When flame dies down, remove chops and vegetable mixture, and serve, if desired, in preheated individual casseroles or ramekins. *Serves 4, or 8 if the chops are large.*

CHULETAS DE PUERCO CHIHUAHUA
(Pork Chops Chihuahua)

I first encountered this dish in Mexico's northern state of Chihuahua, which is known not only for hairless little dogs but also for some spectacular scenery and a consistently exciting cuisine. Pork chops prepared in this manner are usually served with hot rice, a crisp green salad, and perhaps some of the unusual fruits of the region and cubes or wedges of delectable local homemade cheese.

6 pork chops (not too lean) cut ½ inch thick
Water
1 large clove garlic, thinly sliced
¼ cup coarsely chopped onion
1 teaspoon salt
Chopped seeded chili pepper, hot pepper or Tabasco sauce to taste
2 firm ripe tomatoes, or an equivalent quantity of husked tomatillos, cut into wedges
3 hard-cooked eggs, cut into wedges
Finely chopped fresh parsley

In a sizable saucepan with a cover, place pork chops, water to cover, garlic, onion, and salt. Cover the container and bring to a boil. Reduce heat and simmer until meat is just tender, about 45 minutes. During last minutes of cooking, add chopped chili pepper or Tabasco sauce (the original recipe is very fiery, as is much Chihuahuan cuisine).

Remove the chops with a slotted spoon, drain, and pat dry with paper towels. Remove all fat from the chops, cut it into dice, and fry it in a sizable skillet until almost crisp. Drain off all but about 2 tablespoons of fat, add the pre-cooked chops, and brown thoroughly over high heat. Serve very hot, garnished with wedges of tomato or tomatillo and hard-cooked eggs, and sprinkled liberally with parsley. *Serves 4.*

SANCOCHO
(Tropical Vegetable Stew)

This grandiose, all-purpose vegetable stew appears in the cuisines of virtually all Latin American countries. Although vegetables in marvelous variety dominate, shrimp, fish, chicken, beef, pork, sausage, pig's tail, and ham bone, or combinations of these, are sometimes incorporated for their flavors. This is an especially hearty version.

- 1 *pound lean beef or pork, cut into neat 1-inch cubes*
- 1 *large, rather meaty bone from a baked ham*
- 1 *chorizo, butifarra, longaniza, or lingüiça sausage, thickly sliced*
- 1 *cup coarsely chopped onion*
- 1 *or* 2 *large cloves garlic, minced*
- 2½ *cups coarsely chopped ripe tomatoes*
- ¾ *to* 1 *cup coarsely chopped green bell pepper*
- *Chopped cilantro, or ground coriander, to taste*
- *Salt and freshly ground black pepper to taste*
- 2½ *quarts cold water*
- 1½ *pounds potatoes, peeled and cut into sizable pieces (dasheen can be substituted)*
- ½ *pound calabaza or other squash, peeled and cut into sizable pieces*
- 4 *ears tender sweet corn, cut into 2-inch lengths*
- 1 *green banana, sliced*
- 1 *medium-ripe plantain, sliced*
- *Chopped seeded red chili pepper, or hot pepper sauce, to taste*

In a large, heavy pot with a cover, place the beef or pork, ham bone, chorizo or other sausage, onion, garlic, tomatoes, green pepper, cilantro or ground coriander, salt, and black pepper. Add the water and bring to a boil. Reduce heat, cover, and simmer until meats are tender and ham falls from the bone. Remove bone and add the potatoes or other root vegetables, calabaza or squash, corn, banana, and plantain, mixing thoroughly. Season with the chili pepper or hot pepper sauce. Cover and simmer until vegetables are tender. Correct seasoning, and serve in large heated bowls. *Serves 6 to 8.*

SPARERIBS TROPIQUE

Meaty pork spareribs are prepared in a great many handsome fashions in all parts of Latin America. Here is my favorite recipe for these tasty ribs. Sometimes I serve them hot as an entrée, with rice, salad (such as vinaigrette-dressed fresh bean sprouts, widely enjoyed by both Chinese and Occidentals in Latin America), and warmed Arab or Syrian *pita* bread, also widespread in international Latin America. More often I offer them as a special appetizer at room temperature.

1½ *to 2-pound rack of pork spareribs*
¾ *cup good soy sauce (preferably the Japanese Kikkoman brand)*
¼ *cup warm water*
1 *cup tart orange marmalade*
2 *large scallions finely chopped (include the green tops)*
1 *large clove garlic, minced*
Freshly ground black pepper to taste

Separate spareribs and arrange in a shallow heavy pan with a cover. Combine soy sauce, water, marmalade, scallions, garlic, and black pepper and pour over spareribs. Marinate 4 hours, turning occasionally with tongs.

Cover and cook over medium heat, turning often, about 1½ hours, until meat is very tender and sauce is considerably reduced. Serve hot, or drain off marinade, cover, and chill for several hours. *Serves 4 to 6.*

MONDONGO JUANITA
(Nicaraguan Tripe Stew Juanita)

During a memorable series of botanical expeditions in Nicaragua, I indulged in as many of the indigenous culinary delights as possible. One of the most satisfying dishes was the following version of the traditional Latin American tripe stew, Mondongo. This was prepared for us at Monte Fresco, in the shadow of Volcán Santiago, which periodically wafts fetid fumes.

1½ pounds tripe
2½ quarts boiling water
2½ quarts cold salted water
¾ cup fresh uncooked corn kernels, or frozen kernels, thawed
2 small bay leaves
1 cup coarsely chopped onion
1 large clove garlic, peeled and halved
1 tablespoon coarse salt
6 to 8 tablespoons olive oil
3 cups coarsely chopped peeled tomatoes
¾ cup coarsely chopped green bell pepper
1 to 3 chili peppers, seeded and chopped
2 large firm ripe bananas, chopped
2 whole cloves
1 teaspoon paprika
½ teaspoon bija
3 cups parboiled peeled cassava, cut into sizable chunks
¾ cup coarsely chopped fresh parsley

Carefully immerse the tripe in boiling water, scraping it thoroughly and cooking for about 20 minutes. Drain, cut into large pieces, place in the cold salted water in a large kettle, bring to a quick, rapid boil, then reduce heat. Simmer, covered, adding the corn, bay leaves, onion, garlic, and coarse salt during the cooking. After 1 hour, remove tripe with tongs from the hot broth, and set aside until cool enough to handle. Reserve the broth.

Cut tripe into small dice, and fry in a skillet in about 4 tablespoons of the olive oil, stirring often, until it browns lightly. Return tripe to the broth.

In the same skillet, using remaining olive oil, sauté tomatoes, green and chili peppers, and bananas, along with the cloves, paprika, and bija, about 8 minutes. Turn this into the tripe kettle, cover, and simmer 1 hour, or until tripe is tender. Add chunks of cassava 20 minutes before end of cooking time, and parsley just at the last moment. Serve very hot in large bowls. *Serves 6 liberally.*

SOUSE

Souse appears in diverse fashions in English-speaking islands of the Caribbean from the Bahamas to Trinidad. In Barbados, it is typically accompanied by blood pudding, and the Spanish blood sausage, *morcilla,* an unusually interesting combination. Elisabeth Lambert Ortiz provides this comprehensive recipe for souse, which is one of the numerous pickled dishes, like escabeche, Poisson Cru, and ceviche, that are popular in Latin America.

Head of a young pig
4 pig's feet
Cold water
1 tablespoon salt

PICKLE:

1½ cups fresh lime juice
2 or 3 fresh chili peppers, seeded and sliced
1 tablespoon salt

GARNISH:

1 medium cucumber, peeled and thinly sliced
1 medium onion, chopped
1 red bell pepper, seeded and sliced
1 green bell pepper, seeded and sliced
Watercress (if desired)

SAUCE:

1 cup reserved stock (from cooking pig's head)
½ cup fresh lime juice
1 teaspoon salt
1 medium cucumber, peeled and thinly sliced or coarsely chopped
1 fresh green chili pepper, seeded and chopped

Thoroughly wash the pig's head and feet and place in a large kettle with cold water to cover and 1 tablespoon salt. Bring to a boil, lower heat, cover, and gently simmer until meat is tender, 2 hours or longer, depending on the age and size of the pig. Drain; if sauce is desired, reserve 1 cup liquid. Plunge meats into cold water. Cut all meat from the head, skinning and slicing the tongue. Halve the pig's feet. Put all meats into a large bowl. Combine the 1½ cups lime juice, chili peppers, and 1 tablespoon salt, and pour over the meats, along with enough water to cover. Allow to steep overnight, covered and refrigerated. The following day, drain meats and arrange on a platter with the garnish. Or, if preferred, mix the reserved cup of stock, ½ cup lime juice, salt, cucumber, and chili pepper to make a sauce. Omit the garnish and serve the meats accompanied by the sauce in a separate bowl. *Serves 4 to 6.*

Vegetables

Being the author of a book on vegetable cookery, I am obviously exceptionally interested in vegetables, and I am particularly intrigued by all vegetables used by my culinary colleagues throughout the Western Hemisphere.

Many people in Latin America are essentially vegetarians, not because of religious or other restrictions but because they simply cannot afford to buy meats except on rare occasions. These people have created many superlatively flavorful and nutritious vegetable medleys, which have become popular with compatriots who can well afford the finest, most costly seafood, poultry, and meats.

An astronomical number of vegetables are grown in Latin America. Many of these are well known throughout the world, while the rest are rarities in any other cuisine. Cassava, for instance, affords the principal starch for several millions of people in Latin American lands, and yet, except for the commercial tapioca that is made from it, this root vegetable is virtually unknown outside the tropics.

I enjoy the ingenious ways in which Latin Americans prepare and serve their varied vegetables. Mexicans make several subtle dishes with the tuberous morning-glory relative jícama. The cabbage family furnishes virtually all countries with differing varieties; bok-choi or Chinese cabbage, reminiscent of Swiss chard, flourishes in Jamaica. The arum family affords not only edible tubers and rootstocks but some nutritious and tasty leaves which after judicious cooking are used to stuff turnovers (often with the addition of minced hot peppers, onions, and other seasonings) or are cooked until a purée can be made for lovely green-colored soups. The tubers or rootstocks vie with potatoes, which occur in an extraordinary number of forms, colors, and textures, as favorite starchy foods. And corn, from Mexico southward, provides a large roster of culinary creations for a considerable percentage of the populace.

Almost all vegetables save those which require cold climates are found in Latin American cookery, and temperate-zone species can sometimes be grown in the mountain regions.

FRIJOLES BORRACHOS
(Drunken Beans)

Beans in seemingly infinite variety appear as staples at tables throughout the American tropics. This flavorful dish can be made with several different kinds of peas and beans, although pinto beans or red kidney beans or the smaller *frijoles colorados* are those most frequently used. With this dish, I enjoy grilled small steaks or hamburgers, a light tossed green salad, and toasted slices of cornbread. As is usually the case with bean dishes, this tastes even better when reheated.

2 cups dried pinto beans or red kidney beans or frijoles colorados, picked over and rinsed thoroughly
Water
2 tablespoons olive oil
¼ pound lean salt pork, diced
1½ cups coarsely chopped onion
2 or more large cloves garlic, minced or mashed
¾ cup coarsely chopped green bell pepper
1½ cups peeled and coarsely chopped ripe tomatoes
Chopped seeded chili pepper, or Tabasco sauce, to taste
1 cup or more stale beer
Salt and freshly ground black pepper to taste

In a large kettle with a cover, bring beans to a quick boil in water to cover. Place cover on kettle, remove from heat, and allow to stand 1 hour.

Meanwhile, in a skillet or heavy saucepan, heat the oil and cook the salt pork, stirring often, until rather crisp; remove with a slotted spoon and keep warm. Add the onion, garlic, green pepper, tomatoes, and chili pepper or Tabasco sauce, and sauté until vegetables are soft but not browned. Combine vegetables with beans, and cook, covered, until beans are tender, approximately 1½ hours, adding water as needed.

Drain off all but about ½ cup of bean liquid, stir in the beer, salt, and pepper, and simmer beans 15 to 20 minutes longer. Serve beans very hot, ideally in commodious soup bowls. *Serves 4 to 6.*

HAITIAN BLACK BEANS

Black beans—*frijoles negros* in Spanish, *feijoes* in Portuguese—appear regularly on the menus of many good Latin American cooks. In some cuisines, the legumes are simply boiled in salted water until tender, without additional flavoring and seasoning, but not so in this marvelous Haitian version, which has long been a staple at my home.

1 ***pound dried black beans***
Water
2 ***cups chopped onion***
1 ***cup chopped green bell pepper***
2 ***large cloves garlic, minced or mashed***
2 ***medium bay leaves***
1 ***tablespoon salt or more***
½ ***teaspoon freshly ground black pepper or more***
¼ ***teaspoon oregano or more***
¼ ***to*** ½ ***teaspoon mixed herbs***
3 ***tablespoons cider vinegar***
½ ***cup cooking or salad oil***
4-***ounce jar or can pimientos, drained and chopped***

Pick over and rinse the beans and place them, with fresh water to cover, in a large heavy kettle. Cover kettle and bring to a quick boil. Remove from heat and allow to sit 1 hour. Return to the heat and cook, adding water as needed, 30 minutes. Add onion, green pepper, garlic, bay leaves, salt, black pepper, oregano, and mixed herbs, and continue to cook over medium heat until the beans are tender, usually several hours, depending upon age of beans. Add the vinegar, mixing thoroughly, and return to the heat. About 15 minutes before end of cooking time, stir in the oil and pimiento. Stir frequently during these final 15 minutes to avoid scorching. Serve atop or alongside hot rice. *Serves 6 liberally.*

BROWNED CABBAGE

In Latin American markets one can find small, almost immature cabbages, seldom larger than a man's fist, which are almost as tender as lettuce, with a refreshing flavor and texture. Whenever I see these vegetable jewels, I acquire them; to shred for slaws, to steam quickly and serve with lots of butter and freshly ground black pepper, or to use in this dish, which is sublime served with pork or perhaps a rather peppery beef stew. More mature cabbages, cut into wedges, can be used if the small ones are not obtainable.

4 to 6 tiny, tender heads cabbage, well rinsed
1½ quarts lightly salted water
2 to 3 slices lean bacon, diced
¼ cup melted butter
Freshly ground black pepper to taste

Place cabbages in a large kettle with a cover, along with the salted water and bacon; cover and bring to a boil. Remove from heat, drain, and allow to steam, still covered, about 5 minutes; the tiny cabbages then should be rather tender.

Cut cabbages lengthwise into halves, and arrange, cut sides up, in a shallow ovenproof serving dish. Top with bacon bits and some of the melted butter. Place in a preheated 375° oven and bake, basting occasionally with remaining melted butter, until cabbages are lightly browned and nicely tender. Serve very hot, sprinkled with black pepper. *Serves 4.*

CASSAVA CROQUETTES

Latin American dishes of African ancestry are usually spicy, indeed even "hot." But there are occasional recipes that are designed to cool off the happy diner, for example these croquettes, which go well with almost any meat course, and particularly with fish or poultry.

2 *cups peeled grated cassava*
3 *large eggs*
2 *tablespoons grated lime peel (without any white)*
⅛ *teaspoon fresh grated nutmeg*
1 *teaspoon or more salt*
⅛ *teaspoon freshly ground black pepper*
2 *tablespoons finely chopped fresh parsley*
½ *cup fine breadcrumbs*
3 *tablespoons butter and/or cooking oil*

Moisten the cassava with water, then squeeze dry with your hands. Add 2 of the eggs, the lime peel, nutmeg, salt, pepper, and parsley, and mix thoroughly. Beat the remaining egg in a bowl. Shape the cassava mixture into croquettes or flattish cakes and dip in the beaten egg, then in the bread crumbs.

Melt the butter and/or oil in a skillet over medium heat and fry the croquettes, without crowding, until well browned on both sides. Drain and serve hot. *Serves about 6.*

TORREJAS DE MAÍZ TIERNO
(Corn Fritters)

These Colombian fritters are made from mature but tender sweet corn. I find them delectable with fried fish, perhaps served with a piquant peppery sauce such as the Brazilian one on page 190.

3 cups sweet corn, cut from the cob, with its milk
About ¼ cup flour
2 tablespoons granulated or light brown sugar
½ teaspoon salt
Dash or more hot pepper sauce
1 large egg, lightly beaten
2 tablespoons grated sharp cheese, such as Cheddar
Melted lard or other fat for deep-frying

Gently but thoroughly combine the corn and its milk with the flour, sugar, salt, and hot pepper sauce. Blend in the egg and cheese. Heat the lard or fat to 265° and drop in the batter by teaspoonfuls. Deep-fry until golden brown on both sides. Drain on paper towels and serve very hot. *Makes about 2 dozen 2-inch fritters.*

HUMITAS
(Stuffed Cornhusks)

Cornhusks are widely used in Latin America as handy envelopes for all sorts of savory or spicy stuffings. After being boiled or steamed, these preparations are unwrapped at the table, or in the forest on a picnic, where nothing could be nicer than these Humitas from Argentina and Uruguay.

8 fresh tender ears sweet corn in their husks
2 to 3 quarts boiling water
6 tablespoons butter
¾ cup finely chopped onion
1½ cups coarsely chopped peeled ripe tomatoes
1 teaspoon light brown or granulated sugar
Salt and freshly ground black pepper to taste
¼ cup milk
2 large eggs, lightly beaten
Dash or more hot pepper sauce
1 pound lean ground beef or beef and pork mixed

Strip husks and silk from the corn, discarding the silk. Cut kernels off cobs, and reserve kernels, their milk, and the cobs. Place the largest husks in a large pot of boiling water until softened and pliable; drain and set aside.

In a sizable skillet, melt 3 tablespoons of the butter and sauté onion until soft; add tomatoes, sugar, salt, and pepper, mix well, and cook about 5 minutes. Add kernels and their milk, the eggs, the hot pepper sauce, and the ¼ cup of milk, and cook over lowest heat, 10 minutes, stirring constantly.

Meanwhile, in another skillet, melt the remaining 3 tablespoons butter and sauté the meat, stirring often, until rather well done. Add to the corn mixture, combine gently but thoroughly and correct seasoning if necessary.

Make certain that cornhusks are thoroughly dry, then place about 3 tablespoons of the mixture in the center of each (you may have to overlap two husks in some instances). Fold sides of husks over stuffing, making an envelope; tuck in ends and tie up with kitchen twine or thread.

Place the corncobs on the bottom of a large, deep pot, and just cover with boiling water. Arrange the Humitas on the cobs, cover container tightly, and cook 30 minutes over medium heat. Carefully remove the Humitas and allow your guests to untie them at the table. Or chill them to take on a picnic. *Serves 4 to 6.*

CROQUETAS DE BERENJENA
(Eggplant Fritters Mayagüez)

These little fritters come from Puerto Rico, where they are particularly popular with pork and poultry dishes. Eggplant appears in the cuisines of almost all the Latin American lands, often in ingenious fashion.

3 small eggplants, peeled and sliced
Salted water
½ cup flour
¾ teaspoon salt
⅛ teaspoon freshly grated nutmeg
¼ cup freshly grated Parmesan or Romano cheese
3 tablespoons butter
2 eggs
⅛ teaspoon freshly ground black pepper
⅔ cup fine cracker crumbs
2 cups (1 pound) lard for deep-frying (no substitutes)

Boil the eggplants until tender in heavily salted water to cover. Drain thoroughly and mash in a large bowl. Add the flour, ½ teaspoon of the salt, the nutmeg, and the cheese, mixing well. Melt the butter in a skillet and cook over low heat 5 minutes, stirring constantly. Remove from heat and let cool, then add to fritter mixture.

Break the eggs with a fork but do not beat; blend in remaining ¼ teaspoon salt and the pepper. Form tablespoonfuls of the eggplant mixture into balls; roll these first in the cracker crumbs, then in the eggs, and again in the cracker crumbs. Heat the lard (do not use any other fat for this recipe) to 380° and deep-fry 2 or 3 fritters at a time until just golden brown. Drain on paper towels and serve hot. *Makes about 12.*

BERENJENA CON PLÁTANO Y TOMATES
(Eggplant with Plantain and Tomatoes)

This dish, an unusual combination of flavors and textures, is popular in Costa Rica and is also found in Panama and Nicaragua. It goes well with roast lamb, lamb chops with a touch of oregano grilled over charcoal, roast pork, or fried chicken.

4 small to medium-sized eggplants, cut lengthwise into ½-inch slices
Salt
¼ cup olive oil
1½ to 1¾ cups finely chopped onion
1 medium to large clove garlic, minced or mashed
½ cup finely chopped green bell pepper
2½ cups coarsely chopped ripe tomatoes
1 tablespoon finely chopped fresh parsley
Chopped seeded red chili pepper or hot pepper sauce to taste
Freshly ground black pepper to taste
2 tablespoons butter
1 or 2 large ripe black-skinned plantains, diagonally sliced into pieces ⅓ inch thick

Sprinkle the eggplant slices with salt and allow to drain 20 to 30 minutes; then pat dry. Heat the oil in a large skillet and sauté eggplant slices on both sides, without crowding, turning carefully with a slotted spatula; remove to an ovenproof casserole and set aside. To the same skillet add the onion, garlic, and green pepper, and sauté, turning occasionally, until vegetables are soft. Stir in the tomatoes, parsley, chili pepper, and salt and black pepper to taste. Mix well, cover skillet, and simmer until sauce is well cooked and flavorful.

Separately, in the butter over medium heat, sauté plantain slices until lightly browned on both sides, turning with care. Arrange the plantain slices on top of the eggplant in the casserole and pour the tomato sauce over all. Heat through briefly in a 400° oven and serve at once. *Serves 4 to 6.*

TROPICAL-VEGETABLE-STUFFED GREEN PEPPERS

6 medium-sized green bell peppers
4 tablespoons unsalted butter
½ cup shredded crisp cabbage
½ cup shredded Swiss chard, bok-choi, or kale
½ cup finely chopped green bell pepper
¼ cup finely chopped onion
½ cup coarsely chopped parboiled chayote
¼ cup finely chopped parboiled calabaza
½ teaspoon salt
¼ teaspoon freshly ground black pepper
Hot pepper sauce to taste
½ cup coarsely grated Edam cheese

Parboil the peppers for 15 minutes, then drain. Melt the butter in a skillet and sauté the cabbage, chard, bok-choi, or kale, the pepper, and the onion. Combine vegetables with the parboiled chayote and calabaza, then season with the salt, pepper, hot pepper sauce, and a little of the cheese. Stuff the peppers with the vegetable mixture, then top with the remaining cheese. Bake in a preheated 350° oven for approximately 30 minutes, or until topping is melted and crusty. *Serves 6.*

LIMA BEANS WITH HAM HOCKS

Smoked ham hocks or pork hocks are generally available throughout Latin America, and when I can acquire them, they form the basis for many of the most savory dishes offered at my table. Variants of this tasty, hearty soup that is close to being a stew are found in many of these countries. I almost always accompany this main-dish medley with freshly made cornbread or leftover cornbread that has been sliced, toasted, and buttered; marinated cucumber salad, when I cannot get sour or dill pickles; tossed salad with a garlicky vinaigrette dressing; dry red wine; and for dessert a compote of fresh fruits of the season, perhaps touched with rum or grenadine.

- 1 ***pound lightly smoked ham hocks or pork hocks***
- 1 ***quart or more water***
- 2 ***cups coarsely chopped onion***
- 2 ***large cloves garlic, minced***
- ¾ ***cup coarsely chopped green bell pepper (optional)***
- 1 ***pound dried small or large lima beans, picked over and rinsed***
- ½ ***teaspoon or more oregano***
- 1 ***teaspoon or more salt***
- ½ ***teaspoon or more freshly ground black pepper***

Put the ham hocks or pork hocks in a large heavy kettle with a cover, add 1 quart water, cover pot, and bring to a quick boil. Add the onion, garlic, and, if desired, the green pepper, reduce heat, and cook, covered, until meat almost falls from the bones.

Add the beans, mix well, cover the kettle, and continue to cook until beans are tender, adding water as needed. When beans start to become tender (test them), add oregano, salt, and black pepper. Finish cooking and correct seasoning. The mixture should be rather soupy.

Serve very hot in large preheated bowls, in small portions; replenish with frequency from the hot pot on the stove. *Serves 4 to 6.*

COO-COO
(Okra and Cornmeal Mush)

Guyanese cookery is an interesting blend of English, East Indian, American, and African. The antecedents of this Coo-Coo are probably more African than anything else. It is a very filling dish, generally served as the starch of the meal, garnished with fried plantains and rice.

1 *cup sliced raw okra (preferably small pods)*
2 *to* 3 *cups salted water*
1 *cup cornmeal*
½ *cup coarsely chopped onion*
Dash or more Tabasco sauce
¼ *pound cooked corned beef, diced*
2 *tablespoons butter*

Place the okra in a pot with 1 cup of the salted water and boil until tender. While the vegetable is boiling, combine the cornmeal, onion, another cup of salted water, and the Tabasco sauce, and add to the pot, along with the corned beef. Mix well and cook, stirring frequently, until mixture thickens, adding more water if necessary; be certain that the cornmeal does not scorch.

Turn into a buttered baking dish, dot with butter, and bake in a preheated 350° oven 30 minutes. Serve very hot. *Serves 4 liberally.*

PIONONOS
(Meat-Stuffed Plantain Circles)

These sumptuous Puerto Rican meat-stuffed plantain circles make a superb light repast along with hot rice, perhaps a crisp cabbage slaw, heated crusty bread, and for dessert cheese and fresh tropical fruits. They are a bit complicated to make, but eminently worthwhile.

1 *pound lean ground beef or pork*
1 *large clove garlic, minced or mashed*
1 *cup minced onion*
½ *cup minced green bell pepper*
1 *cup finely chopped ripe tomato*
½ *teaspoon or more oregano*
Salt and freshly ground black pepper to taste
1 *teaspoon wine, cane, or cider vinegar*
2 *tablespoons plus* 1 *cup lard flavored with achiote*
2 *tablespoons chopped seedless raisins*
6 *pitted green olives, finely chopped*
1 *teaspoon chopped drained capers*
½ *cup tomato sauce*
6 *ripe plantains*
6 *large eggs, separated*
½ *teaspoon salt*

Very thoroughly combine the ground meat, garlic, onion, green pepper, tomato, oregano, salt, black pepper, and vinegar. In a skillet, over rather high heat, melt 2 tablespoons of the achiote-flavored lard, and cook meat mixture, stirring often, until nicely browned. Mix in the raisins, olives, capers, and tomato sauce, and simmer a few minutes, stirring. Set aside.

Peel the plantains and cut into rather narrow lengthwise slices. Melt ½ cup achiote-lard in another large skillet, and brown plantain slices on both sides, turning carefully as needed. Remove from skillet and form each slice into a circle, fastening with toothpicks.

Beat the egg whites until stiff. Beat yolks, add to whites, and gently beat until well combined. Stir in ½ teaspoon salt. Fill the plantain circles with the meat mixture, then dip them in the beaten eggs. Heat the remaining ½ cup achiote-lard in the same skillet in which the plantains were cooked. Fry the circles until well browned on both top and bottom, being careful not to let meat mixture slip out. Drain on paper towels, and serve hot or at room temperature. *Serves 6.*

LLAPINGACHOS
(Potato-Cheese Cakes)

These cakes are a favorite fare in Ecuador, and variants are found in Peru and Bolivia, where potatoes appear at virtually every meal. I often serve them with roast pork or sautéed lamb chops. They are sometimes served with a fried or poached egg atop.

2 *pounds potatoes (unpeeled)*
Salted water
Butter, salt, and black pepper to taste
½ *cup finely chopped onion*
1 *small to medium clove garlic, mashed*
⅓ *cup butter*
2½ *cups or more cottage or cream cheese or tart homemade cheese*
Fried or poached eggs (optional)

Boil the potatoes in salted water to cover, peel, and mash thoroughly, seasoning well with butter, salt, and black pepper.

In a skillet, sauté the onion and garlic in 2 tablespoons of the butter until soft, stirring often, then blend in the cheese and heat through. Thoroughly mix the mashed potatoes with the onion-cheese mixure and form into smallish cakes. Fry in the remaining butter, turning carefully with a spatula as needed, until nicely browned on both sides. If desired, top with fried or poached eggs and serve hot. *Serves about 6.*

BUÑUELOS DE ESPINACA
(Spinach Fritters)

These fritters are made with just about every imaginable ingredient to be found in the cuisines of Latin America, from fruits and vegetables to meats to nuts. This recipe is from Uruguay, though closely allied versions occur in Argentina, Brazil, and Paraguay. The chopped green vegetable can be spinach, kale, Swiss chard, turnip greens, bok-choi tops, or even finely sliced green scallion tops.

1 *tablespoon butter*
1 *tablespoon olive oil*
1½ *to* 2 *cups finely chopped uncooked or quickly blanched spinach or other green vegetable*
¾ *cup peeled, finely chopped tomato*
1 *to* 1½ *cups finely chopped onion*
1 *large clove garlic, minced or mashed*
¼ *cup finely chopped green bell pepper*
¼ *teaspoon or more minced seeded chili pepper, or hot pepper sauce to taste*
Salt and freshly ground black pepper to taste
2 *tablespoons freshly grated sharp cheese, such as Parmesan, Romano, or Cheddar*
2 *cups flour*
2 *teaspoons baking powder*
1 *large egg, well beaten*
1 *cup milk*
Oil or other fat for deep-frying

Combine the butter and olive oil in a skillet and sauté the spinach or other green vegetable, the tomato, onion, garlic, green pepper, chili pepper or hot pepper sauce until soft, stirring constantly. Blend in the salt and pepper and cheese, remove from heat, and allow to cool.

Combine the flour, baking powder, egg, and milk and stir into the spinach mixture. Heat the oil or fat to 360° and drop the mixture by teaspoonfuls to deep-fry until golden on all sides. Remove with a slotted spoon, drain well, and serve hot. *Makes 36 fritters.*

KIVEVE
(Paraguayan Mashed Squash)

During my visits to Paraguay I found the indigenous cuisine both inventive and attractive. The first time I encountered this Kiveve was in a small town some distance from the capital, Asunción, where it was served with roast tapir. The Kiveve was delectable, and so was the tapir, though I have an aversion to consuming beasts with plaintive expressions, such as this one wore.

1 *pound calabaza or other firm yellow or orange squash, peeled and cut into small chunks*
Water
1 *teaspoon salt*
4 *to* 6 *whole black peppercorns*
3 *to* 4 *tablespoons butter*
½ *cup cornmeal (preferably yellow)*
1 *tablespoon light brown sugar*
2 *cups freshly grated mild Cheddar or other cheese*

In a heavy covered pot, cook the squash in water to cover, with salt and peppercorns until tender. Drain, discard the peppercorns, and mash the squash or put it through a ricer.

Place it in the top of a double boiler over boiling water; add the butter, cornmeal, and sugar, mixing well, and cook about 5 minutes, stirring constantly. Reduce heat under double boiler to low, and cook, covered, until cornmeal is tender, stirring once or twice. Stir in the cheese, heat until cheese is melted, and serve very hot. *Serves 6.*

DAUBE DE PATATE
(Haitian Sweet Potato and Banana Pudding)

Although this hearty, flavorful pudding originated in Haiti, variations of it appear in many parts of Latin America. When hot from the oven the dish is served as a vegetable with all kinds of entrées; chilled and thinly sliced, it makes a delicious dessert with Salsa de Naranjas (see index).

2 *cups mashed cooked sweet potatoes*
2 *medium-ripe bananas, mashed*
1 *cup milk*
1 *to* 2 *tablespoons light brown sugar, or to taste*
½ *teaspoon salt*
⅛ *teaspoon freshly grated nutmeg*
⅛ *teaspoon ground cinnamon*
2 *egg yolks, beaten well*
3 *tablespoons or more chopped raisins*

In a large mixing bowl thoroughly blend the mashed sweet potatoes and bananas. Blend in the milk gradually, mixing until very smooth; add the sugar, salt, nutmeg, cinnamon, egg yolks, and raisins, and mix well. Pour into a well-buttered 1-quart casserole, and bake in a preheated 300° oven until pudding is well set and rather firm and top is golden-brown, usually about 50 minutes. Serve hot or chilled. *Serves 4 to 6.*

CAZUELA
(Sweet Potato and Calabaza Pudding)

This delightful creation is encountered, with variations, in many parts of the Caribbean, though it is especially Puerto Rican.

1 pound mashed cooked sweet potatoes
1 pound mashed cooked calabaza
1 to 1½ cups Coconut Milk (see index)
¼ cup sweet sherry (optional)
4 large eggs, beaten
¼ cup flour
½ teaspoon or more salt
¾ cup granulated or light brown sugar
2 teaspoons ground cinnamon
¾ teaspoon ground cloves
Whipped cream, flavored if desired with a little rum (optional)

In a large bowl, blend the sweet potatoes, calabaza, Coconut Milk, sherry if desired, and eggs. Force through a sieve, or whirl in a blender until very smooth.

In a smallish bowl, thoroughly mix together the flour, salt, sugar, cinnamon, and cloves. Add to the purée, blending thoroughly. Turn into a lightly greased or buttered shallow baking dish, and bake in a preheated 350° oven about 40 minutes or until a toothpick inserted in the center comes out clean. Serve hot as a hearty vegetable dish, or cooled and chilled as a dessert, with whipped cream if desired. *Serves 8 to 10.*

LOCRO
(Ecuadorian Vegetable Stew)

In most Spanish-speaking South American lands, one encounters Locro, a thick vegetable soup or stew, on occasion seasoned with a bit of pig's tail, salt beef, salt pork, or fish. Here is a luscious version from Ecuador, where a number of variations of this creation can be found. The addition of Coconut Milk is coastal Ecuadorian and provides a delectable touch. Potatoes occur in many distinct varieties, and indeed flavors, in Ecuador, especially at high elevations, where they thrive particularly well.

2 to 3 tablespoons butter or lard or a combination of oil and butter
1½ cups coarsely chopped onion
2 large cloves garlic, minced or mashed
½ to 1 teaspoon crushed achiote or bija
2 to 3 tablespoons tomato paste
½ cup water
1 cup tender fresh corn kernels
1 large bay leaf
2 whole cloves
Salt and freshly ground black pepper to taste
3 pounds medium-sized potatoes, peeled and diced or cut into eighths
2 cups diced peeled calabaza
1 cup Coconut Milk (see index) or cow's milk
Cold water
¾ cup freshly grated mild cheese, such as Gruyère
1 cup cooked fresh or drained canned green peas
1 large egg, beaten well

In a large pot with a cover, heat the butter or lard over medium heat, and sauté the onion and garlic with the achiote or bija until soft. Blend the tomato paste with the water, and add to the pot along with the corn kernels, bay leaf, cloves, salt, and pepper. Cover and bring to a boil, then lower the heat and simmer 10 minutes. Add the potatoes, calabaza, Coconut Milk or cow's milk, and cold water to cover. Simmer, covered, over very low heat, stirring once or twice gently, until all vegetables are just tender. Stir in the cheese, peas, and egg, and barely heat through, stirring gently. Serve hot or at room temperature. *Serves 6 liberally.*

Salads

Salads using a very wide variety of ingredients are regularly offered on Latin American menus, on occasion as a main dish, more commonly as a special accompaniment either along with or following the entrée. As a serious salad aficionado, I often make an entire luncheon or supper from one of these culinary delights.

The main-dish salads include superb fresh lobster, shrimp, or mixed seafood, grandiose tossed assemblages, and Caesar salads, which in all probability originated in Mexico. Potatoes and cold meats—tongue, roast beef, suckling pig, or ham—figure in many Latin salads, and other pleasant ingredients include assorted cheese and garlicky croutons. Cold vegetable salads are highly popular. A sort of tropical Russian salad (which originally was not Russian at all) of chilled cooked beets, potatoes, green beans, and just about anything else appropriate and available, bound with homemade well-seasoned mayonnaise or vinaigrette dressing, appears on many buffet and luncheon tables.

The Latin Americans have available a good variety of salad greens, including several kinds of lettuce as well as celery, scallions, chives, watercress, and sometimes escarole and chicory. Ingenious combinations of fresh fruits are often served, either with crisp lettuce or shredded cabbage, or, diced or cut into julienne strips, and chilled, with cooked meats and cheese.

At my home, I often serve a mixed tossed salad, consisting of whatever greenery I can obtain at the local market, along with seeded cucumber, maybe a touch of either white or red radishes, and flavorful cherry or plum tomatoes (the latter are called "apple tomatoes" in Jamaica). For this I make a vinaigrette dressing in which I blend a bit of dry mustard and oregano with the customary seasonings prior to adding the oil and vinegar or lemon juice or lime juice, and mixing.

ENSALADA DE AGUACATE RANCHERO
(Avocado Salad Ranchero)

I was introduced to this salad by Mrs. Bertha Cochran Hahn, former food editor of the *Miami News*, who encountered it in Mexico. I like it with Puerco Asado al Estilo

Cubano (see index), garlic bread, and a bottle of dry red wine; dessert can be thinly sliced, chilled Cocada (see index).

16-ounce can chickpeas, drained
5 tablespoons wine vinegar
¼ cup olive oil
½ teaspoon salt
¼ teaspoon paprika
¼ teaspoon or more oregano
Dash or more hot pepper sauce
½ teaspoon minced garlic
¼ cup minced white onion or scallions
1 pound fresh spinach
3 cups cubed peeled ripe avocado (prepared just before serving)
Salt and freshly ground black pepper to taste

Place the chickpeas in a saucepan with the vinegar, oil, salt, paprika, oregano, hot pepper sauce, garlic, and onion. Bring to a boil, then remove from heat and allow to cool. Pour into a large salad bowl, and chill at least 1 hour.

Thoroughly wash and drain the spinach, trim off coarse stems, and tear leaves into large pieces; dry and chill well.

At the last moment, just before serving, add the spinach and the avocado to the chilled chickpeas in their sauce. Toss lightly, season with salt and black pepper, and serve at once. *Serves 6.*

ENSALADA COLOMBIANA
(Chorizo and Vegetable Salad)

Colombian cuisine is interesting and unusual, incorporating a variety of ingredients artfully and attractively; this hearty salad, with perhaps heated garlic bread and chilled beer, makes a most pleasant repast.

3 chorizo sausages
About 6 tablespoons olive oil
1½ cups cooked tender corn kernels
1 cup cut-up cooked green beans (1-inch pieces)
2 medium-sized or large tomatoes or several cherry or plum tomatoes, sliced
¼ cup finely chopped fresh parsley
Minced or grated onion to taste
4 to 5 cups bite-sized pieces crisp lettuce
Salt and freshly ground black pepper to taste
⅛ to ¼ teaspoon dry mustard
Wine vinegar, cider vinegar, or cane vinegar, to taste

In a skillet, fry chorizos in 2 tablespoons of the oil until nicely browned, turning with tongs as needed. Drain on paper towels, and cut into rather thin slices. In a large serving bowl, combine the sausages with the corn kernels, green beans, tomatoes, parsley, and onion, mixing gently but well. Chill, covered, and separately chill lettuce pieces, also covered.

Prepare a dressing by blending salt, black pepper, and mustard, then adding the remaining 4 tablespoons of oil and finally vinegar, mixing very well. Just before serving, gently mix the lettuce through the salad, pour the dressing over all, and toss gently but thoroughly. *Serves 6.*

ENSALADA DE PAPAYA
(Papaya Salad)

The papaya is one of the tropics' most extraordinary plants. Despite its appearance, it is not a tree, but rather one of the fastest growing herbaceous plants known. I have long been inordinately fond of papaya and wherever I have gone in Latin America, I have tried any new variants that were offered for sale. Incidentally, the coagulated juice of *Carica papaya* forms the basis for many commercial meat tenderizers.

2 cups or more firm ripe papaya cubes, with pith and seeds removed

1 to 1½ cups ripe fresh pineapple cubes

1 cup firm ripe orange or tangerine segments, with pith and seeds removed

1 large firm ripe banana, peeled and diced

1 tablespoon grenadine

Fresh lime or lemon juice to taste

Sugar to taste, if necessary

1 cup homemade toasted Coconut Chips (see index), or canned Coconut Chips

In a serving bowl, combine all the fruits gently but thoroughly. Sprinkle with the grenadine and lime or lemon juice, and if necessary add a tiny touch of sugar. Chill, covered, at least 1 hour. Serve in suitable cool containers, topped with canned or homemade Coconut Chips. *Serves 4.*

ENSALADA DE PAPAS Y MANZANAS
(Apple and Potato Salad)

In Cuba and Puerto Rico one finds this unusual and delicious salad, which apparently had its origin in Spain. Sometimes the potato salad is used to stuff large apples, but I rather prefer all the ingredients mixed together and served on crisp lettuce leaves.

6 firm unpeeled apples, tart or sweet but not mealy, diced or sliced

2 cups or more diced or sliced peeled boiled potatoes

3 stalks crisp celery, thinly sliced or diced

1 cup mayonnaise or boiled salad dressing

Salt and freshly ground black pepper to taste

½ teaspoon dried tarragon

Crisp lettuce leaves

1 tablespoon finely chopped fresh parsley

Gently but thoroughly combine the apples, potatoes, and celery with the mayonnaise or boiled dressing in an attractive serving bowl. Season with the salt and black pepper and sprinkle with the tarragon. Arrange the lettuce leaves around the edge, and chill, covered. Serve individual portions on the lettuce leaves, with a sprinkling of chopped parsley. *Serves 6 liberally.*

ENSALADA DE RÁBONES
(Radish Salad)

Radish Salad is popular in many Latin cuisines, and I find it refreshing.

¼ cup olive oil
2 tablespoons lime juice
1½ teaspoons salt
¼ teaspoon freshly ground black pepper
1 cup peeled, chopped ripe tomatoes
3 cups sliced red radishes
⅓ cup finely chopped onion
Crisp lettuce, torn into pieces

In a small bowl, beat together the oil, lime juice, salt, and black pepper. Drain tomatoes slightly, then combine with radish slices and chopped onion. Add oil mixture and toss until blended. Chill in the refrigerator. Before serving, toss with the lettuce pieces. *Serves 6.*

YAM SALAD

Here is a rather unusual salad with strong African antecedents, which is popular in several Latin American countries, served with meats and fish.

1 pound yams, diced
Boiling salted water
4 large scallions, finely sliced (include the green tops)
2 tablespoons grated or finely minced onion
1 cup finely chopped ripe tomato, peeled if desired
Mayonnaise
Salt and freshly grated black pepper to taste

Cook the diced yams in boiling salted water until just firm-tender; drain well and chill, covered, about 1 hour. In a serving bowl, gently but thoroughly combine the yams with all but about 1 tablespoon of the scallions, the onion, tomato, mayonnaise enough to bind the salad, salt, and black pepper.

Arrange the salad in a neat mound, cover, and chill thoroughly. Before serving, sprinkle with the reserved 1 tablespoon of scallions. *Serves 3 or 4.*

GADO-GADO WITH KATJANG SAUCE

The famous Indonesian multicourse rijstafel ("rice table") appears throughout the Netherlands Antilles, and particularly in Surinam (formerly Dutch Guiana), where one may encounter as many as twenty side dishes with the large bowl of rice that forms the basis of the repast. Here is one of my favorite rijstafel recipes, crisp-boiled vegetables with a peanut sauce.

1 medium-sized firm cabbage, cut into small wedges
1 pound green beans, cut into 1½-inch lengths
1 medium-sized cucumber, peeled and cut into pieces measuring about 2 inches by ¾-inch
1 large eggplant, peeled and cut into pieces about 2 inches square by ¾-inch thick
Boiling salted water
10-ounce package fresh bean sprouts, or a 10-ounce can bean sprouts, rinsed and drained
1 medium-sized ripe tomato, thinly sliced
3 hard-cooked eggs, sliced
Katjang Sauce to taste (see following recipe)

In separate containers, cook the cabbage, green beans, cucumber, and eggplant in boiling salted water, until each vegetable is just tender—overcooking will ruin the dish. Drain and let cool slightly. Arrange vegetables individually and attractively on a large platter, and garnish with bean sprouts, slices of tomato and egg. Chill, covered, if desired.

At the last moment, dress with Katjang Sauce to taste. *Serves 6 as part of a rijstafel menu.*

KATJANG SAUCE

2 tablespoons grated white onion
2 tablespoons olive oil
1 tablespoon dark brown sugar
Fresh lime juice to taste, typically about 1 teaspoon
¼ cup peanut butter
1 cup coconut water (see index)
Salt to taste

Sauté the onion in the oil in a heavy saucepan, stirring, until soft. Blend in the brown sugar, lime juice, and peanut butter, stirring until thoroughly mixed. Gradually add coconut water, stirring constantly, then add salt. Cook, stirring, until sauce is thick and smooth. *Makes* 1¼ *cups.*

SALADE HAITIENNE
(Haitian Vegetable Salad)

Haiti has a fascinating cuisine, and because of the hot climate, cooling but hearty salads are to be found on many a menu. This showy vegetable salad is a favorite dish at elegant Haitian tables, accompanied perhaps with cold roast chicken or a seafood creation.

1½ cups thinly sliced cooked small carrots
1 cup thinly sliced cooked small turnips
1 to 1½ cups peeled and diced cooked potatoes
1 cup peeled and diced cooked beets
2 large ripe tomatoes, cut into neat wedges
½ cup thinly sliced red radishes
2½ to 3 cups crisp watercress, rinsed and picked over
3 hard-cooked eggs, thinly sliced
½ cup olive oil
Wine vinegar or cider vinegar to taste
Dry mustard to taste
Salt and freshly ground black pepper to taste

Chill all the vegetables and the eggs. Meanwhile, prepare a vinaigrette dressing by thoroughly blending the oil, vinegar, mustard, salt, and black pepper, until a pleasant-tasting piquant mixture is obtained. Let stand at room temperature about 1 hour.

Arrange the chilled vegetables in attractive rings on a large platter, with the radish and egg slices in the center. Surround with a ring of watercress. Stir the dressing well and pour over entire salad; serve without delay. *Serves 6.*

Sauces

Latin American cooks make use of a gratifying number of sauces. Some are unusually peppery, while others are deliciously bland, yet most flavorful.

Mexico has special sauces of parsley and of ground nuts, a sort of Soubise sauce made with minced onions and more than a touch of garlic, and a strong garlic sauce which is so artfully prepared that one does not realize that it is garlic. Salsa fría ("cold sauce") is far from cold in flavor, and in some of its forms in the countryside, where hot chili peppers appear in virtually every dish, it can be formidable, even though it is offered in a separate bowl at the table, to be added to individual taste. Some of the hot pepper sauces sold in the American tropics are also fiendishly hot and should be used with caution. I once got a tiny bit of one of these commercial sauces in my eye, and the pain was memorable for more than a day.

Pasta sauces appear in the cuisines of all the lands that have populations of Italian ancestry. Specialized sauces made from tropical fruits, such as acerola (Barbados cherry) and lime, adorn many a menu. In fact, fresh lime juice, which scarcely can be termed a sauce, may appear at any meal from breakfast to supper; a few drops from a ripe lime can be dribbled over all sorts of edibles with superlative results. Unless I can squeeze fresh, ripe, seeded lime wedges over shrimp or lobster or fish, I do not enjoy them to the fullest extent.

GUASACACA
(Venezuelan Barbecue Sauce)

This marvelous sauce is widely used in Venezuela for barbecues and such pleasant culinary events. I use it during my visits to anoint such diverse things as large pieces of beef, quartered young chickens, and butterfly shrimp. Ideally, the sauce should be used as soon as it is made, since the avocado tends to go "off" a bit if it stands long.

1 ***large firm ripe avocado or 2 small ones or to taste***

1½ ***cups or more peeled, finely chopped ripe tomatoes***

1 ***cup olive oil***

Wine vinegar, cider vinegar, or a combination of vinegar and lemon or lime juice, to taste

1 ***teaspoon, more or less, prepared sharp mustard***

Salt to taste
1 ***red chili pepper, seeded and finely chopped, or hot pepper sauce to taste***
1 ***to*** **1½** ***cups finely chopped onion***
1 ***small to medium clove garlic, minced or mashed***
1 ***to*** **2** ***tablespoons finely chopped fresh parsley***

In a sizable bowl, mash the avocado and tomatoes with a fork. Combine the oil, vinegar, mustard, salt, chili pepper or hot pepper sauce, onion, garlic, and parsley and blend into the avocado mixture. Correct seasoning.

Use as a basting sauce for barbecued or charcoal-roasted meats. *Makes about 4 cups.*

SALSA DE ACEROLA
(Barbados Cherry Sauce)

Barbados cherries thrive in many Latin American lands and have long been used in inventive local cookery. The fruit is known as *acerola* in Puerto Rico, where it is raised commercially, being the greatest source known of fruit ascorbic acid. Serve this pleasant tart sauce over chicken, duck, or pork, or such vegetables as wedges of steamed cabbage, chopped calalu, boiled halved small white onions separated into single shells, or cooked green beans.

1 ***cup puréed Barbados cherries***
Boiling water
¼ ***cup butter***
½ ***teaspoon salt***
¼ ***teaspoon black pepper***
2 ***tablespoons flour***
¾ ***cup Coconut Milk (see index)***
Granulated or light brown sugar to taste
2 ***tablespoons finely chopped fresh parsley (optional)***

To prepare the cherry purée, first mash the fruit thoroughly with a fork and remove seeds. Put into a saucepan, adding a small amount of boiling water, mix well, and bring to a boil. In the top of a double boiler over hot water, melt the butter, blend in the salt, black pepper, flour, and cherry purée, mixing and cooking until thoroughly blended. Gradually add the Coconut Milk, cooking and stirring after each addition, until smooth and thick. Season to taste with sugar—the sauce should remain rather tart. Fold in the parsley, if desired, at the last moment. Serve very hot. This sauce does not stand long, so use it promptly after preparation. *Makes about* 1½ *cups.*

SALSA FRÍA
(Cold Sauce)

Salsa Fría appears on virtually every Mexican table, no matter how elegant or humble, at every meal. The name is rather misleading—though the sauce may not be heated, it assuredly will heat one's innards with promptness because of the chili peppers and liquid hot pepper sauce which it often contains. It should be used, naturally, with discretion.

1 *to* 3 *small red chili peppers, seeded, veins removed, and finely chopped*

½ *cup or more finely chopped green bell pepper*

3 *or more firm ripe tomatoes, peeled if desired, and rather coarsely chopped*

About* ½ *cup finely chopped onion

1 *to* 2 *medium to large cloves garlic, minced or mashed*

1 *tablespoon minced fresh parsley*

1 *teaspoon salt*

1 *teaspoon or more chopped fresh cilantro, or* ½ *teaspoon ground coriander*

Tabasco or other hot pepper sauce to taste (optional, but typical)

Thoroughly combine all ingredients and allow to mellow several hours before using as a hot condiment with Mexican, Guatemalan, or other tropical dishes. Serve in a bowl at room temperature or warm briefly. *Makes about 2 cups.*

SALSA DE NARANJAS
(Orange Sauce)

This finds favor in a number of Latin countries; it is used to top sweet-potato puddings, various kinds of cakes, and other pastries.

½ cup granulated or light brown sugar
1 tablespoon cornstarch
1 cup strained fresh sweet orange juice
2 to 3 tablespoons strained fresh lime or lemon juice
3 tablespoons butter
1 teaspoon finely grated lime or lemon peel (without any white rind)
Pinch of salt

In a heavy saucepan, combine the sugar with the cornstarch and blend in the orange juice thoroughly. Cook over low heat until mixture thickens, usually about 5 minutes, stirring constantly. Blend in the lime or lemon juice, butter, lime or lemon peel, and salt, and simmer briefly. Serve hot. *Makes about* 1½ *cups.*

SALSA DE PEREJIL
(Mexican Parsley Sauce)

One of a wide range of interesting Mexican sauces, this is delectable on just about every kind of fish or meat and is well-nigh perfect on sliced ripe tomatoes.

½ cup finely minced fresh parsley
¼ cup finely chopped blanched almonds
3 tablespoons white distilled or cider vinegar
⅓ cup olive oil
Salt to taste

Combine all ingredients, mixing thoroughly. Chill before serving. *Makes about 1 cup.*

MOLHO DE PIMENTA E LIMÃO
(Hot Pepper and Lemon Sauce)

As this book shows, hot peppers and hot pepper sauces are very common in Latin American cookery, though the cuisines of some countries are much "hotter" than those of others. Here is a popular sauce from the state of Pernambuco, Brazil, to be added with some discretion to almost any meat, fish, or shellfish.

2 to 4 chili peppers, seeded and chopped
6 tablespoons grated onion
¼ teaspoon minced garlic
Fresh lemon or lime juice to taste

Place all ingredients in a bowl and stir until well mixed. Allow to stand at room temperature for a couple of hours before serving. *Makes about 1 cup.*

OLD SOUR

Old Sour is said to have originated in Key West, Florida, but I have encountered a comparable delight in Cuba and Puerto Rico. Marvelously flavorful limes are generally available in the American tropics, but when they are not, this makes a superb substitute. In fact, I find it an admirable shaker-bottle addition to all sorts of fried fish and seafood at any time.

To each pint of strained freshly squeezed lime juice, add 1 tablespoon salt, blending well. Allow to stand at room temperature 1 hour or more, then strain through double layers of muslin or cheesecloth. Place in shaker bottles with firm-fitting tops, and store in a dark, cool spot (not in the refrigerator) for at least 1 month before using as a seasoning liquid.

Fruits & Nuts

A truly extraordinary number of species of both fruits and nuts occur in Latin America. Fresh tropical- and temperate-zone fruits can be obtained everywhere. Especially notable are the luscious apples, pears, peaches, and grapes of southern South America, in particular Argentina and Chile; the extraordinary Brazilian *jabuticaba*; the tart, tasty cashew "apple" (whose attached nuts are toxic until thoroughly roasted); papaya, found everywhere; and certainly the myriad members of the genus *Annona*, which includes the guanabana (soursop).

Fruits are used for snacks, in chilled soups, in beverages and wines and even on occasion in liqueurs, and as ingredients in entrées, salads, jams, jellies, preserves, condiments, and many kinds of desserts. A visit to a Latin American marketplace is invariably a fascinating experience, since the variety of fruits differs from month to month, and new ones are frequently encountered. In the market that I customarily patronize in Jamaica, papayas (called pawpaws here although not the same fruit as the North American papaw or pawpaw) are almost always available; Otaheite apples, pineapples, sweetsops, soursops, and naseberries (*sapodillas*) are much more seasonal. I enjoy offering fruits, chilled or not, as a dessert course, combining selected species with grated dry coconut to make ambrosia; or accompanying one or more fruits with cheese and fresh crisp crackers.

Tiny wild strawberries from the Andes and yellow raspberries afford savory jams. Quinces and guavas are made into textured pastes, which, served with cream cheese or some other cheese, provide a favorite dessert in many countries. Most fruits and nuts (as well as many vegetables) are preserved or pickled, sometimes in a steamy hot mixture, or in one in which native cane vinegar predominates.

The coconut, although certainly the best-known tropical "nut," is technically not a nut at all, but the specialized fruit of a towering palm tree. The clear liquid found in the green fruit is refreshing, and the grated flesh of the dry "nut" forms the basis for Coconut Milk and Cream, both widely used in Latin American cuisines.

Nuts range from the familiar cashews, peanuts, and Brazil nuts to rather esoteric species seldom encountered outside their natives habitats. Packaged or canned nuts of many varieties are found in supermarkets and other shops throughout the area. Mexican cooks probably use nuts in their cookery more often than any other Latin Americans; nut soups and fine walnut and other nut sauces appear with frequency.

Condiments include a remarkable number of chutneys; my own specialty is made from bananas. The coconut relish invented by Calvin Grant is a fine accompaniment, not only for curries but for numerous other entrées.

OTAHEITE APPLE PICKLES

Otaheite apples (pomarrosas) are favorites throughout Latin America. The magnificent large fruiting trees bear big pompoms of luminous magenta blossoms in clusters along the major, generally lower branches; the later clumps of large, vaguely pearlike, vivid scarlet fruits glisten almost as much as the blossoms.

2½ ***pounds ripe Otaheite apples***
1 ***teaspoon whole cloves***
1½ ***sticks cinnamon, broken into ½ inch pieces***
1 1-***inch piece fresh ginger (unpeeled), rinsed and crushed***
2¼ ***cups dark sugar***
1 ***cup cider vinegar, cane vinegar or white distilled vinegar***
1 ***cup water***

Rinse fruit but do not peel; cut into halves or quarters, core, and remove blossom ends and blemishes. Tie the cloves, cinnamon, and ginger loosely in a piece of cheesecloth. Combine the sugar, vinegar, and water in a kettle, add the spices, and boil about 5 minutes. Add the fruit and cook until tender, then let stand at least 12 hours in the syrup.

Drain the syrup into a saucepan, bring to a boil, and pour it over the fruit and spices. Let cool, then repeat the draining, boiling, and pouring process three more times, allowing syrup to cool thoroughly each time but the last. Retain the spices until desired flavor is obtained, then discard.

Pack the fruit into hot sterilized jars, then pour in the boiling-hot syrup, being sure to fill every hollow, and seal. Allow pickles to stand at room temperature 2 weeks or longer; chill well before serving. *Makes about 2 pints.*

GINGERED BANANA CHUTNEY

In the tropics, chutneys are made from all kinds of things—not just mangos! This luscious Jamaican chutney features sweet bananas and either fresh or crystallized ginger.

1 *pound small white onions, minced*
2 *large or medium garlic cloves, minced or mashed*
¾ *pound pitted dates, minced*
6 *ripe bananas, mashed*
1½ *cups malt vinegar*
½ *pound raisins*
Grated or finely chopped fresh ginger to taste (probably not more than 2 tablespoons), or ¼ pound crystallized ginger
1 *cup unsweetened pineapple juice*
¼ *cup fresh lime juice*
1 *tablespoon whole mustard seed*
1 *teaspoon salt*
3 *whole cloves*
Tabasco sauce or other hot pepper sauce or chopped seeded chili pepper to taste

In a large heavy enamelware kettle with a cover, combine the onions, garlic, and dates, and cook over moderate heat 3 minutes stirring often. Stir in the bananas and vinegar, bring mixture to a boil and simmer, covered, 20 minutes.

Add raisins, ginger, pineapple juice, lime juice, mustard seed, salt, cloves, and hot pepper sauce or chili pepper (Jamaican cooks prefer their chutneys volcanically hot!). Bring to a boil over moderate heat and cook mixture, stirring, until it is thick, 10 to 15 minutes.

Pour chutney into hot sterilized jars, allow to cool, then seal jars with lids. Store in the refrigerator at least 2 days before serving as a condiment with all kinds of meals. *Makes about 2 quarts.*

BANANADA COM QUEIJO
(Banana Paste with Cheese)

One of the favorite desserts in Latin America is guava paste served with cream cheese or a tart dry cheese. Here is a marvelous Brazilian variation, in which bananas form the principal ingredient of the paste. Quinces or guavas can be substituted.

- 2¼ ***cups light brown or granulated sugar, or to taste***
- ½ ***cup water***
- 3 ***medium-sized ripe bananas, sliced and coarsely mashed***
- ¼ ***cup fresh lemon or lime juice***
- 1 ***pound cream cheese or a tart dry cheese, such as goat's milk cheese, cut into cubes, slices, or balls***

In a heavy saucepan, combine sugar and water, and cook, stirring constantly with a wooden spoon, until the mixture forms a thick syrup. Add bananas, and cook carefully, stirring constantly, until syrup forms a thread. Add lemon or lime juice and continue to cook, still stirring, until mixture is thick.

Pour into a bowl and allow to cool, then chill. Cut into attractive slices or cubes, and serve with a cheese of your choice. Crisp crackers are a perfect accompaniment. *Serves 6 to 8.*

BREADFRUIT PUDDING OCHO RIOS

The breadfruit was introduced into Jamaica by Captain William Bligh and is today a widespread and highly important food tree in many parts of Latin America. This tasty pudding is served warm, typically as a distinctive dessert, but also as a vegetable, with chicken, duck, or pork.

1 large ripe breadfruit
2 firm ripe bananas, thickly sliced
4 medium-sized dasheens
3 medium-sized sweet potatoes
⅓ cup, or less, dark or light brown sugar
Salt to taste
2 cups Coconut Cream (see index)
2 to 3 ripe limes, seeded and cut into wedges

Boil the breadfruit, bananas, dasheens, and sweet potatoes until each ingredient is just tender—do not overcook. Drain, peel if needed, and cut into uniform slices or cubes. Place in a sizable heavy saucepan, sprinkle with brown sugar and salt to taste, then fold in Coconut Cream. Simmer over lowest heat, stirring with care occasionally, until ingredients are very tender yet still retain their shapes.

Serve warm, accompanying each portion with a lime wedge. *Serves 6 to 8.*

DULCE DE PAJUIL
(Cashew Preserves)

Cashew preserves are popular in all countries in Latin America in which the awkwardly attractive *cajú* (cashew) tree occurs. The red or yellow fruits are called cashew apples in the English-speaking countries, and in addition to preserves, wine is made from them, notably in Belize and Brazil.

24 ripe cashew fruits (remove nuts)
Water
8 cups light brown or granulated sugar
½ teaspoon ground cinnamon or allspice
¼ teaspoon ground cloves

Cut cashew fruits in halves lengthwise, and soak 12 hours in salted water. Drain, add fresh water to cover, and heat quickly to a boil. Drain, peel, and rather coarsely chop the fruits. Combine with 6 cups water, the sugar, cinnamon or allspice, and cloves, and bring to a boil. Reduce heat to medium and cook until syrup forms a thread and fruits are tender. Turn into hot sterilized jars and seal tightly. Serve as a preserve or condiment. *Fills about 8 pint-sized jars.*

TROPICAL CITRUS MARMALADE

I very much like the tart orange marmalade made from the sour peel of Seville oranges, and also lime and grapefruit marmalades, and I especially delight in this exceptionally flavorful tropical marmalade, which is a combination of all three. In several Latin American lands, this is offered with toast to accompany coffee or tea or served as a condiment with meat or poultry.

2 *ripe limes*
1 *ripe Seville (sour) orange*
1 *ripe grapefruit*
1 *cup or more water*
1 *small package powdered pectin*
6 *or more cups light brown or granulated sugar*
½ *teaspoon salt*
¾ *teaspoon minced fresh ginger*

Thoroughly rinse all the citrus fruits, which must be unblemished. Using a sharp knife or vegetable peeler, cut off the rind in thin strips, and cut these into thin slivers. Reserve flesh of fruits. Add slivered rind to a saucepan, along with the water. Cover pan and simmer 20 minutes, stirring once or twice, adding more water if needed.

Cut citrus flesh into halves or quarters, and carefully remove sections, discarding pith and seeds. Add to the saucepan, and simmer, covered, 10 minutes, stirring once. You should now have 3½ cups of rind, fruit, and liquid; if the measurement is less, add water. Stir in the pectin, and bring to a boil, stirring frequently. Add sugar, salt, and ginger; stirring constantly, bring to a rolling boil, then remove from heat and let cool.

Turn into hot sterilized jars and seal tightly. Allow to mellow at room temperature at least one week before using. *Makes 3½ cups.*

COCONUT MILK AND COCONUT CREAM

The liquid contained in the coconut and also liquids prepared from grating the coconut flesh are important in Latin American cookery. The liquid that comes from the cracked green "nut" is often erroneously called "coconut milk," but its correct name is "coconut water." This water has a pleasant taste, and few things are as refreshing on a hot day as a "water coconut" sliced open with a perilously sharp machete. However, true Coconut Milk and Coconut Cream are used far more often than coconut water in Latin American cooking.

Break the shell of the coconut, drain off the liquid (reserve if desired), remove the meat, and peel off dark outer skin. Grate the meat from the outside in (for some reason this gives more body to the grated product).

In a saucepan, combine 2 cups of the grated coconut and 3 cups of water; bring to a quick boil, stirring, then remove from heat and allow to stand 30 minutes. Using your hands, squeeze out the liquid, straining it if desired to remove bits of coconut. The heavy liquid is true Coconut Milk. When it is allowed to stand for a while, a very thick, extremely rich, delicious cream forms on top, which is called Coconut Cream.

A weaker batch of cooking liquid can be obtained by

covering the grated coconut meat, after boiling, with an additional 3 cups water and continuing the process as described.

According to some authorities, Coconut Milk and Cream are manufactured by using cow's milk rather than water, but that is not the traditional process in Latin America.

CALVIN GRANT'S COCONUT RELISH

Every possible kind of condiment is offered with authentic curry tables in Latin America, from Bombay duck (a fish) and chopped ripe bananas to chopped salted nuts of divers species. One condiment that automatically appears at my curry tables in Jamaica is this relish developed by my friend Calvin Grant. For the best effect it must be freshly made and served without appreciable delay.

Half the flesh of 1 *coconut, peeled and coarsely chopped*
½ *cup seedless raisins*
½ *cup salted cashews or peanuts*
1 *teaspoon ground cinnamon*
¼ *cup Coconut Milk (see previous recipe) or cow's milk*

Place all the ingredients in a blender and whirl until a delicious, rather nicely textured brown relish is obtained. Serve at room temperature, or lightly chilled if desired. *Makes about 2 cups.*

GINGER PRESERVES

When fresh ginger is readily available, as it often is in Latin American lands (especially Jamaica, one of the world's largest producers), jams and preserves are often prepared from it.

1 pound fresh ginger
Water
2 cups or more light brown or granulated sugar
½ teaspoon cream of tartar
Chopped chili pepper to taste (optional)

Carefully pare ginger and cut into small pieces. Place in a heavy kettle and cover with water. Bring to a boil and cook about 5 minutes. Drain, add fresh water to cover, and bring to a boil again. Cook until ginger is tender but still retains some texture, then drain.

Meanwhile, in another kettle, boil the sugar and 1 cup water, stirring often, until thick and syrupy. Add the ginger, cream of tartar, and, if desired, chili pepper. Boil about 2 minutes, stirring occasionally.

Pour into hot sterilized jars, seal, and store at least 3 weeks in a cool location before serving. This unique condiment is delicious with many dishes. *Makes a little over 1 pint.*

STEWED GUAVAS

The guava is a favored fruit in most Latin American countries, where the small trees frequently abound. The fruits are eaten fresh, out of hand, or made into jams and jellies, pastes and conserves, and even ice creams. In this case, they have been stewed and can be served as a dessert with cream-cheese cubes or homemade tart cheese, and unsalted water crackers.

2 pounds ripe fresh guavas
Granulated or light brown sugar to taste
⅛ teaspoon or more salt
Fresh lime juice to taste (optional)

Rinse guavas, peel carefully, and cut into squares. Scoop

out seedy centers and press them through a sieve to remove all seeds, retaining the juices.

In a saucepan with a cover, combine guava juice, pulp, and quartered flesh. Stew, covered, over lowest heat until just tender, adding sugar during cooking. Add salt toward end of cooking time, and, if desired, blend in a small amount of lime juice at the same time, for extra piquancy. *Serves 4 to 6.*

ALEJANDRO'S MANGO CHUTNEY

There must be hundreds of different methods of preparing mango chutney, but this one is my favorite—perhaps because it is my own creation. It is not one of the fire-engine hot chutneys, but it can be made so by adding more chopped chili peppers.

1¼ *quarts cider vinegar*
2 *pounds granulated sugar*
2 *pounds or less light brown sugar*
3 *or more chili peppers, seeded, and finely chopped, or Tabasco sauce to taste*
3½ *pounds green mangoes, peeled and diced*
3½ *pounds hard-ripe mangoes, peeled and diced*
6 *to* 8 *large onions, chopped rather fine*
7 *large cloves garlic, minced or mashed*
1 *pound raisins, chopped*
6 *large green bell peppers, seeded and chopped*
2 *to* 3 *tablespoons grated fresh ginger, or* 6 *ounces minced crystallized ginger*
1 *cup fresh lime juice*
1 *cup tamarind pulp (available in Near Eastern foodshops)*
4 *tablespoons salt*
1 *tablespoon whole mustard seed*
1 *tablespoon celery seed*
1½ *teaspoons whole cloves*
2 *teaspoons ground allspice*

In a large heavy pot with a cover, combine the vinegar, granulated and light brown sugar, and chili peppers or Tabasco sauce. Bring to a boil, stirring often, then add remaining ingredients, mixing thoroughly. Remove from heat, cover, and let stand at room temperature for 12 hours or overnight.

The next day, mix well, and cook, covered, until mango pieces become just tender, usually about 3 to 4 hours. Do not overcook. Stir mixture frequently as it cooks, to prevent sticking; keep heat low enough to avoid scorching.

Pour hot chutney into hot sterilized jars and seal at once. Allow to mellow at least a week. Serve chilled, as a condiment. *Makes several quarts.*

PAPAYA SAUCE

This luscious sauce made with green papayas is closely akin to applesauce and has fully as many uses.

6 cups diced, peeled, firm, green papayas
½ teaspoon salt
Cold water
Granulated or light brown sugar to taste (optional)
⅛ teaspoon ground cinnamon or allspice (optional)

In a heavy saucepan with a cover, place papayas, salt, and water to cover; bring to a boil. Cover, reduce heat, and simmer, stirring occasionally, until fruit is very tender. Most of the water will be absorbed. Press through a sieve, or mash with a fork. If desired, stir in granulated or brown sugar, and perhaps cinnamon or allspice, while papaya is still hot. Let cool, then chill, covered. *Makes about 2 cups.*

RED PEPPER JAM

Often flavored, sometimes rather potently, with seeded, chopped chili peppers or Tabasco sauce, this jam is guaranteed to open one's sinuses. With or without the hot seasoning, it is a delicious condiment with all kinds of meats and many casserole dishes.

12 ***red bell peppers, seeded***
1 ***tablespoon salt***
2 ***cups distilled white vinegar***
3 ***cups light brown or granulated sugar or to taste***
Chopped seeded chili pepper or Tabasco sauce to taste (optional)

Cut red bell peppers into slivers with a sharp knife, sprinkle with salt, and allow to stand in a covered bowl at least 10 hours at room temperature, stirring occasionally. Drain thoroughly.

Place in a heavy kettle with the vinegar and sugar, mixing well. Cook uncovered, stirring often, until reasonably soft in texture, but do not overcook. Add chili pepper or Tabasco sauce, if desired, during the last few minutes of cooking time.

Pour into hot sterilized jars and seal. Let mellow at room temperature for at least 2 weeks. *Makes about 2½ pints.*

PIÑA CON QUESO
(Cheesy Pineapple)

Sharp Cheddar marries admirably with pineapple, especially the juicy fresh kind common in Latin America. This delightful creation may be served either as a dessert or as an unusual appetizer for a tropical menu.

1 large ripe pineapple
Cheddar cheese to taste, grated, slivered, or cut into julienne strips
½ teaspoon salt
Candied or fresh ginger to taste, diced coarsely

Cut pineapple into lengthwise halves, and scoop out the flesh. Dice or slice it rather coarsely, reserving all juice. Combine cheese, salt, and ginger with the pineapple, and chill, covered, until ready to serve. *Serves 6 to 8.*

Baked Goods

Breads, cakes, pies, cookies, and a number of other baked products appear with some frequency on Latin American menus, whether with tea or coffee in the late afternoon, as snacks at other times of the day, or as desserts.

I found Latin Americans to be admirable bakers; exceptionally good breads, rolls, biscuits, and the like are found in city and country bakeries and in private homes. Some of the firm breads served with afternoon tea or coffee are simply superb; these are thinly sliced and lightly buttered or made into watercress or cucumber sandwiches.

In the Spanish-speaking lands in particular, one encounters elegant sweet cakes, incorporating all kinds of local fruits, as well as raisins, dates, and wines. Pies are made from lime juice, papaya, puréed tiny strawberries from the mountains, and many other fruits. Meat pies are often accompanied by grated sharp cheese and sautéed seasoning vegetables, such as onions and green bell peppers. In Jamaica and other places, one can even find hearty versions of *quiche lorraine.*

The stuffed turnovers, known by so many different names, and containing such a variety of fillings, are always baked; they are delicious as snacks or as a light main dish, served with a crisp green salad, for a luncheon or supper or picnic repast.

I am inordinately fond of cookies in all varieties, and happily my Latin colleagues feel the same way. Cookies are made from molasses, from grated dry coconut, from fresh or dried fruits of many species, and from just about every other conceivable ingredient. Rare is the day when freshly made cookies are not in my kitchen larder.

TORTA CASTANAH DO PARÁ
(Brazil-Nut Loaf)

Brazil nuts are among the most highly prized and costly of all nuts. They grow packed with marvelous precision into immense woody pods weighing many pounds; if one of these falls from the heights of the Amazon's 150-foot trees onto the head of an incautious gatherer, it can split his skull asunder. Heating the nuts in their rough shells on a baking sheet in a preheated 400° oven for about 10 minutes will make cracking them open much easier.

1 pound Brazil nuts, shelled and finely chopped
1 pound pitted dates, finely chopped
½ to ¾ teaspoon grated fresh ginger
¾ cup granulated sugar
½ teaspoon salt
¾ cup sifted flour
½ teaspoon baking powder
3 large eggs

In a large bowl, thoroughly combine the nuts, dates, and ginger. In another bowl, combine sugar, salt, flour, and baking powder. Sift dry ingredients twice, then sift over nut mixture, and mix well.

Beat the eggs until foamy, then mix well with other ingredients. Turn mixture into 2 or 3 small lightly buttered loaf pans. Set these into a shallow pan or pans, and add hot water to reach halfway up the level of the batter in the loaf pans. Bake in a preheated 300° oven until a toothpick plunged into the center of loaves comes out clean, usually about 1 hour. Remove from oven and let cool in pans. Serve in thin slices, perhaps with cubes of cream cheese or homemade cheese on the side, or buttered, with hot coffee or tea or maté. *Makes 2 to 3 small loaves.*

CASHEW TARTS

These tasty tarts are popular in Jamaica, where cashew trees are common in the drier parts of the island. The nuts, which are attached to the apex of the fruit as a sort of afterthought, are covered by a poisonous skin, the toxins of which are removed by careful roasting.

Enough pastry for 12 4-inch tarts
2 cups rather finely chopped roasted cashews
2 cups light brown or granulated sugar, or to taste
2 cups light cane syrup
4 large eggs, beaten
½ teaspoon ground allspice
2 teaspoons vanilla extract

Line twelve 4-inch tart pans with pastry. Combine the cashews, sugar, cane syrup, eggs, allspice, and vanilla, mix well, and divide mixture evenly among the lined tart pans.

Bake in a preheated 300° oven until filling is firm, usually about one hour. Serve tarts chilled or at room temperature. *Makes 12 tarts.*

BAHAMIAN COCONUT BISCUITS

Coconut in cakes and pies is well known throughout Latin America but here is a delightfully different way of using this popular palm-tree product. These biscuits from the Bahamas are especially good as an accompaniment to seafood and chicken, but they make excellent breakfast fare as well.

2 cups flour, sifted
1 teaspoon salt
3 teaspoons baking powder
4 tablespoons butter or shortening
1 cup coconut water (see index)
Small amount of milk (optional)
1 cup freshly grated dry coconut

Sift flour, salt, and baking powder together three times. Cut in the butter or shortening (lard is often used), and add coconut water (and if desired, a little milk) to make a soft dough.

On a floured board, roll out to ½-inch thickness; cut with a biscuit cutter. Arrange on a baking sheet and sprinkle with the grated coconut. Bake in a preheated 450° oven until biscuits are lightly browned, usually about 10 to 12 minutes. Serve very hot. *Makes about 24 1½-inch biscuits.*

PÃO DE GOÍABA
(Brazilian Guava Bread)

Once when I was in Brazil, botanizing and browsing around in the markets and friendly kitchens, I came across a superlative moist bread, the principal flavoring of which was Stewed Guavas. It was served with afternoon coffee at a handsome old colonial home in Olinda, overlooking one of the world's most glorious beaches. We had just returned from a totally exhausting trek to the marvelous Paulo Affonso waterfalls in the interior of the state of Pernambuco; this bread and thick, sweet black coffee boosted our flagging energies to carry on until we were afforded a spectacular seafood repast under coconut palms and a full moon.

⅓ cup butter, softened
⅓ cup light brown sugar
⅓ cup granulated sugar
2 large eggs, beaten
2 teaspoons fresh lime juice
2 cups drained, coarsely chopped Stewed Guavas (see index)
1¾ cups sifted flour
2¼ teaspoons baking powder
½ cup finely chopped, peeled Brazil nuts

Cream butter with light brown and granulated sugar, then beat in the eggs. Combine the lime juice with the guavas. Sift together the flour and baking powder. Sift the flour-baking powder mixture into the creamed mixture gradually, alternating with the guava mixture and stirring thoroughly after each addition. Gently fold in the nuts, and again mix well.

Turn into a well-buttered 9-by-5-inch loaf pan and bake in a preheated 350° oven until a toothpick inserted in the center comes out clean, usually about 1 hour; the top should be nicely browned. Allow to cool in the pan, then turn out carefully. Slice thinly to serve. *Makes 1 loaf.*

TORTAS DE GUAYABA
(Guava Tarts)

Recently developed varieties of guava have fruit that is far more fleshy and less seedy than that of their antecedents; these are often raised on a commercial scale, and made into a range of different edibles, including guava paste. The tarts here are from Cuba, and are prepared with guava paste, called guava cheese on some islands.

Pastry for a 2-crust pie
1 15-*ounce bar prepared guava paste (guava cheese)*
2 *teaspoons or less ground cinnamon*
2 *teaspoons or less freshly grated nutmeg*
8 *teaspoons butter*

Make the pie pastry and roll out on a lightly floured board to ⅛-inch thickness. Cut out 8 circles, each 6 inches in diameter. Butter 8 muffin cups and arrange pastry circles in them. Cut guava-paste bar into 8 equal pieces, and place one in each pastry-lined muffin cup. Sprinkle each tart with about ¼ teaspoon cinnamon and ¼ teaspoon nutmeg and put 1 teaspoon butter on top. Lightly moisten edges of pastry and seal tightly by pinching moistened edges together. Bake in a preheated 400° oven about 30 minutes, or until tarts are nicely browned.

Serve warm, on a warmed, buttered dish to which the rather sticky tarts will not adhere. *Makes 8 tarts.*

GUNGO PEAS BREAD

Gungo peas are known in islands other than Jamaica as *gandules* or pigeon peas. They are rather flavorful, and in many places exceptionally popular. Not long ago, Jamaica's Culinary Arts Competition featured gungo peas as one of its special products. I assisted in the judging that year, and we were amazed by all the different ways in which island cooks use the plebeian gungo pea—in soups, breads, and salads, and even a rather odd ice cream. Here is a nice bread from Jamaica.

3 *to* 3½ *cups flour*
1 *package compressed yeast, or* 1 *envelope active dry yeast*
¼ *cup lukewarm water*
1 *tablespoon granulated sugar*
1½ *cups scalded milk, or* ¾ *cup water and* ¾ *cup milk*
2 *tablespoons salt*
¼ *cup light brown sugar*
⅔ *tablespoon melted butter or shortening, cooled*
3½ *cups gungo peas cooked in water to cover*

Sift the flour. Crumble compressed yeast, or sprinkle dry yeast, into lukewarm water, and stir in granulated sugar; let dissolve 10 minutes. In a 5-quart mixing bowl, combine the hot milk or water-milk combination, the salt, and the brown sugar. Let cool to lukewarm, then stir in the yeast. Beat in 2 cups of the flour thoroughly, then the butter or shortening; add the remaining flour and the gungo peas, mixing well. Turn out onto a lightly floured board, cover with the bowl, and let rest 10 minutes.

Knead dough until smooth and elastic, using no more flour for kneading than necessary. Place dough in a greased bowl, turning to bring greased side up. Cover bowl with a pastry cloth and let dough rise until nearly doubled in size. Cut into quarters, and shape gently into balls. Cover these with the bowl, and let rest for 10 minutes.

Shape into loaves and place in four 9-by-5-inch loaf pans. Bake in a preheated 400° oven for 40 minutes or until bread is nicely browned on top. Remove from pans to racks and let cool, uncovered, out of any draft.

This bread is particularly tasty with butter and tart orange marmalade. *Makes 4 loaves.*

ELISABETH ORTIZ'S MANGO PIE

Elisabeth Ortiz is well known for her books on Mexican and Caribbean cookery, classics in their field. Her mango pie is one of the best mango recipes I know.

1½ *pounds fresh mango (a big meaty one, or two smaller, but none especially juicy)*
3 *tablespoons plus* 1 *teaspoon (approximately) fresh lime or lemon juice*
½ *cup light brown or granulated sugar*
¼ *cup plus one teaspoon water*
1 *tablespoon arrowroot*
1 9*-inch pie shell (see following recipe)*

Peel the mango. Cut two slices lengthwise down the sides, as close to the pit as possible. Slice these lengthwise about ¼ inch thick. Sprinkle with a few drops of lime juice and set aside. Cut all the remaining flesh off the pit; there should be about 1 cup of pulp. Put pulp into a saucepan with the sugar, the 3 tablespoons lime juice, and the ¼ cup of water, and cook until soft, about 20 minutes; do not overcook.

Purée part of mango pulp. Return to pan and stir in the arrowroot mixed with the teaspoon of water, and cook until thickened, only a minute or so. Cool slightly.

Arrange mango slices in baked, cooled pastry shell in an overlapping pattern, using the shorter pieces to fill in at the sides. Spoon purée evenly over mango slices, and chill.

Serve pie with rum-flavored whipped cream, hard sauce, rather thin custard, or ice cream, if desired. *Serves 4 to 6.*

PIE SHELL

1½ cups flour
¼ teaspoon salt
1 tablespoon light brown or granulated sugar
6 tablespoons sweet butter, chilled and cut into small pieces
2 tablespoons lard, chilled and cut into small pieces
3 tablespoons cold water

Sift flour, salt, and sugar together into a large bowl. Rub butter and lard into flour with your fingertips until mixture is crumbly. Sprinkle water over mixture and mix lightly to make a rather stiff dough. Wrap in wax paper or aluminum foil and chill until firm enough to roll.

Turn onto a floured board and roll out into a circle large enough to fit a 9-inch pie plate. Arrange pastry in the pan, pressing lightly into sides of pan and over the rim; trim away excess and crimp edges if desired. Prick pastry on pan bottom all over with a fork.

Bake the shell on the middle rack of a preheated 350° oven until golden, usually about 25 minutes. Let cool before filling. *Makes 1 9-inch pie shell.*

MANGO UPSIDE-DOWN CAKE

Most people are familiar with pineapple upside-down cake, but in this version luscious juicy ripe mangoes are featured. It is a delectable dessert.

2 tablespoons lemon juice
2 cups sliced peeled ripe mangoes
¼ cup plus 1 tablespoon butter
⅓ cup light brown sugar
¾ cup granulated sugar
1 large egg, beaten
1½ cups flour
2 teaspoons baking powder
¼ teaspoon salt
½ cup milk
Rum-flavored whipped cream, or lemon or lime sauce (optional)

Pour the lemon juice over the mangoes, allow to stand 15 minutes, then drain. Melt 1 tablespoon of the butter in a shallow casserole or 8-inch round cake pan, swirling it to coat the sides. Sprinkle with the brown sugar and cover the bottom of the pan with the marinated mango slices.

Cream together the remaining ¼ cup butter and the granulated sugar until fluffy, then stir in the beaten egg. Sift the flour, baking powder, and salt together, and add alternately with the milk to the creamed mixture. Pour this batter over the mangoes. Bake in a preheated 375° oven 50 to 60 minutes. When done, carefully turn cake upside down and serve warm, with, if desired, rum-flavored whipped cream or a lemon or lime sauce. *Serves 4 to 6.*

ORANGE-COCONUT BREAD

This bread originated in Trinidad and Tobago, but now is found in almost all the Caribbean islands and mainland countries. It is delicious thinly sliced and buttered, served with tea or coffee or maté.

3 *cups flour*
1 *tablespoon baking powder*
1 *teaspoon salt*
1 *cup granulated or light brown sugar*
2 *cups finely grated dry coconut*
1 *tablespoon grated orange peel (without white rind)*
⅓ *cup fresh orange juice*
(3) **1 *large egg, well beaten***
⅔ *cup evaporated milk*
1 *teaspoon vanilla extract*
½ *cup butter, melted and cooled*
Additional granulated sugar

Sift together the flour, baking powder, and salt. Mix in the 1 cup sugar, the coconut, orange peel, orange juice, egg, milk, vanilla, and butter, mixing lightly but well. Divide dough between two greased loaf pans (9 by 5 inches), filling each about two-thirds full. Sprinkle with additional sugar.

Bake in a preheated 350° oven until a toothpick inserted into center comes out clean, usually about 55 minutes. Let loaves cool a little in the pans, then turn out on cake racks. *Makes 2 9-inch loaves.*

PAPAYA MUFFINS

These exceptional muffins, served with Papaya Honey, are favorite fare with hot tea or coffee in many a Caribbean home. The Papaya Honey is also delicious on buttered crisp toast.

2 cups sifted flour
2 teaspoons baking powder
1 teaspoon salt
2 tablespoons granulated or light brown sugar
1 large egg, beaten
1 cup milk
3 tablespoons melted butter, cooled
1 cup mashed ripe papaya
Papaya Honey (see following recipe)

Sift together the flour, baking powder, salt, and sugar. Separately, in a small bowl, mix together the egg, milk, melted butter, and mashed papaya. Fold this mixture lightly into the dry ingredients, taking care not to stir too much.

Turn the batter into small greased muffin tins, filling about two-thirds full. Bake in a preheated 375° oven until muffins test done and are lightly browned. Serve hot or at room temperature. *Makes 12 small muffins.*

PAPAYA HONEY

2 cups peeled and diced ripe papaya
¼ cup fresh lime juice
¼ cup honey

Place all ingredients in a blender and purée, or rub papaya through a fine sieve and whip with the lime juice and honey until thoroughly blended. Chill and serve with Papaya Muffins or on buttered crisp toast.

PAPAYA SAUCE COOKIES

If you enjoy cookies as much as I do, these are guaranteed to appeal to you. They are particularly delectable with steaming cups of freshly brewed Latin American coffee.

¾ cup butter
1 cup granulated sugar
1 large egg, lightly beaten
2½ cups sifted flour
½ teaspoon baking soda
½ teaspoon ground cinnamon or allspice
¼ teaspoon ground cloves
¼ teaspoon salt
½ cup chopped cashews, peanuts, or other nuts
½ cup Papaya Sauce (see index)

Cream the butter and sugar, and stir in the egg. Sift together the flour, baking soda, cinnamon or allspice, ground cloves, and salt, and stir the nuts into these dry ingredients. Mix into the creamed mixture, along with the Papaya Sauce. Shape the resulting dough into long rolls, wrap in waxed paper or aluminum foil, and chill.

Slice well-chilled dough rolls thinly and arrange on lightly buttered baking sheets. Bake in a preheated 350° oven until lightly browned, usually about 10 to 12 minutes. Remove cookies with a slotted spatula. Either cool them on racks before storing in tightly covered containers, or better, eat them while they are hot, with coffee. *Makes about 24 cookies.*

PLANTAIN TARTS

Plantain tarts are an insidious specialty of Jamaica and a few other Caribbean isles. Here is a delicious version from Mrs. Doreen Kirkcaldy of Grace Kitchens in Kingston. These tarts are really turnovers.

***1** pound very ripe unpeeled plantains (about **2** fairly large fruits)*
Boiling salted water
½ cup light brown or granulated sugar
½ teaspoon freshly ground nutmeg
***1** teaspoon vanilla*
Red food coloring to obtain desired shade
***1** tablespoon butter*
*Enough of your favorite pastry to make about **15** 4-inch circles*

Cook unpeeled plantains in boiling salted water. When done, drain off liquid, peel, and mash pulp fine while still hot. Add the sugar, nutmeg, vanilla, food coloring, and butter, mixing well.

Roll out pastry about ⅛ inch thick on a lightly floured board, and cut into 4-inch rounds. Place 1 teaspoon or more plantain filling on each round. Moisten edge of pastry with cold water, fold over, and seal, pressing edges together. Prick top with a fork. Bake in a preheated 400° oven 10 minutes, then reduce heat to 350° and continue to bake until pastry is a delicate brown, about 15 minutes longer.

BIZCOCHO CON CREMA
(Spongecake with Rum Custard Filling)

As a finale to a great many Latin American menus one is offered this dessert. You may wish to prepare the spongecake at home; I suspect that you will enjoy it more than the customary restaurant version.

7 large eggs, separated
2 or less teaspoons grated lemon peel (without white rind)
1 cup or less granulated sugar
½ teaspoon salt
1 tablespoon plus 3 drops fresh lemon juice
1 tablespoon light or dark rum
1⅓ cups flour
Rum Custard Filling (see following recipe)
¼ cup confectioners' sugar, plus a little more

Beat egg yolks with grated lemon peel until light yellow. Add sugar and salt, and beat until thick. Add 1 tablespoon of the lemon juice and the rum, mixing well. Add flour, and mix lightly but thoroughly.

Separately, beat egg whites until stiff peaks form when beaters are raised, adding the 3 drops of lemon juice as eggs begin to turn white. Fold into batter and spread evenly in two 8-inch shallow cake pans which have been liberally buttered and sprinkled with flour and/or lined with waxed paper. Bake in a preheated 425° oven approximately 30 minutes, until cakes are lightly browned.

Turn each layer upside down on paper sprinkled with a little confectioners' sugar, and let cool. Remove waxed paper, if used. Unless waxed paper liners are used the layers will not come out of pans easily until they have cooled. Spread the Rum Custard Filling liberally on the bottom layer, put the other layer on top of it, and sprinkle top of cake with ¼ cup confectioners' sugar just before serving. *Serves 4 to 8.*

CREMA PASTELERA AL RON
(Rum Custard Filling)

2¾ cups milk
1 teaspoon vanilla
¼ cup light or dark rum
½ cup sugar
3 tablespoons cornstarch
3 large egg yolks
2 tablespoons butter

In a heavy saucepan, bring milk, vanilla, and rum to a boil; boil, stirring, for a few minutes, until mixture starts to thicken. Allow to cool 5 minutes.

Beat sugar, cornstarch, and egg yolks until creamy and thick, then strain milk mixture into yolk mixture, beating constantly. Cook over low heat, stirring constantly, until custard thickens, usually about 20 minutes. Do not let it come to a boil. Add the butter just before removing from heat, and stir until blended through.

SPEKULAAS
(Dutch Spiced Cookies)

In Curaçao and Sint Maarten and other parts of the Netherlands Antilles one is frequently treated to big cups of strong South American coffee and an array of tasty cakes, cookies, and pastries. My favorite cookies from this part of the world are Spekulaas, which originated in the Netherlands.

About ⅓ cup shelled whole almonds, or one whole almond for each cookie (about 48)

4 cups flour

1 cup softened butter

1 cup firmly packed light brown or dark brown sugar

4 teaspoons baking powder

1 teaspoon salt

1 teaspoon ground cloves

1 teaspoon freshly grated nutmeg

½ teaspoon freshly ground black pepper

⅓ to ½ cup milk

Pour boiling water over the almonds, and let stand 5 minutes or until skins rub off easily. Combine the flour, butter, sugar, baking powder, salt, cloves, nutmeg, black pepper, and milk, and knead into a soft dough, adding a bit more milk if necessary. Roll out dough on a lightly floured board to ½-inch thickness, and cut out circles about 1½ inches in diameter, pressing an almond into each one.

Place on greased baking sheets, and bake in a preheated 350° oven until cookies become golden brown, usually about 25 minutes. Allow to cool, then store in containers with tight-fitting lids. *Makes about 4 dozen cookies.*

Desserts & Confections

I have never been a great one for desserts, preferring to fill up on the main courses of the meal, but there are certain delightful Latin American desserts which I prepare and serve at home and order whenever I encounter them on a menu.

Probably the most widely served desserts are caramel custard flan and Bizcocho con Crema, the former pleasantly light, the latter, in my opinion, a bit heavy. I enjoy both, though I prefer Flan de Piña to the plain caramel variety, and I would rather have guava paste or guava shells with cream cheese than the Bizcocho.

The frequently served dessert of fresh fruits, usually chilled, often accompanied by cheese and unsalted crackers, has already been mentioned; this is a most satisfying finale to any hearty menu.

Some of the many Latin American recipes for sweet pastries, cakes, and pies are given in the preceding section; some of the fresh fruit pies are without equal anywhere in the world.

In spite of my indifference to desserts, I do enjoy confections very much. Candies and sweet preserved fruits delight me. Other excellent Latin American confections incorporate such ingredients as grated coconut, minced ripe fresh pineapple, and various citrus juices.

MATRIMONY

The star apple is one of the handsomest fruit trees of tropical America, occurring widely throughout the West Indies and in its native Central America, where it sometimes attains a height of more than fifty feet. The large, rich green leaves are a lustrous golden brown on their undersides, and the three- to four-inch fruits, globular in shape, vary in color from green to purple when ripe. The flesh, rather latex-filled, is white or lilac. When a ripe fruit is cut in half, the reason for the English vernacular name becomes apparent, for the brown, glossy seeds form a starlike pattern at its center. The flesh, peeled, chopped, and chilled, makes a nice dessert in itself, but in Jamaica it is also used in combination to make Matrimony, which I find extravagantly delicious.

4 or 5 ripe star apples
1 sweet orange and 1 sour (Seville) orange
Canned sweetened condensed milk to taste
Freshly grated nutmeg

Peel star apples, remove seeds and pith, and cut into small pieces. Peel oranges, remove all pith and seeds, and divide into sections. Gently mix with star apples. Add condensed milk and mix gently but well. Cover and chill.

Serve attractively displayed, lightly sprinkled with nutmeg. *Serves 3.*

BANANA DELIGHT

This creamy ice comes from Barbados, but counterparts are to be found in many other parts of the American tropics.

3 fully ripe bananas
2 tablespoons fresh lime juice, or to taste
½ cup granulated sugar
1 cup heavy cream
⅛ teaspoon salt

Thoroughly mash the bananas, and blend in the lime juice and sugar. Beat cream until stiff, adding salt. Gently fold the banana mixture into the whipped cream. Pour into an ice-cube tray from which the sections have been removed, and freeze without stirring until moderately firm but not hard. *Serves 4 to 6.*

CHURROS CON BANANA
(Banana Doughnuts)

Churros and similar doughnut-like affairs abound in Latin American cuisines. Some of them have a special touch, such as these with a delicate banana flavor.

¼ cup vegetable shortening
1 cup sugar
1½ teaspoon vanilla extract
3 large eggs, beaten well
¾ cup mashed ripe banana
½ cup milk
½ cup buttermilk or sour milk
5 cups flour, plus ½ cup
3 teaspoons baking powder
1 teaspoon baking soda
2 teaspoons freshly grated nutmeg
2 teaspoons salt
Fat or oil for deep-frying

In a large bowl, cream the shortening, blend in the sugar, then add the vanilla and eggs, beating the mixture until light and fluffy.

In another bowl, combine the mashed banana, milk, and buttermilk or sour milk, then stir this into the creamed ingredients, mixing well.

Sift together the 5 cups flour, the baking powder, baking soda, nutmeg, and salt. Add the sifted dry ingredients, about a heaping cupful at a time, stirring thoroughly after each addition. Cover and chill the dough.

Roll dough out on a well-floured board (use about ½ cup flour) to ¾-inch thickness. Cut into rings with a doughnut cutter. Heat the fat or oil to 380° and deep-fry the doughnuts. Drain well and serve hot or warm. *Makes about 40.*

BANANA SOUFFLÉ

This extraordinarily tasty soufflé made with ripe bananas is one of my favorite desserts.

Confectioners' sugar
5 large eggs at room temperature, separated
⅛ teaspoon salt
1 teaspoon grated lemon or lime peel (yellow or green part only)
2 tablespoons lemon or lime juice
2 medium-ripe bananas, mashed
3 tablespoons butter
2 tablespoons flour
1 cup milk
½ cup granulated sugar
1 teaspoon vanilla extract
Sweetened whipped cream (optional)
Freshly grated nutmeg (optional)

Lightly butter a 1½-quart soufflé dish up to the inside ridge. Sprinkle the buttered surfaces with confectioners' sugar and set aside.

Beat the egg yolks until thick and lemon-colored. In another bowl, beat the whites until stiff but not dry, adding the salt. Reserve.

Combine the lemon or lime peel with the juice and the mashed bananas. Reserve 1 cup of this mixture.

Melt the butter in a saucepan and blend in the flour, then gradually stir in the milk, and cook, stirring constantly, until sauce is smooth and thickened. Stir in the granulated sugar, vanilla, and the banana mixture; remove from heat. Gradually fold in the beaten egg yolks, then add this mixture slowly to the beaten egg whites, lightly folding together with a rubber spatula.

Turn into the prepared soufflé dish, and bake in a preheated 375° oven 30 to 35 minutes. When done, sift confectioners' sugar over the top and serve immediately, topped if desired, with sweetened whipped cream and sprinkled with nutmeg. *Serves 6 liberally.*

BAKED BANANAS WITH ORANGES

The luxuriant island of Jamaica is one of the largest producers of bananas in the Western Hemisphere, most of its supply being shipped to Great Britain. Jamaica also grows quantities of exceptionally flavorful citrus fruits, several of which have a particular affinity with bananas, as proved by this baked dessert, which should be served following a main course of roast pork, suckling pig, chicken, duck, or turkey.

6 *firm ripe bananas, peeled*
¼ *cup butter*
1 *cup fresh orange juice, strained if desired*
¾ *cup firmly packed light or dark brown sugar*
2 *teaspoons dark Jamaican rum*
½ *teaspoon Angostura bitters*
½ *teaspoon ground allspice*
½ *teaspoon grated orange peel (colored part only)*
1½ *cups crumbled coconut macaroons*
⅓ *cup slivered blanched almonds, lightly toasted, or chopped roasted cashews or Brazil nuts*
6 *peeled, seeded, sweet orange slices, cut ¼ inch thick and halved*

Cut bananas into lengthwise halves, and sauté in the butter in a skillet until golden, turning them carefully with tongs or a spatula. Place bananas in a buttered shallow baking dish.

Combine the orange juice, brown sugar, rum, bitters, allspice, and grated orange peel and pour over the bananas. Top with crumbled macaroons and nuts.

Bake in preheated 350° oven for 10 minutes. Arrange orange slices on top of the bananas, and bake 5 minutes longer, or until the oranges are heated through. *Serves 6.*

BANANADA DOCE
(Sweet Banana Loaf)

This interesting medley of very ripe bananas, brown sugar, ginger, and other spices is a favorite dessert in Brazil.

5 very ripe bananas
Dark brown sugar to taste
½ teaspoon or more grated fresh ginger
¼ teaspoon or more ground cinnamon
⅛ teaspoon ground cloves

Mash the bananas coarsely, and thoroughly beat in the sugar, ginger, cinnamon, and cloves, until a spicy mixture is obtained. Simmer mixture, covered, in a heavy pot for about 1½ hours, stirring very often to avoid scorching.

Allow to cool, shape into a loaf, and chill, covered. Serve thinly sliced, with an assortment of cheeses. *Makes 1 loaf.*

POLVO DE AMOR
("Powder of Love")

This confection is West Indian in origin, but its fame has spread throughout most of the Western Hemisphere. Though its name means "powder of love," I have not been able to ascertain whether it works.

Grate enough coconut meat to make 2 cups, mashing out as much of the liquid as possible. In a large skillet, over very low heat, cook the grated coconut, stirring often, until it becomes lightly browned. Sprinkle with 3 tablespoons light brown or dark brown sugar, mix well, and continue to cook, still stirring, until sugar is partly melted.

Remove from heat, allow to cool slightly, and form into small balls. Chill and serve as a confection. *Serves about 6.*

GUYANESE COCONUT FUDGE

One of the most pleasant confections I know is this easily made fudge from Guyana.

2 cups milk
2 to 2¼ cups (1 pound) light brown or granulated sugar
2 tablespoons butter
1 teaspoon vanilla
¼ teaspoon baking powder
½ cup grated dry coconut

In a heavy saucepan, bring the milk, sugar, and butter to a slow boil, stirring continuously; boil until mixture becomes granular. Remove from heat and stir in vanilla, baking powder, and grated coconut, and beat until creamy.

Pour into a buttered 8-inch square pan and allow to cool. Cut into neat squares. *Makes 36 pieces.*

COCONUT ICE

Towering graceful coconut palms abound throughout Latin America.

Among the many delicious Latin American dishes using coconuts is this ice, which appears as a soothing finale to many a spicy meal.

4½ cups Coconut Milk (see index)
1 cup fresh coconut water (see index)
1 teaspoon light rum
Granulated or light brown sugar to taste
½ cup grated dry coconut meat, toasted

To the prepared Coconut Milk add the coconut water, light rum, and sugar to taste. Stir until sugar is dissolved, then pour into ice-cube trays from which partitions have been removed. Freeze until partially frozen, then turn out into a bowl and mix well to break up ice crystals; return to trays and freeze until firm.

Sprinkle each portion with toasted coconut just before serving. *Serves 6 to 8.*

COCADA
(Antillean Coconut Pudding)

Naturally, Cocada is a very popular pudding in all Latin American countries where coconuts grow abundantly. It is often eaten hot, but I prefer it well chilled and thinly sliced, served with squares of cream cheese and unsalted crackers.

6 egg yolks
¾ cup granulated or light brown sugar
1 teaspoon vanilla
¼ cup melted butter
½ cup dry white wine
½ cup coconut water (see index)
Grated meat of 1 large ripe coconut
½ cup slivered blanched almonds or cashews

In a bowl, beat the egg yolks with the sugar; add the vanilla, butter, wine, and coconut water. Mix with the grated coconut and nuts (reserve a few nuts for garnish).

Turn into a buttered baking dish and decorate with the remaining slivers of nuts. Bake in a preheated 325° oven until pudding is firm, usually about 30 minutes. Serve hot, or chilled and thinly sliced. *Serves 6.*

CREMA DE GUANABANA
(Soursop Cream)

For this cream, one of the most popular of the unusual desserts found in Latin American countries, one needs a fully ripe soursop (guanabana), a big, strange-looking prickly fruit which appears on the major branches and sometimes the trunks of a small tree of the species *Annona muricata.* Canned guanabana nectar is now available from Puerto Rico and makes a rather good substitute for the fresh fruit. A marvelous ice cream is also made with this fruit.

1 *ripe soursop (guanabana), or* 1 *medium-sized can of guanabana nectar*
Heavy cream
Granulated or light brown sugar to taste (optional)
Freshly grated nutmeg (optional)

Remove the objectionably flavored skin of the soursop, and press the flesh through a fine sieve, discarding the seeds and coarse pulp. Blend in enough heavy cream to make a smooth paste and sweeten lightly, if desired.

Chill thoroughly, and serve in small ornamental crème pots, with a very light sprinkling of nutmeg if desired. *Serves 4.*

GELADO DE JACA
(Jakfruit Ice)

The jakfruit is one of the most extraordinary tropical fruits, often weighing fifty pounds or more. The fruits grow directly from the trunk of the densely leaved tree, or from its major branches and rather resemble a huge prickly green balloon. The young fruits are curried or sautéed in oil, and mature ones are made into a flavorful ice which is exceptionally popular in Brazil.

4 to 8 cups sliced unpeeled jakfruit
Water
1½ cups fresh orange juice
¼ cup fresh lime juice
Granulated or brown sugar to taste
1 teaspoon salt

Cook the jakfruit in water to cover in a covered container. When tender, peel the fruit and purée the flesh with the orange and lime juices, adding sugar and salt. If necessary, add a little of the cooking liquid to dilute the mixture slightly.

Pour mixture into ice-cube trays and freeze until ice crystals form. Remove trays and beat mixture, then return to freezer and freeze until firm. *Serves 4 to 6.*

FLAN DE PIÑA
(Pineapple Caramel Custard)

Caramel flan is one of the most commonly served desserts in Latin America. I enjoy it when it is well prepared, but I do get a bit weary of having it meal after meal after meal. This variant flavored with pineapple juice makes a most refreshing change.

2 cups pineapple juice
2 cups sugar
About ¼ cup water
5 large eggs

Heat the pineapple juice with 1 cup of the sugar, and boil over medium heat until the syrup forms a thread about 2 inches long when a little is dropped from a spoon (222° on a candy thermometer). Allow to cool.

In another saucepan, boil the remaining sugar with the water for 8 minutes, stirring. Pour this syrup into a 9-inch round cake pan or fireproof dish, and caramelize over lowest heat, swirling container to coat sides and bottom evenly.

Gently beat the eggs and combine with the cooled pineapple syrup. Pour the mixture into the pan with the caramel. Place the container in a larger pan, and add 1 inch hot water to the latter. Bake in a preheated 350° oven until set, usually about 1 hour. Let cool thoroughly, then unmold upside down on a serving plate, and serve at once. *Serves 6 to 8.*

AREPITAS
(Plantain Griddle Cakes)

These distinctive pancakes, nicely flavored with mashed ripe plantain, sugar, and cinnamon, come from the U.S. Virgin Islands; they are particularly popular on St. Croix.

2 large eggs, separated
¼ teaspoon salt
1 teaspoon baking powder
1 tablespoon vegetable shortening, softened
1 cup milk
1 cup boiled, peeled, mashed ripe plantain
1 cup flour
1 tablespoon light brown or granulated sugar
¼ teaspoon ground cinnamon
Butter
Honey, cane syrup, or guava jelly

Combine the egg yolks with the salt, baking powder, and shortening, and beat well. Add milk and beat again. Add the plantain, flour, sugar, and cinnamon. Beat the egg whites and add to the plantain mixture. Blend into a smooth batter.

Pour batter by tablespoonfuls onto a lightly greased griddle or skillet, and brown pancakes, turning once. Serve hot, with butter and a sweetening, such as honey, cane syrup, or guava jelly. (You might wish to melt the guava jelly and serve it hot.) *Serves 4.*

BOLLITOS CON RON
(Rum Balls)

Rum Balls generally are served in Latin American homes during the Christmas season, but I see no reason why they should not be offered to friends at any time of the year. They freeze very well.

2 tablespoons butter, softened
1 egg yolk, beaten
¼ cup sifted confectioners' sugar
2 tablespoons dark rum
4-ounce bar sweet cooking chocolate, finely grated
Chocolate sprinkles

Cream the butter until light and fluffy. Blend in the egg yolk, and gradually beat in the sugar. Beat in the rum and the grated chocolate, and beat until smooth.

Shape mixture into balls about ½-inch in diameter. Roll the balls in chocolate sprinkles, coating evenly. Place on waxed paper and chill very thoroughly. *Makes about 2 dozen.*

BUDÍN DE FRESAS
(Chilean Strawberry Pudding)

Chile is known for its superb wild strawberries, which are frequently used in desserts not only in the high Andes, where they grow, but in elegant restaurants and private homes in the large cities. In Santiago, this dish is sometimes also called a *bavaroise,* but by any name it is lovely.

2 envelopes (2 tablespoons) unflavored gelatin
⅓ cup cold water
⅓ cup boiling water
2 cups fresh strawberries (preferably wild), hulled and coarsely mashed
4 egg whites
¾ cup granulated sugar
2 tablespoons water
Fresh whole strawberries, chilled

Soak the gelatin in ⅓ cup cold water, then add the boiling water and dissolve; blend into the mashed strawberries. Chill until strawberries start to jell.

Beat the egg whites until stiff but not dry and set aside. In a small heavy saucepan, cook the sugar with 2 tablespoons of water, stirring constantly, until mixture forms a soft ball in cold water. Remove from heat, and fold gradually into the beaten egg whites. Allow to cool, beating gently.

Fold the slightly jelled strawberries into the egg-white mixture and pour it into a 1½-quart bowl or 6 to 8 individual molds. Chill until well set. Unmold and garnish with whole strawberries. *Serves 6 or more.*

TROPICAL CHRISTMAS PUDDING

Christmas is celebrated grandly in most Latin American countries, usually with specialties from the kitchen to help spread the glad tidings. One, this delectable pudding, typically served with a superb Coffee Hard Sauce, I encountered in Jamaica, an island which still retains much of its colonial heritage.

¾ cup chopped raisins
¾ cup whole sultanas (golden raisins)
½ cup chopped dates
¼ cup finely chopped candied or preserved citron
¼ cup finely chopped candied orange peel or grapefruit peel
1½ cups, or less, dry red wine
4 large eggs
1½ tightly packed cups light brown sugar
½ cup coarsely chopped cashews, peanuts, or Brazil nuts
½ cup or more grated dry coconut
¼ pound minced suet
1 cup sifted flour
1 teaspoon salt
1½ teaspoons baking powder
¾ teaspoon baking soda
½ teaspoon freshly grated nutmeg
½ teaspoon ground allspice
Pinch of ground cloves
Coffee Hard Sauce (see following recipe)

Combine the raisins, sultanas, dates, citron, and orange or grapefruit peel, and marinate in the wine for about 1 hour, stirring occasionally so that all ingredients are covered. Beat the eggs with the sugar and add to the fruit-wine mixture, along with the nuts, coconut, and suet.

Sift together the flour, salt, baking powder, baking soda, nutmeg, allspice, and cloves; blend into fruit mixture gently but thoroughly. Turn into 6 to 8 well-greased pudding molds, filling not more than three-quarters full; cover with aluminum foil and tie firmly.

Place molds on a rack in a large deep kettle so that they are not sitting on the bottom of the pot, and water can circulate beneath them. Add enough boiling water to reach halfway up the molds. Cover kettle securely, and steam 2½ hours, adding boiling water as needed. Check puddings, and if they are done, remove the molds from the kettle and take off foil coverings. Let cool, then cover with foil again and refrigerate. If possible, allow puddings to mellow in the refrigerator for at least a week. To serve, reheat, covered, about 45 minutes. Serve with Coffee Hard Sauce. *Serves 6 to 8.*

COFFEE HARD SAUCE

½ cup butter
1½ cups light brown sugar
3 to 4 tablespoons strong black coffee, preferably made from a fine, dark roast
⅛ teaspoon freshly grated nutmeg

Cream the butter and gradually beat in the sugar. Slowly add the coffee and nutmeg, beating until sauce is thoroughly blended. Chill thoroughly before serving over Tropical Christmas Pudding. *Makes about 2 cups.*

Beverages

In all the Latin American countries one encounters a wide variety of drinkables. Some of these are potently alcoholic; others not at all. Many beverages are offered to refresh—indeed, there is a special category of fruity beverages known as *refrescos*.

In almost all the islands and mainland countries, we find rums, frequently of superb caliber, in infinite variety; these are used in the production of a tremendous number of drinks, such as the tall Planter's Punch, hot buttered rum, and the tasty Jamaican liqueur, Rumona. In South America, sugar-cane distillates include wild potions such as the Brazilian *cachaça,* which is generally drunk neat in water glasses.

All Latin American lands have their own specialties. Peru has *pisco,* Mexico has *tequila, mescal,* and *pulque,* and many of the countries have fiery *aguardiente,* made from all kinds of fruits.

Some of the finest beers to be had anywhere in the world are made in Latin America. I am especially fond of Jamaica's Red Stripe, often considered one of the world's finest brews, and several of the Mexican beers, Dos XX (Equis) in particular, and those from Yucatan. Brazilian Brahma Chopps comes in a large bottle and packs a distinct punch. In the high Andes, there is a beverage called *chicha,* made from fermented crushed corn and in my opinion very much an acquired taste, and in tropical areas there are others made from esoteric ingredients such as palm fruits or palm sap.

Nonalcoholic drinks made in Latin America, include a great range of soft drinks, some very good, some very poor. The unique Brazilian Guarana is, assuredly, the most pleasant of such beverages anywhere in the world.

In the English-speaking lands tea is a favorite beverage, but little tea is raised. Coffee, though, abounds almost everywhere at the higher elevations; Jamaica's Blue Mountain coffee is often pronounced the finest in the world, yet it is rarely available (and terribly expensive) in its home island because the bulk of the crop presently is being exported to, of all places, Japan. Brazilians probably drink more coffee than anyone except the Arabic peoples, often happily consuming ten or more tiny sweet, thick *cafézinhos* every day of the week. *Café con leche* is a favorite breakfast drink, the coffee hot and thick, the milk likewise.

Maté, or Paraguayan tea, is the principal hot beverage of millions of people in Paraguay, Uruguay, Argentina, and southern Brazil. This is a rather bitter but refreshing brew made from the dried leaves of a species of holly tree. Maté is typically sipped from a handsomely carved or embossed gourd through a special silver-colored metal straw with a filter at the bottom. Because of its rather high caffeine content, it is a marvelous breakfast or pre-breakfast drink, ideally served without sugar or milk.

Beverages made from fruits are found almost everywhere. The thick, often sweetened and spiced Brazilian *batidas* are closely allied to the *refrescos,* but are usually less thick and on occasion made with Coconut Milk rather than cow's milk or water. (Rum is sometimes added.)

A considerable number of good wines are produced in Latin America, with some truly exceptional varieties produced in great quantity in Argentina and Chile. Homemade wines of diverse sorts, such as the intriguing and rather insidious cashew-fruit beverage of Belize and others made from citrus and palm fruits elsewhere, are also of some interest.

PONCHE DE PIÑA
(Hot Pineapple Punch)

In Tegucigalpa, Honduras, Managua, Nicaragua, and several other cities in Central America, I have enjoyed this spicy heated punch on festive occasions, especially around Christmas time. Ripe fresh pineapples are best, but one can substitute canned crushed pineapple or even shred pineapple chunks or slices for the desired effect. The quantity of rum can be increased, of course.

3 large fresh ripe pineapples
Cold water
3 1-inch pieces stick cinnamon
2 teaspoons whole cloves
2 teaspoons whole allspice
Granulated or light brown sugar to taste
1 cup Coconut Milk (see index)
½ cup or more light rum

Peel pineapples and chop fine or shred; add water to cover, and let stand overnight in the refrigerator. The next day, put the pineapple into a large pot with the cinnamon, cloves, allspice, sugar, and Coconut Milk. Mix thoroughly, and bring to a boil; boil, stirring, 5 minutes. Add rum to taste, heat through but do not boil, and serve very hot. *Serves 8 to 10.*

GINGER BEER

Ginger is produced in a considerable number of Latin American lands, Jamaica being perhaps the most famous supplier. Those of us who delight in the authenticities of the cuisines of these countries much prefer to use fresh ginger, now available almost everywhere, as opposed to ground or powdered ginger, which, though powerful, has none of the spicy charm of the fresh root.

1 to 2 ounces peeled and grated fresh ginger
⅓ cup fresh lime juice
Grated peel of one large ripe lime (green part only)
Granulated or light brown sugar to taste
4 cups boiling water
1 teaspoon active dry yeast
¼ cup lukewarm water (105° to 115°)
Light rum to taste (optional, but very typical)

In a large nonmetallic bowl, combine the grated ginger, lime juice, lime peel, and sugar (the beverage should not be too sweet). Pour the boiling water over all.

Separately, in a small bowl, stir the yeast into the lukewarm water, and let stand in a warm place until it begins to bubble. Add to the ginger mixture, mixing well.

Cover bowl and allow to stand in a warm spot 1 week, stirring occasionally and adding rum, if desired, toward the end of the week. Strain well, pour in a bottle or bottles, and allow to mellow at room temperature for about a week longer, checking to be sure it does not explode.

Chill well, and serve with cracked ice. *Makes 1 quart.*

SANGRÍA

Sangría, a delectable wine-based drink made with fruits of diverse species, has long found exceptional favor throughout most of Latin America and other parts of the world as well. The fruits should be fresh and the red wine a dry variety. When apples have been unavailable in Jamaica, as is often the case, I have used to excellent advantage Otaheite apples. Vivid scarlet outside, white and crisp within, they made a marvelous substitute. Some aberrant recipes for Sangría call for the addition of a good slug of gin, which I find rather offensive for this special purpose. The drink originated in Spain.

3 ***ripe fresh peaches, peeled and thinly sliced (or an equivalent amount of ripe papaya)***
2 ***rather tart apples, peeled if desired, cored, and thinly sliced***
1 ***large ripe sweet orange, thinly sliced (unpeeled)***
2 ***bottles dry red wine***
Granulated sugar (optional)
Ice cubes

Place the peaches, apples, and orange slices in a large glass container and add the red wine and the sugar, if desired. (Sugar is usually not needed, since the sangría should be rather tart.)

Mix fruits and wine, mashing a couple of fruit slices, if desired, though usually the drink is clear. Add ice cubes and stir gently until well chilled. Serve in chilled glasses. *Serves 8 to 10.*

PISCO SOUR

Pisco, a seaport in Peru, has given its name to an unusual alchoholic beverage, most often used in this singularly insidious yet refreshing drink. Of course, the best place to try a Pisco Sour is in Peru.

9 *ounces Pisco brandy*
1½ *ounces honey or simple syrup*
1½ *ounces lemon or lime juice*
½ *teaspoon Angostura bitters, or to taste*
1 *egg white*
Crushed ice

Combine the brandy, honey or simple syrup (I prefer the former), lemon or lime juice, and bitters in a cocktail shaker. Stir to mix well. Add the egg white and crushed ice and shake vigorously. Strain into well-chilled cocktail glasses. *Serves 6.*

PLANTER'S PUNCH

Planter's Punch is certainly one of the most famous and widely served rum drinks in the Caribbean, and many other parts of Latin America as well. Every good bartender has his own subtle interpretation of the basic recipe. Here is mine.

1½ *ounces light rum*
1½ *ounces dark rum*
3 *ounces or more fresh orange juice*
¾ *ounce fresh lime juice*
Simple syrup to taste
Cracked ice
Garnish:* 1 *orange slice (unpeeled),* 1 *ripe fresh pineapple "finger," and* 1 *maraschino cherry

Combine both kinds of rum (I prefer the Jamaican varieties) with the orange and lime juices, simple syrup, and cracked ice. Shake well and pour into a prechilled 12-ounce glass. Impale the orange slice with the pineapple finger and add the cherry to garnish the glass (or use your imagination). Serve with straws, if desired. *Serves 1.*

PIÑA COLADA
(Pineapple Juice with Coconut Milk and Rum)

This drink, which is exceptionally popular in the Bahamas and Cuba, certainly should be better known throughout Latin America, where the basic ingredients are commonplace. It is a lovely soothing beverage.

- ⅔ ***cup light or dark rum***
- ½ ***cup Coconut Milk (see index)***
- **1 *cup chilled unsweetened pineapple juice***
- **2 *cups crushed ice***
- **6 *ripe fresh pineapple "fingers" and* 6 *maraschino cherries, for garnish (optional)***

Thoroughly chill 6 cocktail glasses. Combine the rum, Coconut Milk, pineapple juice, and ice in a blender. Blend at high speed until smooth and frothy, usually about 30 seconds. Pour into the chilled glasses, and add garnishes, if desired (I do not). Serve without delay. *Serves 6.*

CHOCOLATE MEXICANO
(Mexican Chocolate)

Several kinds of packaged Mexican chocolate are already sweetened and flavored with ground cinnamon and cloves; sometimes ground almonds are blended in. The word chocolate comes from two ancient Nahuatl words, *xoco* (bitter) and *atl* (water). If you happen to have a *molinillo,* a very old wooden beater that is twirled rapidly between the palms of your hands, to produce the needed froth here, then so much the better; otherwise use a whisk or rotary beater.

4 *cups milk*
4 *ounces unsweetened chocolate, grated*
1 *egg yolk*
½ *cup light or heavy cream or Coconut Cream (see index)*
Sugar or honey to taste
½ *teaspoon or more ground cinnamon*
¼ *teaspoon or more freshly grated nutmeg*

In a saucepan, heat ½ cup of the milk, add the grated chocolate, and stir over low heat until dissolved; add remaining milk and, stirring almost constantly, gently bring to a boil.

Combine the egg yolk with the cream, sugar or honey (if Coconut Cream is used, cut down on sugar or honey), cinnamon and nutmeg. Stir well, and blend into the hot chocolate, stirring constantly.

Heat mixture thoroughly, but do not allow to boil. Remove from heat and beat until a froth appears. Serve at once. *Serves 6.*

PONCHE DE TAMARINDO
(Tamarind Punch)

The tamarind, one of the more commonly cultivated trees of Latin America, has extensive culinary uses. Both the attractive fernlike foliage and the fresh flowers are used in curries and other dishes. The copious sticky pulp within its lumpy brown pods figures in diversities such as commercial Worcestershire sauce, most chutneys, India relish, jams, jellies, hard candies, a variety of refreshing beverages, and cookies, cakes, and other desserts.

½ pound fresh tamarind pods
Water
Sugar to taste

Peel pods, place in 4 cups water, and soak at room temperature several hours.

Mash pulp with a fork or, more easily, your fingers. Discard seeds, and strain the thick liquid through a fine sieve or layers of cheesecloth. Dilute the liquid with water as desired, sweeten to taste, and serve well-iced as a most refreshing beverage. (The residual pulp can be tightly covered, refrigerated, and used as seasoning later.)

BATIDA JANEIRENSE
(Batida, Rio de Janeiro Style)

In Brazil and several other South American countries, batidas are made with cow's milk, or a combination of cow's milk and Coconut Milk, fresh tropical fruits, and sometimes a judicious dash of rum; in Brazil, the last would generally be the potent cachaça.

1 cup cow's milk
1 cup Coconut Milk (see index)
½ cup mashed ripe papaya
1½ ounces fresh lime or lemon juice
1½ ounces cachaça or light rum (optional, but typical)
3 or 4 ice cubes, cracked

Place all ingredients in a cocktail shaker or blender, and shake or blend thoroughly. Serve at once. *Serves 4.*

Glossary

aceituna (Spanish). Green olive.

acerola (Spanish); also called Barbados cherry, West Indian cherry, garden cherry, Malpighia. A fruit of the tropics; a very rich source of Vitamin C. Botanical name, *Malpighia punicifolia.*

achiote (sometimes called annatto). The dried seed of the annatto tree, a small tree of the American tropics (*Bixa orellana*). The round form of these seeds is called bija. Both are used extensively for flavoring and food coloring, especially in Puerto Rico.

aquacate (Spanish). Avocado.

aguardiente (Spanish). Literally, "burning water"; strong liquor distilled from grapes and molasses and bottled without aging.

ají (Spanish). Chili pepper; chili pepper sauce.

ajo (Spanish). Garlic.

akkra. Black-eyed peas; called calas in Curaçao.

albondiguita (Spanish). Small Mexican meatballs.

annatto. See **achiote.**

annona. A genus of tropical fruit trees that includes the soursop.

anticuchos (Spanish). Broiled meat served on skewers as an appetizer.

arepitas (Spanish). Pancakes made with plantain.

arroz (Spanish). Rice.

asado (Spanish). Barbecue; roast meat.

bammies. Thick cassava wafers.

bananda (Portuguese). Dessert made with bananas.

Barbados cherry. See **acerola.**

batida (Portuguese). Brazilian drink made with fruit juices, milk, and sometimes rum.

berenjena (Spanish). Eggplant.

bife (Portuguese). Beefsteak.

bija. See **achiote.**

bizcocho (Spanish). Cake, spongecake.

bok-choi; also called pak-choi, bok-toi, Chinese cabbage. A dark green leafy cabbage. Botanical name, *Brassica chinensis.*

breadfruit. A starchy tropical fruit that resembles a green melon in size and shape but has the taste and texture of a white potato.

budin (Spanish). Pudding.

buñuelo (Spanish). Fritter.

bussu. A blackish mollusk found in Jamaica.

butifarra (Spanish). Fatty pork sausage prepared with white wine.

cacerola (Spanish). Saucepan, casserole.

cachaça (Portuguese). A very strong Brazilian rum distilled from sugar cane.

cafèzinho (Portuguese). A very strong Brazilian coffee served in small cups.

caju (Portuguese). Cashew nut.

calabaza (Spanish). West Indian pumpkin.

calalu. A leafy green vegetable sometimes called Chinese spinach or bhaji. Botanically, *Amaranthus gangeticus;* also a species of *Colocasia.*

caldo (Spanish). Broth; soup.

camarón (Spanish). Shrimp.

canja (Portuguese). Brazilian chicken soup.

cardoon. A vegetable related to the globe artichoke.

carne (Spanish). Meat.

carne seca (Spanish). Sun-dried salted beef; jerky.

carnitas (Spanish). Crisp roasted cubes of lean pork.

cassareep. A seasoning made from the root of the cassava.

cassava; also called manioc; sometimes referred to as yucca. A tropical plant cultivated for its root, which is the source of tapioca and cassareep. Botanical name, *Manihot utilissima.*

cazuela (Spanish). Candied, baked sweet potatoes with spices. A specialty of Puerto Rico.

cerdo (Spanish). Pork. (Also called **puerco.**)

ceviche (cebiche, seviche). Raw fish pickled in lime juice.
See **poisson cru.**

chayote; also called xuxu or christophine. A pear-shaped squash found in the Central American and Caribbean countries.

chicha. A South American drink made from fermented corn.

chili con carne. Spicy meat and beans, most common in Mexico.

chili pepper. See **peppers.**

choclo. Stewed corn kernels; an ear of corn.

chorizo (Spanish). Pork and pork liver sausage, seasoned with cayenne pepper and juniper berries.

christophine. See **chayote.**

chuletas (Spanish). Cutlets or chops.

churrasco (Spanish). Meat broiled or barbecued over an open fire.

churros (Spanish). Mexican crullers or sweet fritters.

cidra. A cider wine of Cuba.

cilantro. See **coriander.**

cocada (Spanish). Coconut pudding.

cocido (Spanish). A stew found in the Dominican Republic.

cocina (Spanish). Cuisine; cooking style; kitchen.

coco (Spanish). Coconut.

conch (pronounced "konk"). A large edible shellfish with a strong flavor.

coo-coo. An okra and cornmeal mush of African origin.

coquilles (French). Scallops.

coriander. An annual herb with delicate foliage, native to Asia and the Mediterranean countries of Europe and grown throughout tropical Latin America. Prized as a spice, its seeds are used either whole or ground. Fresh coriander leaves are also called cilantro and are used as a seasoning or garnish.

crapaud (French, toad). Large bullfrog native to Dominica and Montserrat.

cui. South American guinea pig.

cumin; also called comino, cummin. The dried fruit of a type of parsley plant, used as a seasoning for curries, soups, stews, and as a flavoring for breads and rice.

dasheen; malanga; taro in Polynesia and parts of Latin America; yautia in Puerto Rico; eddo in Barbados. A starchy tuber that is a dietary staple in many tropical countries.

dashi (Japanese). Fish stock prepared from seaweed and dried flakes of bonita and used as a soup base.

daube de potate (French). A Haitian pudding of potatoes and bananas.

dendê (Portuguese). Brazilian palm oil.

djon-djon. Black mushrooms of Haiti.

dulce de cajuil (Spanish). A cashew preserve.

empanada (Spanish); also called empanadilla, empanaditas, empadinhas, empada (Portuguese). A small pastry turnover filled with fish or meat.

enchilada. A rolled tortilla filled with cheese or meat. Mexican.

ensalada (Spanish). Salad.

ertensoep (Dutch). Pea soup seasoned with chili peppers.

escabeche (Spanish). Pickle, pickling solution.

espinaca (Spanish). Spinach.

farofa (Portuguese). Toasted cassava flour.

feijão (Portuguese). Dried beans.

feijoada (Portuguese). Brazilian national dish of rice, beans, and meat.

flan. Custard.

fresa (Spanish). Strawberry.

frijoles (Spanish). Beans.

frijoles colorados. Red peas or kidney beans.

frijoles negros. Black beans.

frigideira (Portuguese). Frying pan.

fruta (Spanish). Fruit.

fruta bomba. Cuban name for papaya.

gado-gado. A crisp boiled vegetable dish served as part of a **rijstafel.**

gallego. A term referring to the Gallician region of Spain.

gandules; also known as Gungo peas. Pigeon peas.

garbanzos (Spanish). Chick peas.

gazpacho (Spanish). Cold raw-vegetable soup.

ginger. Spice derived from the root of a colorful tropical plant. Used as a dry powder with a sweet and pungent flavor, or sliced, chopped, or grated from the fresh root. The flavors of these two forms are very different. Fresh ginger is also preserved in a syrup and eaten as candy.

guacamole. Mashed avocado spread or dip of Mexican origin.

guajolote. Mexican name for wild turkey. Also pavo (Spanish).

guanabana. See **soursop.**

Guarana. Bottled Brazilian soft drink made from a paste derived from a local plant.

guasacaca. Venezuelan barbecue sauce made with avocados.

guava; guayaba in Cuba; gioaba (Portuguese). A sweet or slightly acid tropical fruit that is made into a paste by boiling the fruit pulp until it is a solid mass that can be sliced. This paste tends to crystallize with age.

Gungo peas. See **gandules.**

huevos (Spanish). Eggs.

huachinango. Red snapper.

humitas. Cornhusks stuffed with meat.

jabuticaba. Round, blue-black, pulpy fruit of the jabuticabeira (*Myceara cauliflora*).

jakfruit; also known as jackfruit or jaca. A very large fruit of a tree in the rubber family, cultivated for both the seeds and the pulp. Botanical name, *Artocarpus integra.*

jalapeño. A small green chili pepper used to make a fiery sauce.

jenjibre (Spanish). Ginger.

jícama. Tuberous vegetable grown in Mexico and Guatemala.

jonga. Small crawfish found in the Negro River of St. Thomas.

Katjang sauce. Sauce made from peanuts, originating in Surinam and the Netherlands Antilles.

kiveve. Mashed squash.

langouste (French); **langousta** (Spanish). Large crawfish, and some clawless varieties of lobster.

leche (Spanish). Milk.

lechosa. Puerto Rican name for papaya.

legumbre (Spanish). Vegetable.

limão (Portuguese); **limón** (Spanish). Lemon.

llapingachos. Potato cheese cakes.

lleno or **relleno.** Stuffed or filled.

locro. A thick vegetable stew.

longaniza (Spanish). Sausage of pork, garlic, herbs.

maize or **maiz.** Corn.

malanga. See **dasheen.**

mango. A long oval fruit whose flesh is very juicy when ripe and usually orange-colored. The flavor combines those of the peach, pineapple, and strawberry. The large seed or pit may be roasted and the kernel eaten.

mangrove snapper. A tropical fish found in the Caribbean.

manioc. See **cassava.**

manzana (Spanish). Apple.

marisco (Spanish). Shellfish.

matambre. A rolled slice of beef stuffed with peppers, vegetables, and often hard-boiled eggs.

maté, or **yerba maté.** A Paraguayan tea made from the dried leaves of a species of Holly tree, the *Hilea paraguaiensis.* A favorite drink in many parts of South America.

mayonesa (Spanish). Mayonnaise dressing.

môlho (Portuguese). Sauce.

molinello. Wooden utensil used to whip chocolate.

morcilla. Blood sausage.

morcilla blana. Sausage of chicken, bacon, and hard-boiled eggs.

morro crab. A large meaty salt-water crab.

nacatamales. Nicaraguan tamales, banana leaves filled with a medley of fried meats and vegetables.

naranja (Spanish). Orange.

naranjilla. A type of orange with bright green pulp, native to South America, especially Ecuador.

naseberry; also called sapodilla. A plum of West Indies from a large tropical evergreen that produces chicle. The fruit resembles a pear both in appearance and taste.

Otaheite apple. See **pomarrosa.**

paella (Spanish). Rice dish of Spanish origin, also found throughout Latin America.

paellero. A shallow pan from which paella gets its name.

palm oil. See **dendê.**

pão (Portuguese). Bread.

papa (Spanish). Potato.

papaya; also called papaw, or pawpaw. A large tropical fruit that resembles a watermelon, with pinkish flesh, many seeds, and a somewhat soapy sweet flavor. Not the North American papaw or pawpaw.

pappadum (East Indian). A very thin whole-wheat wafer or pancake, quickly fried in oil until crisp.

páramo (Spanish). A high, bleak plain or cold region.

pastel (Spanish). Pie or pastry roll.

pato (Portuguese). Duck.

pavo (Spanish). Turkey. See **guajolote.**

pejibave. The peach palm fruit of South America.

peppers. A great variety of fruits of the Capsicum family with flavors ranging from very hot to mild or sweet, and colors from vivid green to bright red. The hot varieties are usually called chili peppers and the mild ones bell peppers. A few of the chili pepper varieties are: cayenne (the most familiar), jalapeño, annaheim, country, mulato, ancho, pasilla.

percebe (Spanish). A small shellfish with a delicate flavor, eaten in El Salvador.

perejil. Parsley.

pescado (Portuguese, Spanish). Fish.

pimiento. Sweet red bell pepper. Eaten raw, roasted, or pickled and used as a relish.

piña (Spanish). Pineapple.

pionono. Meat-stuffed plantain.

pisco. Peruvian brandy.

pita bread. Flat round East Indian bread.

plantain; also called Adam's Fig or cooking banana. A tropical fruit that resembles a very large banana and is almost invariably cooked before being eaten. High in starch, rich in vitamins.

poisson cru (French). Raw fish dish similar to ceviche but marinated with tomatoes as well as lime juice.

pollo (Spanish). Chicken.

pomarrosa; also called Otaheite apple. A tree of the Eucalyptus or Myrtle family with scarlet fruit.

puerco (Spanish). Pork. See **cerdo.**

pulque. An alcoholic drink of fermented agave juice.

purple potatoes. A starchy root crop distinguished by its color, and grown in Ecuador.

queso (Spanish). Cheese.

queso de crema (Spanish). A type of cream cheese of Nicaragua.

quince. A hard, acid, yellow, pear-shaped fruit.

rábano (Spanish). Radish.

refresco (Spanish). Refreshment; usually a drink.

rijstafel. Traditional Indonesian rice table.

rumona. A Jamaican liqueur.

saffron. A species of crocus whose stamens are used as a yellow dye and to color and flavor foods.

salchichas. A veal-and-pork sausage flavored with rum.

salmagundi; also called Solomon Gundy. A spicy paste of salty fish used as a spread and in combination with other ingredients. A Jamaican specialty sold commercially in small jars.

salsa (Spanish). Sauce.

sambal. A fiery hot pepper native to South Pacific regions and parts of Latin America.

sancocho. A vegetable stew common throughout Latin America, made with different regional and seasonal vegetables and ingredients.

sangría. A drink made with red wine, fruits, and sugar.

sapodilla. See **naseberry.**

sopa. Soup.

soursop; also called guanabana. A large fruit with aromatic white pulp. *Annona maricata.*

souse. A dish made of pig's feet and head, kept in a pickling liquid.

spekulaas (Dutch). Cookies made with coconut milk or coconut cream.

star apple; also called cainito. A globular tropical fruit varying from green to purple in color, with white or lilac flesh. Botanical name, *Chrysophyllum cainito,* member of the Sapote or Chicle family.

tamales. Mexican cornmeal pastry filled with meat or chicken or other stuffing.

tamarind. A tropical fruit sometimes called the Indian date. Similar in taste to a plum, though slightly more sour; used in curries and other dishes. Botanical name, *Tamarindus indica.*

tapioca. A starchy food obtained by heating the cassava root.

taro. See dasheen.

tequila. A Mexican liquor made from cactus.

Tico. Nickname for Costa Rican.

tomatillo. A small fruit resembling a tomato, used in making sauces and preserves.

torta (Spanish and Portuguese). Tart.

tortilla. Flat, thin, round cornmeal pancake.

turmeric. An herb of the ginger family from which is obtained a yellowish powder, used to flavor and color curries, mustard, and other preparations.

vatapá (Portuguese). A Brazilian shrimp and cornmeal dish.

West Indian pumpkin. See **calabaza.**

xuxu. See **chayote.**

yucca. See **cassava.** Although this is another name for cassava, it is also the name applied to an entirely different wild food plant found in the southwestern United States.

zarzuela (Spanish). A stew of assorted seafood (originally, a light opera or musical comedy).

Index